SAVING GRACE

CRISTINA SLOUGH

Love Cristina Slough x

BLOODHOUND
— BOOKS —

First published in 2023 by Bloodhound Books.

www.bloodhoundbooks.com

Print ISBN: 978-1-5040-8524-3

To Adam, Lucas and Mya for completing me.

'I believe the only way to reform people is to kill them.'
— **Carl Panzram**

PROLOGUE

The lights are on. You haven't pulled across those expensive mechanical shutters yet; what are they for? To shut out the world, or shut out me? It doesn't matter because I see you. I always see you. You're with me every single day. You move with ease around your habitat, like a ballerina, supple and elegant, dancing a story. *Our story*. You've cut your hair, I imagine the snip of the scissors slicing away parts of your golden strands, like a reptile shedding its skin, becoming anew. The choppy bob ages you, but in a good way. It's added an exclamation mark to your sophisticated style, emphasising how you want the world to see you. But they don't know you like I do. All smoke and mirrors. You hold a glass of red wine with those long slender fingers, and you still have that habit of twirling the ends of your hair with your thumb. You are still there. Nobody can erase all of themselves, there are always splintered fragments left behind, built within us like the coding of our DNA. You said you felt sorry for me, but I know who I am. Do you?

You can change who you are on the outside, but you will never change who you are on the inside. Aristotle once said,

'Knowing yourself is the beginning of all wisdom.' Try to remember that, it will help.

You reach for a book; I can't see what it is, but I know you have always preferred real books to e-readers. You always said we need to experience the written word, the smell of the paper, the weight of a story in your hands. I love the way you sniff a book before you dive in and read. I wait a couple of seconds and laugh; there you go, your nose pressed up to the pages like clockwork. The crisp white shirt you're wearing hangs loosely around your slender frame, the memory of what's beneath it takes my breath away. Your soft silky skin; it's one of the things I loved most about you. You set the book down and jump up, reaching for the phone. Who is calling you this late? It must be somebody important to you. I watch you throw your head back and laugh. I miss that sound. We had a lot of laughs, didn't we? Now someone else is firing you up, making your insides light up. You take the phone to another room and slip from view. I let myself imagine I'm on the sofa, waiting while you make us both a drink. I can envision us both in the apartment, it suits the couple we were supposed to be. Your job isn't enough to pay for all of this, but that's the way it's always been for you. Money comes easily. You told me not to worry, that I was enough and money was just a thing, but if that was true then why do you need the leather sofa, the expensive Art Deco bullshit on your walls that could feed a family of four for six months. Why is it so important that your coffee machine has ninety-nine settings? You love to pretend to be humble, and I think you want to be, but you just can't let go of the good life. I get it, I longed for it too, but I deserved it more than your pretentious, spoiled friend did. I'm glad she's gone.

You stay on the phone for a while. A hard lump that I cannot swallow forms in my throat like a piece of coal. I've been replaced. It's painful to watch you for this long, but now that I've finally found you, I don't want to let you go.

What would you do if you saw me?

Run?

Scream?

Hide? But you're already doing that. We've been playing this game of hide-and-seek for a while now. I came close to finding you before, but you always changed tactics, my clever girl.

I have so many questions; how this all came to be, how two people so connected, so in love could have yanked it all away. Just like that. Our love was like a mirror, such a beautiful reflection, but it came under strain. It remained intact until it smashed to pieces, and once a mirror is broken, the cracks will forever be visible, impossible to repair, but I could live with the damage if it meant I still had you. If you still wanted me.

My soul hurts.

You fall away from my view again; it's like I am watching you on the TV and it went to a commercial break. I eagerly wait your return; you're gone for ten minutes. Now the cold has snaked around my body and I feel the bite of the night air. When you come back you walk to the window, dressed in a linen white two-piece pyjama set, your hair pulled away from your face in a neat headband. You return to the sofa and sink into it, you reach for the book again and sink down lower, the book covers your face and I can only see your long, slender legs. So many of our nights were spent with your legs draped across my lap, you enjoyed the way I stroked them so much you'd close your eyes and drift into a deep sleep. Hours later, I'd wake you and take you to bed in your dozy state, your voice drenched with sleep as you'd ask me to put a glass of water next to the bed. It was my duty to look after you. How could you forget that? How was it not enough? I reach out my hand, longing to touch you, but your eyes are fixed ahead. I don't want this to end. I am still immersed in your beauty. I want to get inside your apartment. Get inside you.

Can you feel me?

I'm right here.

CHAPTER ONE

JENNIFER MACK

I stare at the headline:

Police Name Body Found in Briar Bay

But the reporting name isn't mine. Hayley Woolley's name shows up big and bold, and it gives me a headache just looking at it. I imagine her smug little face sharing her delight with her family and friends, even happier her name is taking up the space where mine should have been. The writing certainly isn't riveting; a trained chimp could have churned out that rubbish.

Hoping that they misspelled her name in the byline (something that happens all too often with me) I read on, cringing at each line. The body had been pulled from the water and now awaits examination from the coroner to determine the exact cause of death. The words carved into the victim's back with a sharp instrument tell us this was no accident; it's a message. Whoever did this wants us to know it was deliberate. Terrance Harding, a local fisherman, discovered the body while out on his boat. I guess he didn't expect his early morning catch to be a corpse. Hayley got to Terrance first and that's why Hayley got the headline.

The yellow police tape has now snapped and frayed at the ends, blowing in the wind, disarranged along the coastal path and there's a small team of weary-looking forensic examiners on the beach. The sound of police speedboats hum as they cut through the water, looking for further clues. Someone's phone is ringing, a malapropos jolly little jingle that doesn't belong in the sombre surroundings. There are several of us from the paper here as well, and we gravitate together because we're all part of the same pack. But not really, we all know we want to take the scoop for ourselves, fuck the rest. We are impertinent, with minds that never switch off, we have a reputation, and it's not a good one. But without us, there is no news. We are a necessary evil.

Steve from the camera crew comes toward me, his pale belly spilling out over the top of his jeans forcing me to turn my head. 'Jen, can you hold this?'

'Jennifer,' I correct him.

He rolls his eyes. '*Jennifer*. Hold. Please.' He places a Nikon D3500 in my palms, not the most impressive camera, but one that'll do the job.

My name back in my uni days was Jennifer, not Jen or Jenny or *Jan*, as I'd been known in Cornwall. Jennifer, the Cornish derivation of Guinevere (fair lady). I always typed Jennifer at the end of my emails. Calling me Jen indicated endearment, but I'm not here to be endeared by anybody. *Jen-nif-er*. Not that hard, is it?

The sea breeze whips through my hair, making it a tangled mess. Cornwall has been home to me all my life, although I had a brief break when I attended Oxford. Back then I had big plans, huge plans to work for the BBC reporting news from all over the world, making a difference. I believed Oxford would be the skeleton key to open any door, believing I had hundreds of possibilities neatly set out before me. Maybe I was arrogant, maybe naïve, but I believed I would dip directly into the waters of the fast-paced news scene. When offers didn't come my way, I worked for free, even sweeping the floor at newsroom offices. After endless applications, I was given one offer: *The Cornwall Chronicle*. Head hung low, shame pulsing through my veins, I swallowed my pride and came back to my home town to work for the local rag. The more I think about the first days of being back in Cornwall, the more my ambitions slip away. Within months of moving back, Mum got sick and then she was gone, just like that. And now, there was a murder.

It had been twenty-four hours since the body was discovered and the breaking news sent a ripple of fear amongst the local community, because things like this didn't happen in Cornwall. Newsflash: bad things happen everywhere because bad people are everywhere.

The sun disappearing behind the hills and the darkness setting in makes the crime scene feel even more ominous, as though the sea could whisper its secrets from beneath its surface.

Finally, the news crew starts to pack up. There's nothing more to see, nothing more to do. They head away from the beach, their faces flushed, carrying heavy equipment with wires dangling round their bodies. The forensic team remain, the scene now illuminated in sterile white floodlights. It reminds me of a film set, it feels insurmountable. I sit down and take my trainers off, shaking the sand out of them. It's been a long, pointless day and I cannot help but feel defeated. I should have been here first; timing is everything. I reach into my backpack and take out my blue flask which would most likely hold tea, coffee, water... gin. I bring it to my mouth and sip. The burn reminds me of cramming for my finals. I'd take a swig just before my exam, and it would quiet my mind and set the mood I needed to be in. Power. I think that's the best word to use; it gave me power... until it didn't. I reach for yesterday's paper again, the one with Hayley's headline, and smooth out the crumples with my hand. I read her name and take another sip, then another. I don't need to drink, I *want* to; there's a difference and that's why I am not an alcoholic. It's been a bad week, so I, like many other proud Brits, am entitled to reset and reflect.

Elliot Young, the intern with greasy hair, acne, and sardine breath offers me a lift home, but I wave him off and tell him I'm going to stay a while longer. I used to come here as a child and watch the boats come into dock. The swell begins propagating away as faster waves race in and out. I see something wash up on the sand. I get up and find I'm unsteady on my feet and feel light-headed; I should've eaten lunch. I cross the beach and see a forlorn flip-flop with a glittery pink strap that has snapped. It could belong to just about anybody, but this is a crime scene, so I make my way to the forensic team feeling quite triumphant in my find.

CHAPTER TWO

NORTH LONDON

I t was cold for mid-August. The steel-grey sky opened up to let a gentle rain fall before gradually becoming heavier. Wet and shivering, Grant found a shopfront, dirty and neglected, with a To Let sign plastered on the glass with an out-of-date area code and graffiti. The place had the stench of stale urine, but it was a place out of the way, where nobody would ask him to move along and he would be sheltered from the rain. People wouldn't notice him under his ragged coat; not that they would care if they did. He used to sleep in the bus station, but now it was manned by security, all glass and steel, alarm systems and a coffee shop selling overpriced lattes in fancy recycled cups that promote veganism. It made him mad. He'd be grateful for any decent food in his belly, not excluding a thousand different things from his diet because of this New Age kindness bullshit and caring about the fair treatment of animals. All the while he walked the streets hungry and alone, not a single *caring* vegan so much as offered him a hot cup of tea.

The streets were empty because of the weather. It was the afternoon; rush hour wouldn't start until five o'clock. Then the trains would come in thick and fast with hundreds of commuters spilling out onto the pavement and rushing home like their lives depended on it. As he went to make up his bed, he leaned up against the door, and to his surprise, it creaked open. He looked behind him, making sure nobody was watching and slipped in. He felt like he'd won the lottery with walls all around him to shelter him from the rain. He even had reading material; old posters littered the floor, with pictures of films and promotional material promising no late fees, free popcorn, and a soft drink with any two rentals. He laughed at the irony, the old video shop was just like him – discarded, redundant, useless, with the best days long behind it. He looked down at his hands, dry and calloused, worn from the days he worked tirelessly with them. He'd never owned a house. He lived in rented flats, usually above shops, and changed his address often. He was an urban nomad. Wherever there was work, he followed. Marriage and children were for other people, not him. He savoured his independence, never having to answer to anybody. He enjoyed the brief company of women with no strings attached, which meant he'd pay for it mostly; but he felt no shame, he never had to be tied up in pointless chit-chat, pretending to care what they did for a living or whatever bullshit problems they had. Keeping to a simple business transaction was better for all parties involved: he got what he needed, she got paid. But things were different now, and he had nothing but regret and bitterness. Maybe if he had let himself fall in love, found someone to settle down with, then he'd have somebody to share the burden with and he'd still have a roof over his head and food in his belly. Pulling himself from his thoughts, he looked around the shop. The shop looked like it was left in a hurry, nothing carefully packed or thrown away; he thought about how this would have once been such a happy place – families picking out a film on a Saturday night, friends and couples coming in, hoping their favourite video wasn't already rented out. In the front of the shop was an old drop-box now covered in thick black tape. The air was thick from where there had been no ventilation for years. He pulled out some old cardboard boxes and placed them flat on the floor. It wasn't a mattress, but it beat sleeping on cold pavement. The hours passed and he fell into a deep sleep, it had been so long since he found a place to sleep that was so private. His exhausted body welcomed the reprieve away from the elements.

He woke up several hours later to pangs of hunger pulling at his stomach. Reaching into his pocket, he pulled out all the money he had in the world; he counted £4.89. Enough for a loaf of bread and some salted ham. When he opened the door, the orange glow of streetlights illuminated the slick pavement. He stepped out into the night and kept his head hung low. He found a convenience shop on the corner and stepped inside; behind him he could hear hushed laughter, he paid and left not looking back. All he wanted to do was pay for his food and get back to his new home for the night.

————

Crossing the street on the way back to the video shop, he planned to eat and sleep as much as he could before sunrise. He wanted to be able to stay at the shop for as long as he could, but he knew if a member of the public saw him, he'd be reported and he'd lose the roof over his head. As he entered the shop, he noticed the cardboard boxes he set up had moved. He imagined it could be an animal, perhaps a rat, but it would have to be a bloody big rat. He was not the most perceptive of people, but he felt the atmosphere had shifted. *He was not alone.*

CHAPTER THREE

JENNIFER MACK

There was something in the way her eyes smiled, an ominous aura that shrouded her petite frame as though it foretold a tragic fate, a photograph marked for death that would appear on the front page of all the papers. Grace Matthews; the twenty-two-year-old pulled from Briar Bay. The post-mortem revealed Grace had died as a result of asphyxiation which took place prior to her body being placed in the water. She didn't drown, and the markings on her back were consistent with that of a kitchen knife: the non-consensual coercive tattoo etched into Grace's body was a mark of assertion by her killer. Only decomposition would, in time, remove the cruel scar on her otherwise perfect young body.

The police brought Grace's stepfather into custody. The details of his whereabouts the night Grace was last seen hadn't rung true – although not officially named a suspect, his name had already been blackened within the surrounding villages. It's funny how everyone has a story to share about Tim Matthews: the mystery of how he made his money, the affair he had with Vivienne Ellsworth, as well as her sudden disappearance, all of which now called into question. The Matthews family agreed to an interview; it was my biggest breakthrough yet, talking to the family of the *victim*. On the way, my car bumps along the uneven road surface, with every thump my head seems to wobble on my neck as the sunbeams penetrate through the glass and directly through my eyelids. My brain feels like it will explode. Whisky straight before bed – never again. As the road widens, I find myself driving down a tree-lined road with perfectly manicured gardens; the Matthews house is set back from the road, standing prestigiously behind cast-iron gates. I push the intercom and announce myself; the gates seamlessly slide open. As I step out of my car, I note how incongruous it looks next to the luxury cars parked next to the triple garage. I wonder what it feels like to live in a house like this, waking up surrounded by luxury. But it doesn't matter whether Grace's family has money or what Egyptian cotton sheets they cry their tears into because, at the end of the day, their daughter's life has been stolen from them and nothing would ever change that.

Public interest hasn't waned; in a way, I think people love the drama it's injected into this sleepy village. It's all they talk about in the pubs and shops. But with all the excitement also comes worry, especially from the older community. The local security companies have been cashing in on installing new alarm systems.

I press the doorbell, which chimes like an old-fashioned church bell. The large oak door swings open and there stands a woman with a blunt blonde bob framing her defined facial features. She looks like she's had work but not so much that she looks like one of those scary plastic surgery freaks you see on shows like *Botched*.

'You must be the reporter.' Andrea Matthews' voice is as cool as her demeanour.

'Jennifer Mack.' I extend my hand and she reluctantly takes it.

She leaves the door open as an invitation for me to follow her into the grand foyer. An imposing crystal chandelier hangs above our heads, the shadows of the sparkle it gives bounces off the gleaming wood floor. She moves with uncertainty even though she is in her own home. Her shoulders stoop as though they are weighed down with anchors of grief. The living room is a mix of coastal and classic. The décor shouldn't mesh, but it does. There are floor-to-ceiling windows giving breathtaking panoramic views of the ocean. I look out to the distance of the glassy sea; calm on the surface but the depth of the water conceals dark secrets. It knows the truth. It knows what happened to Grace Matthews. I notice a gold-framed photo on the mantle of Grace on the beach. In the portrait, fresh-faced wisps of blonde hair escape from her ponytail. She is dressed in a wetsuit with a surfboard perched at her side wedged into the sand. Andrea Matthews catches me staring at the photograph.

'We will bury her near her grandmother. They were so close, it feels only right she is with her. But who knows when her body will be released back to us.'

I think of how she looks now. Her corpse lying in the confined space of a morgue refrigerator, her body opened, and the organs removed for examination, enduring further uninvited incisions. Her photo is a cruel reminder of her fatal demise.

'It's my fault,' Andrea Matthews says. She stands by the window, her voice loud like she's making an announcement, words so important they need to be heard.

'She was two weeks overdue. I was so fed up and wanted her out of my body. I hated being pregnant, truth be told. I wanted her out. As a child, she never sat still. She talked and talked and talked, and I willed her just to be quiet. I willed it all away and now – now she's gone.'

How do you respond to a grieving mother?

'My husband didn't do it. They need a suspect, of course, to make it look like they're doing something, but Tim isn't capable of murder.'

'Do you know where he was the night Grace went missing?'

'No. But I know he didn't...' Andrea Matthews pauses and pinches the bridge of her nose.

'Are you all, right?' I want to shove the words back in my mouth the moment I utter them.

'Headache,' she says and sits down on the sofa.

I feel out of my depth. I'm here to get a story. A front-page story. But I didn't realise how hard this would be. I practised in the bathroom mirror and my rehearsal was articulate and professional, nothing like the wreck I am now.

I sit opposite and take out a tape recorder. It's retro, but it works. I know the recording will crackle later as I listen to the interview, but I'll never use my smartphone for this kind of thing; I like the feel of analogue machines.

'Are you ready to begin?'

She nods. The irony isn't lost on me that we begin at the end. The last few weeks of Grace's life. Born into privilege but never one to flaunt her parents' status, she had a job and earned her own money; she still studied as hard as she could to achieve good exam results. She was kind to others and volunteered at an animal shelter. I like the sound of Grace Matthews. But I have to ask myself, was she really this perfect? Her murderer certainly didn't think so.

'Did she have any enemies, a jealous boyfriend, anybody you could highlight to the police as a potential suspect or who might know something?'

'She was a lovely girl. I can't think of who or why somebody would want to hurt her. Deep down, I don't think she knew the person. A madman did this. And he will strike again. It's only a matter of time.'

'Why do you say that?'

'The inscription etched into her back. He's made it clear. My Grace is the first. Not only did he kill my daughter, but he used her body as his own message board.'

I find myself apologising, but there is nothing I can say and as I stumble over my words, Andrea fixes me with a firm stare: 'My daughter's body was left with a cruel message.'

CHAPTER FOUR

THEN

K *a-pow*! She walks in, dressed head to toe in black, but not in a morbid way – she's stylish.

I'm attracted to her, but so are all the boys in the room. I watch how they suddenly sit up straighter, talk deeper, and a few brave souls even offer to buy her a drink.

She pretends not to notice the attention and I don't give it to her. If I ignore her, it might make me seem intriguing; she will wonder why I'm the only one who isn't interested.

The air is thick and filled with the scent of fruity booze, perfume, and desperation. We're all here searching for something. The thumping music gives me a headache; before she got here, I was about to leave. Soon she is joined by two other girls who laugh too loudly and try too hard. It astounds me that she's friends with them; she's Gucci while they're Primark.

I don't feel invisible because I'm noticed. What is it they say? 'Any publicity is good publicity.' It's not exactly fun being the one who's the butt of the joke all the time, how the room falls silent when I walk into it followed shortly after by the sound of hushed laughter.

I'm seen, even if sometimes being seen means I'll be tormented.

She's the only girl I've felt instinctively drawn to; most girls aren't worth my time, and most girls in this school are just straight-up bitches.

Daniel Smith isn't particularly good-looking, and he's not all that smart either, but he's never without a girl hanging off his arm. He's the type of guy who gets attention with his silver tongue and twisted sense of humour, like the time he thought it was hilarious to invite Daisy Moretz to the cinema and didn't show up. The next day, photos of her standing alone outside the multi-screen complex emerged on Facebook and she became the school's meme of the year.

When he homes in on her, she takes a step back. This makes me smile. I see how the corners of his mouth turn down and embarrassment washes over him.

I've always told myself I'd be standing close by when Daniel Smith falls, and it looks as though tonight is the night, and I'm so glad the new girl is the one to do it.

Being sixteen is utter shit. Things are stirring in my inner world, and it's been painful. Each day bleeds into the next, and I'm always waiting for something big to happen. Today, I think I may have found it; now I only have to get the new girl to notice me for all the right reasons. I stand and begin to walk towards her, wanting her to see me, but then I feel a harsh shove into my shoulder. It happens so quickly I can't catch myself, and before I know it, I'm flat on my arse.

I feel my heart thud against my chest, time slows, Imogen and Samantha snigger, and one of them coughs 'Loser.'

Her big blue eyes flash apologetically, and she extends her hand, ignoring the ridicule of her two pathetic pals.

'I'm so sorry,' she says and extends her slim, perfectly

smooth hand. 'That was completely uncalled for.' She throws the comment over her shoulder.

'I'm fine,' I say and swallow down the vengeful words I want to hurl out.

'My friends have been drinking and a few too many Cosmos can make them a little psycho.'

This is how things go for me in social situations. I'm lying, I am not fine, but it grabbed her attention so I'm not going to look a gift horse in the mouth.

'Let me get you a drink to apologise for those two.'

She takes me by the arm, my previous anger tapers off and I catch a scent of her perfume, all sweet and expensive.

'I'm Grace.'

And I'm a fucking mess, but right now I'm not going to let anything stop me.

Thank you, Imogen. Thank you, Samantha!

CHAPTER FIVE

JENNIFER MACK

It's 3am and I'm still awake. So far, I've taken the maximum allowance of herbal sleeping pills – taking one more pill will push me over the edge, then I'll have an entirely different problem. But insomnia is an old friend. It comes in periods of stress: the last time I had a spell this bad was after Mum, and before that my exams, oh and when Josh left. People don't understand when I tell them how tired I am. The simple solution is, of course, to sleep. It's not as if I haven't tried. The GP referred me to a counsellor, believing my sleep issues were rooted to a much deeper issue. It wasn't exactly a poor diagnosis, she was onto something, but meeting with the counsellor was painful; not because I explored parts of myself I'd long since buried that had risen to the surface, no, I was fine with that. The problem was that Dr Mary Drake was textbook through and through. She wanted me to follow tick-box criteria and didn't see me as an actual flawed human being who was trying to find out what the hell was wrong with them. I was a mere academic frustration she tried so hard to categorise. After session three and being asked 'how does that make you feel?' for the nine-hundredth time, I ended our short-lived relationship and cancelled the remaining five sessions.

Now I'm back to spending £50 a month on acupuncture treatments and buying the latest pillow sleep mists to promise a good night's sleep. Tonight, or should I say this morning, my thoughts are with Andrea Matthews and how she remained so calm speaking about her only child who'd been murdered. She'd concealed the grief during the interview, but at times it almost bubbled over and exploded. In those moments, she'd look away to catch herself before she erupted. The interview lasted over an hour. Until a phone call came from Tim, her husband and Grace's stepfather, asking to be collected from the police station.

I lean over the bed and grab the tape recorder. Pressing play, I listen to Andrea Matthews' haunted voice:

'I know this question is hard, Mrs Matthews, and I understand if you don't want to answer, so take all the time you need. Who identified the body?'

Pause . . . crackles. . .

'I did.'

'How did it make you feel?'

Long pause.

'It's an image that will never ever leave my mind. . .'

Long pause, heavy sigh.

'I'm sorry. I can't continue.'

Click.

Exhaustion hits me like a freight train. I look in the mirror and see glassy eyes reflecting back at me. My skin feels tight and prickly. I hear the toilet flush and the click-clack of pencil-thin heels walking on the tiled floor. Hayley opens the stall door looking polished and impossibly attractive, her raven hair falling to the slender shoulders of a suit that fits her like a glove. There is an awkward silence. She smiles, but it's not quite whole. I know how I see Hayley; I wonder how she sees me. I bet she looks at me like a frumpy old hag who probably has eight to ten cats to keep me company. I nod at her and smile back. The discomfort between us is overwhelming. Since the sink next to me is broken, she waits patiently behind me while admiring her crimson-red manicure for an unrealistic amount of time. I put my hands underneath the dryer and welcome the blast of hot air to fill the silence between us.

I'm just about to leave when she blocks my path.

'So I heard you got an interview with the mother?' Her mouth moves in the most exaggerated way. 'Just how did you manage that?'

I inhale, wondering if she is annoyed that I got there first or if she's just poking fun at me. It was probably a bit of both.

I smile, half imagining her tripping over her sky-high heels and breaking one of her skinny little ankles.

'You know how it is. Right place, right time.'

She nods.

I smile and turn to leave. From the reflection, I see her pull a face. I'm too tired for a confrontation, but anger bubbles up inside me and I just can't ignore it.

'I don't need to get on my knees to get places!'

She shrugs, looking smug like the true bully she is. Oh how I want to wipe the smirk off her face, how I want to shove her skull against the wall and knee her in the gut. I wait for her answer, but it doesn't come, which only elevates my frustration. I thought this inconsequential behaviour wasn't something I'd have to deal with in adulthood, but it seems some girls never grow up. They only evolve into beings who are more condescending and have free rein to get away with more. It may be more subtle, less of the playground lark of name-calling or cyber-bullying, but it's there, and it's just as hurtful now as it was then.

Then and now. These girls always have a way of finding me.

The door opens. Olivia Manning, the local democracy reporter, walks in and gives us a suspicious look. I don't know much about Olivia; she tends to get on with her job and says very little.

I finally exit the room and feel a breath escape me. I go back to my desk which thankfully has a wall partition between Hayley and I so I can pretend she doesn't exist.

I take a sip of tepid tea when an email notification pings; it's from Olivia:

```
I was waiting for the beat of a drum.
What do you mean? I type back.
There was tension in the air when I walked in
on you and HW.
Oh, it's nothing. Just a bit of healthy
competition, that's all.
Nothing is healthy where HW is concerned.
```

We type back and forth. I am careful what I say to Olivia. A, because I don't know her and B, I am a naturally paranoid person and wonder if Hayley is behind this. I delete the messages, making sure there is no trace left behind because in the world of reporting everybody looks at everything; I should know. In the past, I longed for female friendships. I'd get very jealous of girl groups or those elite enough to have the honour of calling somebody her BFF. I've had friends over the years, but they have never lasted long and before my friendship with Hayley ended – as I suspected it would – I spent much of my time alone and used studying as a way to fill the void. I felt this loneliness every time I saw girls huddling together or heading out for their evening while

I was heading home from the library. I'd say I was like a ghost, moving in and out of the shadows, unseen, unheard. The only way I feel I can communicate is through my writing, it's the only attribute I have to speak to people, but the personal approach is taken out of it; until my interview with Andrea Matthews. My fingers are poised to type another email to Olivia, but I pause as I think of Andrea Matthews and how she is right now. There hasn't been any news on her husband since he was released.

Olivia asks me to join her for lunch, but I feel a tap on my arm just as I try to think of an excuse as to why I couldn't go. Olivia is standing next to me with a persuasive smile.

'There's a new bar in town and they do lovely light lunches, apparently. I've been meaning to try it for ages.'

'It sounds great, and thank you, but–'

'Great, let's head off now. Before Leona comes into the office and bores us all with photos of her newborn and the play-by-play of her day with her new mummy friends and the consistency of little Harry's poop.'

I can't help but let out a hearty laugh.

'Don't you wonder if life was so bloody fantastic then why does she bloody keep coming into the office? Ugh, I cannot imagine having kids, the thought of pushing one of those things out of my vagina and then being expected to care for it for the next eighteen years. No thank you!'

I shrug, and before I've had a chance to log off from the computer, she is bending down picking up my bag.

'What have you got in here, woman? Bricks?'

'Books, and–' I begin, but she was making a statement rather than asking a question.

We step out onto the slick pavement, and the sun burns through the grey clouds to expel the rain from the earlier downpour.

I make pointless conversation about the weather.

When we walk into the bar, there's a large-screen TV, an old Man Utd vs Liverpool game blaring chants of drunk football fans. We are greeted by the bartender. He is neat and clean; his tanned skin setting off his blue eyes.

'What's your poison?' Olivia asks.

'I'll just take a mocktail.'

'Umm... really!' she says.

I feel a burn at the back of my throat desperately begging to be expelled by a cold, crisp glass of white wine. 'Yes, really.'

Olivia secures us two drinks and a bowl of snacks before we order our lunch. She leans in close to me.

'I actually have an ulterior motive for lunch today. I didn't want anybody to overhear us at work.'

I try to keep my voice indifferent. 'Okay?'

'I heard things.'

I want to drag the words out of her mouth and not be subjected to the suspense which she seems to enjoy building up. She clears her throat and tucks a loose dark curl behind her ear. I notice how her nose is dusted lightly with freckles in a way that makes her youth shine through.

'I heard Hayley chatting to Mike about you, and then I saw Mike go to Jacob.'

'What did you hear?'

'It's hard to tell you this, but I feel like I should because I don't actually like Hayley, and I don't trust her.'

I take a sip of my mocktail which is drowned in so much ice I can barely taste the drink.

'Just tell me.'

Olivia takes a swig of her whisky and Coke and sets the glass gently on the bar.

'She said she was concerned about your mental state after

what happened to you at university. Said they should probably remove you from the Grace Matthews case.'

My heart stops. My mouth goes dry. The room sways like I'm on the surface of a stormy sea; the beautiful smell of booze now seems too overwhelming, too pungent. My temples begin to throb with the start of a migraine.

My insides churn, my fists tighten into balls. This is not a side of myself that comes out as often as it used to, and I'm almost surprised it's still there.

'I wish that Hayley wouldn't stoop so fucking low to try and snatch this away from me.' I bang my fist on the bar and feel my chest tighten. My tongue feels rough, I'm trying to fight the overwhelming craving that grows more persistent with every second that passes.

A phone call interrupts us. It's my neighbour, Kitty, who works at the police station. As I pick up the line, she whispers into the phone so quietly I can barely make out her words.

'They found another body in an abandoned video shop in London. Grace number two.'

CHAPTER SIX

JENNIFER MACK

Brooding clouds knit together and turn the sky charcoal to match the mood of the mourners. A group of young women walk with their arms interlinked, as if they are holding one another up for support; their shoulders slumped under the weight of grief and the sudden pull of Death's hand. A sea of people dressed in black circle the gravesite like ravens. Mounds of earth lie piled next to the large gaping hole in the ground, which looks like an open maw ready to devour the beautifully polished coffin. Among the crowd are tear-stained faces. I stand back and wonder how many people would attend my funeral? The thought of being alone even after death terrifies me – is that even possible?

Some people choose death to end their suffering, whether it be physical or mental. My mother believed a spirit goes to its own funeral, the final farewell before they move from earth's plane to heaven, hell, or somewhere in between. I'm not a religious person (even when standing in church listening to prayer and hymns today, I didn't feel connected to God) but I do believe there has to be something greater than us. Otherwise, what's the fucking point? I told myself after Mum was buried that her body was nothing but the vehicle that carried her through life, but I still tell myself she watches over me.

Andrea Matthews is shrouded in the arms of her husband and stares vacantly into space, her skin ashen, like part of her soul has left her. She must know life will never be the same again. I try to imagine what it is like for her, the entire injustice of the situation: a violent murder, burying her child, of all the improbable endings.

I look at Tim Matthews. He looks younger than his wife, and perhaps that's because of the burden of grief she holds, what with being biologically connected to Grace. My mind is riddled with questions today. I'm eager to piece together the facts of this heinous crime, but today my heart won't allow it. Today, my heart is with the family who lost a daughter, a sister, a friend, a colleague. The clouds give way and rain begins to fall. I hear a muffled voice next to me.

'Even heaven is crying today. It wasn't her time.'

Back at the office, daily sounds like the clicking of a keyboard, a phone ringing, and laughter ignite a sobering reality like a slap in the face. Life does go on. 'Today's news is tomorrow's fish and chip paper' as the old saying goes. I enter the staffroom and make myself a cup of tea; I sit quietly at the table and blow the steam from the cup, inhaling the comforting scent of a good English brew. But a cup of tea, no matter how good, isn't going to fix this one. I pull out my old battered notebook and start jotting down the events of today.

The funeral of Grace Matthews, whose body was

found by local fisherman Terrance Harding, was on Wednesday 7 July.

Grace Matthews, 22, is described by her family and friends as a loving, fun girl who was kind and witty and had a heart of gold. Police are treating her death as murder, and an ongoing investigation is taking place. Fears have rippled through the local community that this is not a one-off killing and perhaps something more sinister.

Today, over two hundred people gathered at St Mary Magdalene's C of E church in Truro. Crowds of family and friends braved the harsh weather conditions to bid farewell to Grace. Tomorrow, we will move on, but Grace's family and friends will forever have a gaping hole in their hearts.

I have a deadline and my moral side is telling me I should just write about Grace Matthews, a tribute to her and her grieving family and friends, but that isn't going to grab the headlines.

CHAPTER SEVEN

THEN

My morning breath warms the pillow. I open my eyes and wait for my blurred vision to clear – it is then that I realise it was not a dream: I *am* here. Downstairs, I can hear a barking dog. I walk barefoot to the edge of the steps and stand listening, my feet sinking into the plush carpet. I wonder if I should sneak out of the house, convincing myself it was an alcohol-fuelled evening which brought me here.

I slowly creep downstairs, thinking I should leave, but the house is so warm, so inviting. I feel like I am in one of those shows on MTV where they show beautiful stars' homes. Everything has a place, and everything belongs – except me. I hover in the kitchen doorway, watching her. Her butter-blonde hair is pulled up in one of those effortless ponytails. She pours coffee in a mug that looks like hand-knitted porcelain. The rich aroma of freshly ground coffee beans lures me in a step closer. When she sees me standing there, my curly hair matted and knotted and wearing one of her T-shirts, I expect a look of disgust – instead, she leans against the kitchen worktop and says, 'Sleep well, love?'

My heart skips a beat, and I freeze – *'love'*, the smoothness of her voice echoes in my head – I feel euphoric. I am desperate to stay, but I cannot be late for work. My boss has already given me a warning, and I have done my best to be on time and put in more effort; as much as anyone can serving greasy bacon sandwiches and weak grey tea to sweaty, tattooed workmen. It was a world apart from the home I find myself standing in. The town is split into two parts: council high-rise estates and leafy, prestigious detached homes known as 'rich man's row'. The poor say it's only dirty money that can afford such lavish houses, probably high-class prostitution and drugs. Meanwhile, the rich say the poor can't get ahead in life because they are ill-educated and lazy, relying on government benefits to pay their way and get something for nothing. The divide is real. I need this job to help put food on the table. Mum's health is declining, and her benefits aren't enough to cover the cost of food for the week. Things were so bad last month I had to resort to a food bank: I queued with all the other unfortunates. Mum had been borrowing money from Aunt Lizzy and spending it all on weed, which she claimed was for medicinal purposes to numb the pain. Aunt Lizzy had been generous but now that she's met that creep Alan from The Old Bull and Bush, she needs money to splash out on new clothes and make-up. Aunt Lizzy said Mum owes her close to a thousand pounds; mind you, Aunt Lizzy received a massive inheritance from Uncle Mark, and maybe she could have let Mum off, but she wanted it back, with interest. I should feel jealous of Grace; all the things she has around her. I'm sure this house is filled with wonderful memories – a place where Christmas is magical, and summers are sun-kissed and blissful. I've been stripped of all of that, and I am the one playing the grown-up, worrying about things I shouldn't have to worry about. I promise myself I won't make the same mistakes my mother did: I won't fall in line with the rest of them, claim benefits, complain about the immigrants stealing our jobs, all the while sitting at home watching mindless cooking programmes on food I will never cook, where the highlight of the week is going to Tesco late on a Thursday night when they put out the reduced meats.

Grace's kitchen is a mix of old and new, with cool, grey marble countertops and extravagantly exposed wooden beams. She sits down on a rustic chair the colour of burnt toast and taps her delicate manicured fingernails on the chair next to her.

'Sit,' she says, warmly.

Tra-la. Inside, I am all jitters and butterflies. The most beautiful girl I have ever seen is right in front of me, and she wants me to stay longer. I am so happy. Thoughts of work suddenly melt into the background, and nothing else matters at this moment... For a change, I don't want to play by the rules; I don't want to be responsible. At times I have felt dead. Not even depressed, beyond that – because at least with depression, you feel something. Indifference is worse than depression but sitting with Grace makes all of that disappear.

'Considering how much I drank last night, I don't feel too bad.'

For someone who downed seemingly half her body weight in wine, Grace looks like she has spent a weekend at a spa, all relaxed and clean. I feel damp and clammy under my arms, my eyes feel stingy and tight and my throat itches. I need water, how much did I drink? One bottle... two... three?

I lean my back against the chair and can't find my voice. I'm stumped for what I should talk about, afraid if I am myself this moment will end, and it will be nothing but a memory I will forever long for. It's funny, I fear losing something which is not even mine. If she knew my feelings, she would run and who could blame her? Even I am scared of how intense this feels. I long to run my fingers through her silky hair, let it out of its ponytail, and watch it cascade down to the small of her back, which is exposed from her vest riding up. Smooth skin yields to a taut stomach and a silver hoop shines in her belly button. I try to take in all of her, without making it obvious.

'You're welcome to stay as long as you like, but I have to get ready soon.'

My heart falls into my stomach.

'Plans?' My voice sounds a bit too high-pitched to be casual.

'I have a job interview. I applied for a position in the local nursery.'

'I don't think I could work with kids. They're so unpredictable and they–'

'A garden nursery, as in plants.' She laughs. 'I know it seems to some like a really boring job, but I absolutely love watching things grow from a small seed to a blooming flower.'

I never really cared for flowers, Mum always bought the discount flowers from the old perv, Jim Croker, at the Saturday market, but I just thought the joy from them was too temporary, like everything in my life.

'I didn't think you would have to work.'

'My father came from humble beginnings, he worked really hard to get where he is today, and he taught me to know the value of true graft.' *Graft* – the word sounds foreign on her lips; her articulate tone doesn't carry the meaning of the word with conviction.

CHAPTER EIGHT

JENNIFER MACK

I wedge my body into the tiny space next to the window, sitting next to a man who smells of stale fags masked with cheap deodorant.

It's raining, and everyone looks depressed. More passengers board at the next two stops – they huddle together, taking up every inch of space, soggy umbrellas drip onto the floor. I try to read a book, but I feel so hot I can't concentrate, my coat clinging to my skin and the bumps along the tracks making me feel nauseous. I close my eyes and will myself to tame the anxiety building up inside me. Over the years, I have tried many tactics to loosen the grip of my anxiety, the only thing that works is the one thing I need to control, or it will control me.

As soon as the doors slide open, people spill out onto the concrete platform and swarm like hornets toward the exit. I insert my card in the mouth of the ticket barrier, a red light flashes up: *seek assistance*. People bump up behind me as I disrupt the natural order of the morning sequence. It is nigh on impossible to find a staff member. After what seems like forever, I find a big burly man, whose breathing sounds so laboured, I worry he is going to pass out. He takes my ticket in his huge hands.

'Off peak.' He slaps the ticket back into my palm and points me toward a tiny office to pay the excess fare.

'But I asked for a return . . . and–'

'It's your responsibility to make sure you've been issued the correct ticket. You might have to pay the excess, or maybe a fine. Ticket office will decide.' He begins to cough – a nasty hacking cough – and turns away from me.

I swim against the crowd and make my way to the ticket office which has a long queue. I am hot, flustered, and very pissed off. I'm finally served and bolt for the Tube. I cannot be late.

Outside, it feels cold and unwelcoming. London is bold. I have always wanted a slice of London life, but for a fleeting moment, I long to be back in Cornwall walking along the familiar craggy streets, hearing the hiss of the sea, where there are only two choices for coffee and not ninety-six. Here, everything moves in fast-forward, everybody is in a hurry, and nobody seems happy. The heady aroma of car exhaust fumes feels overpowering and if there was a volume button on London, it's been turned up to the max. Every other shop is a café and I'm lured in to a small Italian Café by the smell of toast and melted butter as I pause in the doorway listening to early morning chatter, plates and cups clinking together and the hiss of milk being steamed. My stomach growls in protest but my nerves won't allow food, it will reject it. This is the capital of the country, the place people long to be; *they'd sell their grandmother to the devil*, as Mum would say, if it bought them a flat the size of a box so long as it came with a London postcode. So far, I was not being drawn into the appeal. It is not matching my fantasy, it would take some getting used to. Cornwall knew my secrets. It was a place of both comfort and pain, but it was always home.

I arrive in High Holborn. It's as I imagined; a long street flanked by tall Victorian buildings and flashy advertising boards, black taxis lining the side of the road, yellow lights on ready and waiting for a passenger.

Lilith Grain is diminutive. Her office seems too big for her; she stands no taller than four feet. Her dark eyes bore into mine; her ultra-short, pixie-style hair sharpening her angular face. When she speaks, she does so with authority, for what she lacks in height, she makes up in confidence. Duncan, who owns Fruits & Roots back in Cornwall, used to talk of short man syndrome; I wonder if the same could be true for women? Grain is a veteran in her field, she's served in the Metropolitan Police for fourteen years, starting as constable and climbing her way to chief inspector and detective chief inspector. She rose to stardom for her role in capturing Derek Johnson, the serial killer known as the King's Cross Ripper, and the South Kensington Strangler. She wrote a book of her account of capturing Johnson called I Found You in the Dark; it featured in a documentary on the BBC and was optioned for a mini-series.

'Thank you for seeing me today, Miss Grain.' I extend my hand out, which she takes but then snaps back just as quickly, like I have a virus. Her fucking name is as bad as her handshake; all starchy and self-righteous. I imagine she has no close relationships and if she does, she'll be a dominatrix with a whip and adopt a Russian accent forcing her mortals into submission. The weight of the journey has started to catch up with me, I do not feel sharp, and I am hoping she will at the very least offer me a cup of tea, water, but she doesn't.

'The connection of the murders. Grace 1 and Grace 2.' I hold my breath as I notice the ghost of a smile curl her thin lips.

There is no room for mistakes. No possibility of a rewrite. Lilith taps her fingers; silence fills the room, and I'm aware that I'm sweating. I hope she doesn't see the inexperience flooding out of my pores.

My stomach turns over with nerves. *Say something.*

'This must be a very big story for you?'

'The biggest!' I want to shove the words back into my mouth – what a childish response!

'A few things I should educate you on, Miss Mack. The relationship between the police and the media should be taken with integrity, impartiality, and it is my job to safeguard the confidentiality of information, as it is also my duty to be open and transparent.'

'I understand.'

'Good. I don't like the media. Too many times our investigations are muddied with inaccurate information all just to grab the headlines. If you are one of those reporters, which I suspect you are, then it is better you leave now. Safe travels back to Cornwall, a lovely part of the world. You can let yourself out.'

I am at a loss for words. I have travelled for hours to get here to see Lilith Grain. I feel heat rise and anger set in. This is something she could have told me on the phone, in an email. Why get me to travel all this way to tell me to leave?

I sit straighter, pull my shoulders back. I know what I need to do.

I hold Lilith's gaze, reset my focus, clear my throat. I catch my reflection in the window behind Lilith, its view of a brick wall, and I don't recognise myself, perhaps it's the unfamiliar surroundings or the voice in my head telling me to grab this opportunity or regret it forever. A smile stretches across my face. I can hear the confidence in my voice as I say, 'Yes, Cornwall is lovely, but a heinous murder has taken place and now a second one. I'm not here for a thrill – I fully respect your position and your reputation, but I also need you to respect mine. I can write any story, I can write a horror even Stephen King would take note of, but that's not why I am here. Yes, the media has a bad rep, but with all due respect, so do the police and wouldn't it be something if we worked together to help get a killer, a potential serial killer, off the streets.'

I take a breath. 'Work with me, Lilith.'

'Impressive speech. I admire your passion, but–'

'No buts and no more bullshit. I haven't travelled all this way for you to send me away. I'm here for a story. I will get it. How many times did you get snubbed, walked over, dismissed because you were a woman? I know this about you, Miss Grain, because you talked about it in an interview with Aaron Priestley. It's not a well-known interview but let me just say, I can do my homework too. Why did you even invite me here if all you intended to do is shove me out? Let's work together.'

Lilith's eyes narrow, and I keep my face set even.

'What do you need?' she asks. I pause long enough to make her ask me again. 'Well?'

'An exclusive. You only talk to *The Cornwall Chronicle* about the London murder; to be clear, just me.'

There have been too many moments when I have asked myself, *What if?*

I leave it there. I thank Lilith for her time and remind her she has my number. It's a bold move, and this could go one way or another. I pick up my bag and leave the office and navigate through the busy police station where the silence is replaced by ringing phones, loud voices, and chaos.

When I'm out of the building, I walk to the corner of the street and take several deep, slow breaths.

CHAPTER NINE

THEN

The deep fryer had formed a waxy substance around the surface just begging to be scraped away; plates dirtied with ketchup and dried egg from the breakfast rush are piled up. The smell of fat hangs in the air, made even worse by it being such a stifling day without the hint of a breeze. I'll carry the stink of the café home with me later. Already I am imagining a cool shower and soap being washed into my skin, cleansing me of this horrible place. It's quiet for now, but soon the pace will crank up into another gear when the workmen arrive for lunch like a gaggle of geese – hungry and impatient, ordering food that will clog their arteries and take them on their first journey to a heart attack before they reach fifty.

When the workers arrive, they will not pay attention to me. I'm just there to take their orders and serve them quickly. They don't know my name, but I've learnt to respond to clicking fingers and the occasional 'love'.

I move through the café, wiping the tables clean and setting cutlery, neat napkins, and bottles of ketchup and mayo while trying to think back to this morning – the house, privilege, wealth, a world I so desperately want to be part of. Ian, *Boss Boy* as he likes to be called, likes to point out errors, his favourite quote being 'missed a spot'. If I had a bloody pound for every time he said that to me, I'd be a millionaire, so I would. I think of Grace and feel a wave of embarrassment over who I am, working in this place, living where I live. She's used to having the best of everything, you can tell, even by her every well-spoken word. I found myself trying to speak better when I was with her, not wanting the real me to penetrate through. See, we are all born into one of two things in this part of the world: wealth or poverty.

Ian emerges from the kitchen in his stained apron, his balding hairline glistening with sweat. 'Got some extra shifts next week.'

I shrug. 'Thanks, can I let you know?'

'You are always begging for extra shifts. Got somewhere better to be?'

'I...' I can't think of an excuse. 'That would be great,' I say, wishing I did have somewhere better to be, but I need the cash. I won't be telling Mum about the extra shifts. She'll spend my money before I've even cashed the cheque. I need to start looking out for myself. Fuck her.

Ian slaps my back and I feel myself stiffen at his touch. It's the first time he's ever put his hands on me, and I don't like it. Sometimes I've noticed him staring at me, but up until now I thought that was just to be an overbearing boss, but there is something in his touch that brings a strong sense of unease. His hands do not belong on me. My mind flashes back:

My bedroom, Queen poster on the wall, the door slowly opening, I pull the covers tightly round my shoulders, a whisper, a shush, a promise I am made to keep it our little secret. Freddie Mercury's smile is what I focus on, he's the one who gets me through it.

When Ian leaves the kitchen, I feel like I can't breathe. I reach for a knife, small but its blade sharp enough; I take a quick look over my shoulder to make sure nobody is watching and slip the knife under my T-shirt. I need to splash cold water on my face, I go to the toilet, which smells of stale urine and bleach. It is clear someone attempted to clean up the mess, but it has done nothing to mask the smell. I pull down my jeans and press the knife into my inner thigh, dragging it along my pale flesh until blood begins to well. Soon it will scar into a thin white line, like the rest, but for now I enjoy the stinging sensation and watch the dark crimson trickle down my leg. I am the one in control of my pain, just for a short while the memories fade. For now, I breathe a little easier.

One Week Later

I wasn't expecting her. She walks into The Coffee Bean. Effortlessly stylish – she looks soapy clean even from a distance. She smiles politely at the barista; it's easy to see that she is a nice person. She runs her hand through that pretty butter-blonde hair, and I wish I were close enough to inhale her scent. I recognise the girl she is with, delightful Imogen. She is not polite; she doesn't look up from her phone as she orders a skinny latte. I'm only here for the free wifi and to cash in on the free coffee voucher I snipped out of the paper.

I sink back a little further, allowing the sofa to swallow me. Beside her is a soft brown leather handbag; simple, expensive. I spy a book, but *what book*? I edge closer, grab my phone and open the camera – full zoom – hoping my one shot gets me the information I need. S*nap*!

Stephen King – oh I never had her down for a horror fan,

the king of horror at that: *A Good Marriage*. Interesting, very interesting. There's a Waterstones on the main high street, what time is it? 3.30pm. I have time. Imogen places a copy of a woman's magazine called *Grazia* next to her tall glass and takes a photo.

Why?

Oh, of course – social media. Art, impression, desperation. I have not jumped on the social media bandwagon; I prefer to remain anonymous, hold my own power and not let other people decide my worth by how many likes I get. That, and there's also the lack of friends in my life – you need to be 'social' to have a network of people to connect with.

Social media belongs to arseholes, that's where you'll find them all; forget a natural pose at Aunt Mary's sixtieth, it's all about lighting, angles, and don't get me started on the whole 'caring is cool' gang, the armchair philanthropists whose only real care is themselves and how much attention their charitable posts will gain – how sweet!

My heart skips a beat. She looks in my direction, curious. I'm all too aware I look like shit in the same pair of jeans I've had on for three days straight, and they're sagging, coupled with a T-shirt that if you look close enough, you'll see a faint tea stain that refuses to wash out. *I'm a mess.*

She walks over, smile fixed; thank God Imogen hasn't followed, but I still see her cold, judgy eyes. I can almost hear her voice 'loser', but I don't care.

'Well, fancy seeing you here.' She puts her coffee next to mine. 'All better?' I don't know what she means. *Was I sick?* Is that why I woke up at her house last week and haven't gotten her out of my mind since. If I made an arse out of myself, she's not letting it show; no, she is acting like a sweetheart.

'I'm good, thanks. You?' My tone comes out a bit too matter-of-fact, but she doesn't seem to pick up on it.

'I'm great! I got the job at the nursery, starting Sunday.'

Sunday. I take note.

'Congratulations.' I don't know what else to say but there is so much I want to say, need to say to keep her talking, keep her next to me. I want her to see me again. Not just bump into, because today, right now must be fated. It must be!

'Thanks, I'm excited.' I can see that she means it, her almond eyes wide and bright. Excited over seedlings and soil? Well, it doesn't match her look, but then people think they know me just by how I look. They couldn't be more wrong.

'Anyway, I better get going. It was really nice to see you.'

She didn't have to come and say hello, but she did and it means something.

She's walking away, and I watch Imogen meet her gaze mouthing her disapproval; I could let it go and I probably should, but that kind of behaviour only transcends me to *loserdom*.

'Hey Grace.' My voice is confident, strong. She turns back, still smiling. *Thank God.*

Imogen looks away.

'Let's catch up after you start your job.'

She raises her eyebrows. 'You really want to hear about photosynthesis?'

'Well, I'm keen.' She has no idea.

'What's your number? I'll drop you a call, then you'll have mine and we can arrange a date.'

A *date*. Did she just say that out loud, in this coffee-house surrounded by above-themselves people, trendy geeks with their thick-rimmed glasses and Apple Macs, and, of course, Imogen with her jaw clenched shut. She isn't even bothering to hide her disapproval; her icy gaze is boring into me. Grace is not her friend; she's her possession and I am a big annoyance. People like Imogen think the world should fall at their feet because of their good looks, their expensive clothing, their privilege. Tough shit.

Our numbers electronically exchange, and my stomach flips in the same way as when you're at the top of a rollercoaster and about to fall – and I know I am falling hard.

Waterstones is quiet for this time of day. Usually when school breaks, it's busy. There is something about the smell of books that is so alluring. You can live a thousand lives through books. I love bookshops; the sensation of flipping through the pages. There is something fundamentally harmonious about choosing a book, or the book choosing you. My gaze travels over the new titles section. My fingertips delicately touch the spines and trace the names of authors, some I have not heard of and some old-timers who have cemented their name in the lit world: Martina Cole, a veteran of crime writing like Mike Tyson is in the world of boxing. Then the young adult section appealing to tweens and women (although they won't admit to it) transfixed into the world of Edward Cullen and Bella Swan's romantic fantasy. I do not know what I would have done if the book in Grace's bag had been Meyer instead of King; would it have piqued my interest in the same way? Would I have thought differently of her? There is something to be said about Meyer though. She has transcended her words to a diverse audience, the woman who had a dream and in her waking world spun it on its head, making her dream a global phenomenon – like it or loathe it, everybody has heard of it. The sleek black bookshelves house something for every taste. I need to get to horror first, but before I do something catches my eye. The book stands like an ornament, waiting to be noticed, to be *touched. Held. Read.* The orange background is hard on the eyes, the woman on the cover holds her cuffed wrists close to her neck as if she herself has surrendered. Even with her eyes closed, she looks euphoric. Then I notice the orange jumpsuit, a garment that identifies her as a prisoner, the dress code of the damned. The last thing I see is the title *Monster*. Yes, yes, I remember the movie with Charlize Theron. It was a long time ago and I only saw it once, but it is one of those stories that stays with you. I didn't see Aileen Wuornos as a devil woman, not the cold-hearted killer she was portrayed to be, if anything I resonated with her. The scene with the baseball bat flashes in my mind, the barbaric cruelty of a man asserting power over a woman, put to death like a dangerous dog, but just like a dangerous dog she was fighting back out of fear, out of pain. Nobody thought about her pain. Didn't try to put her on a pathway to rehabilitation. She wasn't evil, she was broken and she had to pay the price of a judicial system that failed her over and over again, shoving that baseball bat up her arse one last time and executing her by lethal injection.

Rest in peace, Aileen Wuornos.

For those who have failed you, may they pay.

For those who hurt you, may they pay.

For those who have judged you, let them too be judged.

I come across another book about Jeffrey Dahmer. People say he was born evil. He wasn't born into the arms of loving parents, he was isolated, he had no friends and no one to talk to, I resonate with him too.

I often thought of *him* and all the different ways to punish him, most of these thoughts included a knife, sometimes surgical scissors, and the severing of his dick. I imagine the blood. *So much blood.* The pain wouldn't be enough, but at least he couldn't hurt anyone anymore. His weapon, his pleasure – *gone,* but his testicles would remain in place. He could never again satisfy his sick sexual needs, never again darken the doors of my private surroundings. Never again will Freddie Mercury need to save me.

'Can I help you with anything?' A friendly voice interrupts my thoughts.

His fiery red hair sits on his head like a flame; he's kind and he has a round face that softens his features.

'Stephen King,' I say, letting out a long, shaky breath. 'I think... it's called *A Good Marriage*.'

'Right this way.'

I follow him to the horror section. King has his own shelf; why wouldn't he? He is his own genre. His own league. The classics have their place: Carrie, what a goddamn hero. Dear Pennywise, IT, the creepy smile masquerading the evil within.

'Ah, here it is.' Flame Boy hands me *A Good Marriage*. It's different from the rest of King's mammoth books, thinner, so much thinner.

'Thank you,' I say to Flame Boy. He smiles and politely interprets my attention to the book blurb as an invitation to leave.

Aside from an empty carton of milk, half a pack of ham – dry and curling at the sides – and a Dijon mustard bottle at least three years old, the fridge is empty. As usual. I slam the door shut and swear under my breath. My stomach grumbles in protest; I should have popped into Tesco after I left Waterstones, it was only next door, but I wanted to get back, to start reading.

The flat feels especially oppressive today. Mum snores on

the sofa, her long, grimy toenails peep out from her tattered duvet. I can't remember the last time she washed it; it has long since lost the whiteness and has turned tobacco yellow, the corners fraying from where she bites the ends like a child does with their favourite toy. I study her as she sleeps, wondering how I came from her, grew inside her, how her fragile, broken body somehow managed to sustain my life. Next to her is an energy drink, and crumbs of toast and own-brand chocolate spread. The curtains are shut, banishing the last dregs of the sunlight; windows closed shut, trapping in the sickly air. I don't press her on making healthy choices or prompt her to go to the doctor for that hacking cough she's had for weeks. Nor do the blood-spattered tissues she leaves on her bed alarm me. Should they?

Sputter, sputter. Her bony frame wriggles on the sofa like a fish out of water; she bolts upright and holds her throat, gasping to catch her breath. She sees me, waves her arms frantically, pointing to the kitchen. I pause and watch her eyes bulge. Her skin glistens. Bloody mucus expels from her mouth. *I transfix my gaze onto the flowery wallpaper, the bright red blooms which have been a part of these walls for as long as I can remember. Mum is with him, loved up, watching Saturday night game shows under the covers. He watches me with hooded eyes, but she doesn't notice. Eventually she falls asleep and it's just me and him. She doesn't feel him move away, doesn't hear him open my bedroom door. She doesn't keep me safe.* I glance at the kitchen clock – 18:36 – and can't help but think of how the doctors call it on *ER* – *time of death.* Only she isn't dead, she's on her hands and knees crawling toward the kitchen, her body becoming slower with every movement until finally, she falls flat onto her stomach. Then there is silence.

Tick-tock... tick-tock.

Can I call it?

I move towards her, gently roll her over. A gentle pull of her shoulder is all it takes. There is no rise and fall of her chest, her eyes are glassy. I don't need to move any closer to know she's gone.

I call it: 18:38.

CHAPTER TEN

The paramedic chews the side of her mouth and grunts. Her green uniform is so tight it restricts her movement, she reminds me of an overfilled shopping bag, only it's her stomach spilling over. She looks at me as if she's searching for clues.

'Was Mum sick for long?' *Mum*, she says, like we are siblings.

'Cancer!' I say deadpan, at least that's what I think.

'I'm sorry. Do you have any relatives we can call on your behalf?'

'No.' I think of Aunt Lizzy, but I don't want her to come after me for Mum's debt, but I guess it's only a matter of time before she does anyway.

'I want to stay here,' I protest.

'I understand you are under a great deal of stress, but at your age–'

I cut her off. 'I'm sixteen, I can live alone. It's me who pays for everything in this place anyway. Mum was sponging off me.'

Her voice softens and she takes a deep breath. 'But still... it's best you call somebody, a friend perhaps, to come and stay with you. I lost my own mother when I was young, and I'll tell you, it's a shock to the system.'

I don't understand why people feel the need to share snippets of their lives as if we are now bonded by losing a parent at a young age. I can't be 'bonded' with every fucker whose parents croaked. Shit happens. People die.

Watching her take her last breath exhilarated me to the core, as if somehow watching her die freed the resentment I had harboured for so long. The paramedic, named Dawn, fixes her eyes on me and waits. I can tell she is searching for one ounce of emotion because we are all expected to act in a certain way, do certain things. Well, fuck that, fuck it all! I really don't care what people think of me. The sound of the zip of the body bag rips through the air, the exact moment when a person becomes a body. *The end.*

When the buzz of the emergency services dies down and her body is taken away, there is a gentle knock at the door. It interrupts my cleaning session. So far, I have managed to wipe all the surfaces with bleach, open the windows, and fill the flat with fresh air. It feels chilly but comforting, like I had exorcised the demons haunting this place for years. I mentally plan all the things I will do with the flat to make it my own; a lick of paint maybe? Now that she's gone, the possibilities are endless. Another knock, harder this time. I am reluctant to open the door and wonder why they didn't buzz in on the intercom, but it's not as if this block is secure; anybody can push past those hollow wooden doors. There isn't any neighbourly community here, there are so many different tenants, tenants of tenants, illegals. Car alarms go off so frequently they are ignored, we are tower rats, the scum of society. I open the door to see a man and a woman standing there, they both smile but it doesn't quite reach their eyes. Both look past me and into the flat.

'Can I help you?' I ask.

'We're from social services. This is Brian Keith and I'm Sandra Power.'

I almost laugh out loud.

Well, well, well. Social services, here on my doorstep and so quickly too.

Where the fuck were you four years ago?

Sandra waits to be invited in, but Brian steps forward. I block the door with my arm.

'Now is not a good time,' I say.

Sandra looks to Brian; she's new at this, I can tell. I have met enough social workers to pick out the ones who've been on the job for years and the eager new blood who think they're going to change the world one case at a time.

'We were informed of your mother's passing and are here to offer support, especially as you are still under the age of eighteen.'

Support – the word hangs in the air like a bad stench. I stand staring at them both, the couple of misfits that they are, ticking boxes, filing paperwork; at the end of the day, that's what it's all about.

'May we come in?' Brian asks.

'Not a good time, I'm afraid,' I say with a shrug. And I mean it too, these people are making my newly clean air toxic again and I am starting to feel irritated. I feel my body temperature rise and I swallow hard, trying to suppress my thoughts and not let them out in the open.

'We really just want to help.' Sandra looks at me with pleading eyes, she wants in, and Brian is frustrated, reeling off a load of old shit about my safety and welfare which I am blocking out. I feel my lips curl into a smirk because if this wasn't so bloody tragic it would be a fucking comedy.

'Thank you for your concern,' I say, 'but I want to be alone right now. I have a lot to process–'

'We understand it must be hard for you to process, but we have a duty of care.' Brian cuts me off, his tone authoritative and cold. His smirk sours into a sneer.

'Duty of care?' I ask. 'That's interesting. Have the policies changed in the last four years, because I don't really recall you following up on me when I needed your support back then.'

I can feel a vein pulsing in my forehead.

'There is some history we are aware of,' Sandra says. 'We can talk about this inside.' She turns to Brian whose eyes are narrowed, and he sucks his teeth; the nice guy act truly dropping away.

'No. We can't. As I said, I want to be left alone. My mother isn't even a cold corpse on a slab yet, and you think you can come over for some tea and a pat on the head? Leave me alone!' I snap.

Brian turns his gaze on me, barely blinking. He takes a deep breath and says, 'We're here for you, we totally understand the shock and grief you must be feeling.' He pauses, smiles. 'And at times like these, from our experience, getting the right support early on can be very beneficial for you in the long term.' He isn't that great an actor with his faux display of compassion and caring. He's just here because it's how he pays the rent. I know they can't force their way in, they know it too, but it doesn't stop Brian reeling off a load of rehearsed bullshit. Words with no meaning, a heart without a beat. No bloody way was I going to invite them in. It would, inevitably, end horribly.

'Look,' I say. 'You're just too fucking late. Everything I needed from you fuckwits is in the past now, but I am sure you can find some other poor unfortunate and maybe, just maybe you'll help them.' I clench the door handle and with as much strength as I can muster, slam it firmly in their self-righteous faces.

Since Mum's funeral, I've been dancing to my own rhythm. I've stripped every wall of that hideous wallpaper, I've thrown out the curtains which clung on to years of decay, and the bathroom no longer smells of damp and piss. It's no show home, but it looks different, *feels* different. Aunt Lizzy has been hounding me for the money Mum owed her and I tell her it's nothing to do with me. Mum never had a will, never had any savings but she did have life insurance, go figure. Since I am her immediate family, the money goes to me and Aunt Lizzy can go to hell if she thinks she's ever getting her hands on it. I messaged Grace after Mum died, she was kind and has reached out to me every day since, but I am not ready to see her right now. I feel like I need to retreat. Like a caterpillar in a chrysalis, I need to re-emerge when I am a butterfly. I want her to see me in a different light. Not because she ever looked at me in a way that ever made me feel ashamed of myself, not because she ever spoke to me like she didn't want me there. It isn't like that. I want to be better around her and feel good for me. Before Grace, there was Hannah. She was beautiful too. I was into her, but my feelings for Grace are far more intense. It was fun for a while, but our relationship shifted; I guess it was a first crush, maybe first love kind of thing. I'm not sure. The shift happened when she became more into me than I was her, it changed the dynamics. It made it boring. I didn't pull away from her immediately, but she noticed the small, subtle changes and she mentioned them, no, correction, hounded me every single goddam time I saw her and it was just too much. I'd been carrying so much emotional baggage I couldn't carry her too. I did things, bad things, to make her hate me, but she just kept coming back for more. I was as patient as could be. We were at different schools and that helped widen the distance. 'I'd do anything for you. I'd kill for you,' she said on the night I told her I couldn't carry on. She knelt down next to me; I saw her like a leech, a bloodsucking parasite that I couldn't get rid of. That was the first time I ever really thought about it.

'You'd really kill for me?' I asked.

When people say they'd do anything for you, they rarely think you'll take them up on it. It's as if the elaborate gesture is enough. But it isn't enough.

After I asked the question, she was quiet. Silence filled the room and with each passing moment I could feel myself start to crack, my fists tightened into a ball and I was ready to punch something... somebody... her.

'I would,' she finally said.

The call came the next morning. Hannah was dead.

I guess she really did love me after all.

CHAPTER ELEVEN

NEWQUAY

The alarm on Gwen's phone buzzed and vibrated on the bedside table at 7.15am. The cat kneaded his paws into her pillow, his purrs growing louder. Gwen liked to get up early, as she took these quiet moments for herself to stretch and scroll through her phone. She thought of the day ahead, the filth that awaited her. Nobody ever noticed the cleaner, but they noticed when things had not been cleaned. She was an invisible servant. After several headbutts and a tail-slap in the face, Gwen gave in to Darwin's plea for breakfast. As soon as she sat up, the cat leapt to the floor, racing to the door, looking back for confirmation his owner was still coming. She made a cup of tea, wiped down an already clean surface, and took a sip from her mug. In the silence, she observed her hands; they were dry and cracked, her fingernails brittle from the endless chemicals and hand washing. They were the vital, yet worn-out tools for her work, but she was grateful because without them she'd have even less.

She left her flat and ventured out into a miserable and wet Sunday morning. Drizzle clung to her hair, she slipped into her car and gave a sigh of relief when it started first time. She drove through a downpour of torrential rain – she hated driving in weather like this – she carefully followed the blurry orange tail lights of the cars in front and finally made it to the club. Her main cleaning job was the local primary school, but since the new head that joined had fallen by the wayside, she'd pay by invoice only. 'Everything had to be above board,' as she said. It was a huge blow to her income, cleaning the school was decent pay. Soon after, she met Rocco, the manager of The Earth Rabbit in Newquay, by chance. The club was full of surfer types, free spirits, and locals. It used to be an old discotheque, but it still had the sticky floors, cheap beer, and was home to retro eighties Friday night cheese. Rocco, a laid-back fifty-something Scotsman, a giant of a man who wore shorts no matter the weather, allowed Gwen to work under the table. He'd pay her in cash, always in a small brown envelope with a smiley face drawn on the front. She cleaned The Earth Rabbit twice a week, Friday afternoons and Sunday mornings. Sunday cleans were the worst. After the Saturday night carnage, she cleaned vomit, excrement, and semen that had sprayed up the walls in the toilets. She wore a mask, the kind bought from B&Q, to shield the stench and stop her throwing up.

Gwen entered the club through the back entrance and went to the office first. Rocco sat at his desk, his eyes bloodshot, a glass of whisky sitting untouched in front of him. Gwen smiled at Rocco and opened the window to let fresh air in. It smelled of bodies and aftershave. She didn't want to know what happened in the office after hours; she didn't want to think of Rocco in that way. The air was cool, and Gwen's skin prickled. It felt wrong being in Rocco's private space, just the two of them. She could feel him watching her. Now she wished she had started with the cloakroom first. It was the easiest job, picking up discarded tickets, straightening up the hangers, vacuuming the carpet, and spraying air freshener.

Rocco leaned back in his office chair. 'You look tired, Gwenny Girl. You've lost weight.' His tone was caring, but she couldn't help but feel like he was being critical. Rocco was right though. She had lost weight. The stress of being short of money and rationing food to make sure her daughter Bea was taken care of first and foremost had resulted in her shedding a few pounds. Even her smallest jeans fell from her hips.

'I was thinking, you don't earn a great deal with me, do ya?' Rocco said.

'You pay me fine.'

'I'm sure we could work something out, you know. I help you and you help me kind of thing.'

'Rocco!' Gwen said crossly. 'I don't know where you are going with this but if it's what I think...'

'No, no, no. You got me all wrong, Gwenny Girl. My God, *no*. I meant some work behind the bar. Mike walked out on me last night, left me in the shitter.'

'I've never been a bartender before. I'd mess up the orders... and—'

'Gwenny, we just get a bunch of high-as-a-kite, horny drunkards in here. They won't give two shits what you serve them so long as there's booze in it. All I care about is getting the money in the till.'

'And you still want me to clean as well as work at the bar?' Gwen asked.

'If you can manage it, I'll pay you a fair wage for both. I like you, Gwen. You remind me of myself; you're not afraid of some hard graft. And like me, life, well, I dare say, life hasn't been kind to you. It's never too late, y'know, Gwenny. To turn it all around.'

'But...' She frowned, leaned against the wall, started to let her body relax. 'How will I keep this from the government? If they find out, I'll lose everything and I can't afford to...'

'Girl, we'll keep you off the books. Cash in hand, like always. If any of those council bodies come sniffing round here, I got what's called plausible deniability. I'll tell them you're just a mate of mine, a lass I have a lot of time for. Come, I'll show you where the action happens.'

Rocco showed Gwen how to use the till and she was surprised at how easy it all came to her, but she wondered how well she'd cope in a busy club with the crowds around her.

'Let me show you where the kegs are kept. Bart's responsible for changing them, but the more you know the better off you'll be.'

There was far more to The Earth Rabbit than Gwen realised, the back was corridors and rooms. As she walked behind Rocco, she started to feel a bit sick. *Faint and sick.* She began to sway and held the concrete walls to steady herself. Rocco turned to her.

'I'm fine,' she said, before he could ask what was wrong.

'What in the love of God is that smell?' Rocco said, holding his hand over his mouth.

He pushed open the door to the main storage room. It was usually locked but Bart probably forgot because it had been such a busy night.

'It's coming from here. Fuck. Maybe we have rats. I need to deal with this right now. Can't have health and safety shutting me down.'

'Rocco... I don't feel well.'

'You're all right, lass. I'm sure you've dealt with worse, aye?'

Gwen followed Rocco as he investigated like a police dog; there was a shift in the atmosphere, something didn't feel right. The air felt close – stagnant. It felt like a pair of eyes were on them. A pile of cardboard boxes looked disturbed, thrown on top of each other haphazardly, like the person who put them there was in a hurry.

Rocco crossed the room and started picking up the boxes with caution. 'You can't be too careful with rats. Not all cute and fluffy. Evil fuckers they are and...'

Silence.

'Rocco! What is it?'

A gasp, a sob.

'Rocco. Talk to me for fuck's sake! What is it?'

'Stay back, Gwenny! Don't come any closer.'

She ignored him and stepped forward, pushing past him as he tried to hold her back.

A quiet Sunday morning turned into a TV crime show like the ones you see on those documentaries. Police swarming the area, cameras clicking, forensics gathering evidence, and sealed plastic bags being carried away, the contents later to be analysed in a lab. Gwen thought of the victim's final moments; a woman lying face down with an ugly scrawl on her back: the words flashed in her mind on repeat. She would never forget the gruesome text, never forget how the blood drained from Rocco's face. Gwen thought of Bea and how the victim in the storage room could only have been a few years older than her. Sadness swept over her like a storm. She needed to get home to Bea, hold her close, hold her and never let her go. The police wanted to talk to her and Rocco sat at the bar, head in his hands, the shock vibrating through his trembling shoulders. What would she tell the police? She was down there training for a new job, a job she wasn't supposed to have. She couldn't lie, it would make her look like a suspect. She wished she could get Rocco to work something out, cover her tracks. *How the hell did this happen?*

Right now, Gwen was part of a major murder enquiry. The press sniffing around like flies on shit, the photos... it was only a matter of time before her name would be leaked to the press. *What would the parents at the school think?* She always lived a quiet life, keeping to herself and now that was all going to change.

A tall man walked towards her. He wasn't in uniform, but it was clear by the way he held himself upright with an air of authority he was a cop. He didn't smile but he wasn't stern either. Meanwhile, Gwen could feel her body start to shake. *She was fifteen years old again, about to tell her parents she was pregnant and suffer the glare of judgement and disappointment.*

'Gwen Foster?' the officer said.

'Yes?' she replied in a shaky breath, picking her fingernails.

'I'm Detective Matt Burns, we are here to investigate a potential homicide.'

There was nothing 'potential' about it. It was crystal-clear murder. No one body can carve the words *Grace #3* into their own back.

CHAPTER TWELVE

JENNIFER MACK

My dreams are violent lately.

I hear cries, but they're not my own. They belong to the Graces.

I toss and turn, but sleep is out of reach. I blame it on the research. Since digging deeper into the complex minds of murderers and studying the detailed accounts of how the crimes were committed, I've become unsettled. Every time I slot the key in the door and turn it, I have the unnerving sensation the killer will lie in wait. My imagination runs wild: I think a lot about the act itself, the blade pressing into the skin on the victim's back. He walks among us. If I pass him in the street, *will I know?*

I think about last night. I got a takeaway and watched re-runs of *Friends* to lighten my mood. I enjoyed the taste of a long overdue chicken korma and the sound of Janice's woodpecker laugh filling the room. I did these normal Saturday night things all while, just a few miles away, a young woman went to a club in search of a good time but met her end. As soon as I heard about the body, I rushed to Newquay. The Earth Rabbit was off the beaten track, set away from the hustle of the busy bars on the main drag. It is true that you shouldn't judge a book by its cover; the outside appeared small and could be confused with a house or a boutique shop. On the inside, however, it was a different story. The inside was a labyrinth of open spaces leading into narrow, darkened corridors. The main bar, being the centre stage, was lit with an array of multicoloured fairy lights that twinkled against the bottles of spirits. The corridors didn't interlink, making it difficult for a drunken person to find their way round. The killer had to know the club, had to have been familiar with the place to know where the storage was kept. The police were interviewing everybody connected with the club, including the staff who weren't even on duty at the time. They asked the police to help them look for a person of interest, a barman called Mike Lane who left his job and hadn't been heard from since. I interviewed the owner, a real character by the name of Rocco, with a heavy Scottish accent and features so close together that I wanted to pull at his cheeks to widen his face.

'I'll never get that fuckin' image out of my head… that poor lass… dead. In my place o' all places. What sick bastard did this?'

I give up on my bed and head to the kitchen, the tiles cool against my bare feet. The kitchen window faces the road, a streetlamp flickers, soon ready to give up the last of its light and allow darkness to flood the street. I feel a sense of unease; he could be with his next victim right now, at this very moment. I let the tap run and fill the glass with water and take a long desperate gulp, it does little to calm my nerves. Here is what we know about the killer so far: the key fact is that the victims are all named Grace and all have blonde hair, each in their twenties. Serial killers often have a specific type of victim, a very particular taste they crave and need to satisfy.

Jeffrey Dahmer killed men and boys.

Ted Bundy kidnapped and raped young women.
Peter Sutcliffe murdered women.
Steve Wright strangled sex workers.

The police haven't found any DNA linking the killer with anybody on their database; no CCTV images have caught any activity of interest. The puzzle is only in its early stages, building the edges, tiny pieces which are not forming anything close to a clear picture. The movements of the killer are unpredictable, he chooses unseeing places. I wonder if Andrea Matthews is awake, mulling round her big house with big thoughts, and how the latest Newquay club murder will bring back fresh emotions and the strange cruelty of guilt for naming her daughter Grace. I glance at the cooker clock. It's a little after midnight and my report will be going to print, my name now officially affiliated with the murders. I think about the fragile woman I briefly interviewed, how she looked so oddly out of place at the club. She answered questions with one-word answers and avoided my gaze, her unease growing stronger as she began to stutter, her eyes pooling with tears. She was too thin, too pale, and looked as though she needed rescuing in so many ways. Yet, she was being smart not saying too much because, whether I like it or not, a reporter's job is to get the story, no matter the cost. I suppose I can be a bit gentle on those I interview. I try to separate my emotions from doing the job. I need to wise up and be a little more forthcoming. There are reporters (Hayley) who throw anybody they need to under the bus to get ahead. When I was younger, I behaved in the way I was expected to, but slowly as this story takes hold of me, I know I must change. I take a deep breath. Remind myself I am a great journalist and I will be the Saving Grace.

———

Summer has not yet given way to autumn, and the two seasons collide today with warm sunshine and newly fallen golden-brown leaves. September is closing in thick and fast. Three lives taken, three stories, and zero leads. The office is busy, there is a buzz in the air and a hunger for gory details. Nobody likes to admit it, but the dark world fascinates us all. Sure, we show disgust and repel the evil wrongdoings of the killer, but we all want to know, the how, what, and why of it all. It's like seeing a horrific car accident; you can't just drive on by or turn a blind eye – no, we need to stop and absorb every little detail. We need to witness their misery first-hand. It's just after lunch and the team is called in for a meeting. Jacob is the last to come into the meeting room and everybody huddles together to make room for him. He stands, claps his hands firmly and rubs them together.

'Right, kids... we are covering the biggest story this paper has ever seen. We can't afford to fuck it up.' Jacob's face is flushed red from his heavy boozing and it's all too obvious today. He pulls a tissue from his pocket to blot the beads of sweat on his forehead. I wonder how much he has been drinking.

'I interviewed Gwen Foster. She was there when the owner of the club found the body,' I say, my voice sounding too high-pitched, not my own.

'What did she say, I want you to get an exclusive with her and the owner... Rocky?'

'Rocco,' I correct him, unable to shake the image in my head of Sylvester Stallone.

When I jot some notes down, there is an annoying sound that is coming from Hayley tapping her fingernails on the desk. Nobody else seems to notice but I feel the taps are like jabs directed at me. I shouldn't let her get to me. I'm half tempted to call her out, to ask her why she's trying to derail the meeting. Her actions seem harmless, but she gets under my skin and she is trying to pull away my train of thought. I've beaten her to it;

she may have gotten the first write-up to first print, but I am determined to be the one to put this together. Till the bitter end.

'Have you connected with the police in London, Jen?' Jacob asks.

There is a whispering in the background. It's Hayley's voice. I don't look up to see who she's speaking to. I know jealousy is stirring like the beginnings of a storm.

'Lilith Grain is on board.' As soon as the words spill out of my mouth, I feel my cheeks burn and the room closes in on me – voices in the room filter out, becoming more distant.

'Jen... Jennifer!' Jacob's voice snaps me back in the moment.

'Set up a call with Lilith. We can really use her expertise.'

Later, I sit at my desk and continue my research. I look at images of where each body was found, looking for something each place has in common. The two murders in Cornwall suggest this is where the killer resides, but why London? The middle of the sea, an old video store and the back of the club. None of it makes any sense. Whoever the killer is, there is a dark history with a person named Grace, maybe even a scorned lover? If only Lilith Grain would return my phone calls!

CHAPTER THIRTEEN

THEN

A scream startles me out of a deep sleep. Glass shatters. A car alarm shrills. I lie in bed, frozen. The neighbourhood is like a predator lurking on every corner, waiting for prey to sink its blood-hungry fangs into. Drug dealers, domestic violence, gangs, robbery, it's all here in Grahame Warner Park. There's another scream, one that's feral, desperate. It's a piercing sound that rings in the air even after it's finished. I stumble around in the darkness, tripping over my own feet. My hands grip the sofa and I steady myself. I hide behind a curtain, careful not to make any movement; the orange glow of the streetlamps faintly illuminate the grainy pavement. The estate is flanked in a sea of grey and miserable high-rise tower blocks, tall and ugly, reeking of poverty and struggle. The screaming finally stops, and I cast my eyes over the pathway below where I see a thin woman in a short skirt and thigh-high boots. Even from this high up I see her clearly, her eyes wide, mouth twisted downward. Her arms are flailing as a man stalks her.

'Get back here right fucking now, you stupid bitch!' The male voice echoes, bouncing off the walls of crumbling concrete.

The man grabs the woman's arm and yanks her towards

him. After a moment he spits on her and pushes her small frame to the ground.

He's a monster, wild, unhinged, and even if I did intervene, I'd only be putting myself in danger. And was it even worth it saving a *bag bitch*? Maybe the world would be a better place once both freaks dropped dead.

When the couple disappear out of my view, I go back to bed, a knot forming in my gut. I don't want to be here anymore. How it is some people are born into luxury and some – like me – are just not. I am tired of walking through the estate with a quickened pace. I don't want Grahame Warner Park to become a part of me, contaminating who I am. I never wanted to be seen or heard. Lately, when I go out, I've been brandishing a kitchen knife in my belt. I've practised on melons to try and imitate how deep I'd need to penetrate through the skin to cause actual harm; not the superficial kind, but the kind that would leave a person withering in agony, unable to fight back, unable to get back up. I've leaned forward to stab and twist, destroy tissue, and maybe sever arteries. My thoughts slowly flutter away to the back of my head and my body gives in to sleep once again until, for the second time, I am awoken. This time the noise is coming from the front door. *Rattle, rattle!* The door shakes, somebody is trying to break in. My breath pauses.

I swing my legs out of bed. I glance at my rucksack flung open on the sofa, its contents spilling out, including the kitchen knife. I dash across the room and grab hold of my weapon. My grip tightens around the handle and my legs go near limp from fear. In slow, methodical movements I approach the door – a slight movement from my fingertips causes me to drop the knife, the blade clipping the edge of my foot – a small droplet of blood begins to well.

The door is being pushed now, with force. *Bang! Bang!*

I shiver. There's fuck all here to take; nothing of financial value anyway.

I take a deep breath and shout, 'Who the fuck are you?'

It's a bold move.

'Open the fecking door! The key your mum gave me ain't bloody working.'

I'd know that raspy voice anywhere. Aunt Lizzy.

I sigh and slide across the lock and open the door.

'You could have just rung the buzzer, you know?' I say.

'Would you have let me in if I did?' Aunt Lizzy is taller than my mother, heavier. Her red hair is dry and faded with greying roots. She's not just rough round the edges, she's rough inside and out.

Aunt Lizzy steps in the flat like she owns the place and flicks a light on, her gaze transfixed on the surroundings. She takes notice of the fresh paint on the walls with a raise of her drawn-on eyebrows and takes a deep breath, which results in a cigarette-fumed cough. She makes no effort to cover her mouth and lets her splutter and spit escape freely.

'What do you want?' I ask.

'You know what I want. Your mother owes me money.'

'Good luck with that one. She's dead. You were at her funeral!'

I shake my head and feel heat rise to my cheeks. My fists clench, and I begin to feel my temper boil despite a voice in my head telling me to calm the fuck down. But another voice, the less tolerant one, takes over.

You owe her nothing.

She's vermin.

Make her go away.

Do what you have to do.

'But she had life insurance and that means you get a pay-out and by the looks of this place, you already got it. I'll stay here tonight and we can go cash a cheque tomorrow, only cash. If you're anyfink like your old lady, the cheque will bounce to the bleedin' moon.'

'Go. Home. Lizzy.'

'Beg your bloody pardon? What did you just say to me?'

'You heard me. Go. The. Fuck. Home. Now.'

Tiredness has overwhelmed me and robbed me of my patience. Lizzy takes a step back, her expression, disbelieving. She lets out a loud sigh.

'I'm not leaving until I get what I am owed,' Lizzy says in that terrible rasping voice.

Get rid of her.

Take her out.

This is your kingdom now.

'It was your fault.' I end up standing right next to Lizzy, her breath stinks of old fags and cheap wine.

'What are you on?' For the first time, her chutzpah wavers. She stutters, her breathing becomes uneasy. She avoids eye contact, she's breaking down. Inside my head, I hear the merry bells of victory, I am no longer that scared child Lizzy can intimidate.

'Derek. You were the one who brought him into our lives.'

Lizzy shakes her head and takes a step back. But I take another step forward. I won't let her get away from me. I never realised it until now, but if it hadn't been for Lizzy, Mum would have never met Derek and he would have never...

'Who your mother let into her bed ain't naught to do with me.'

'You set them up. You introduced them. It has everything to do with you. You did this... YOU!'

My hand searches for the knife again; it doesn't take me long to find it. Lizzy's head turns into a melon. Big, green, hard.

69

The knife feels light in my hands, it rests easy in my palm, and my fingers wrap around it and tingle with excitement.

'I don't know why you are blaming me for your mother's old boyfriend, your mother had her own fecking life.'

'I know you know...' I say, she needs to be held accountable, admit the fucking truth.

'Ah... not my fault you are such a freak, blame your mother for that one. You ain't never been right in the head, can see it, see it right in your eyes. What is it they say, birds of a feather stick together. No wonder you two invited the devil right into your home.'

She holds my gaze for a moment and the corner of her lips curl into a smile revealing a mouth of decayed teeth.

There is nothing left to say.

So much blood.

And then, right before she collapses, another voice shouts, my voice.

What have you done?

CHAPTER FOURTEEN

THEN

You never know how heavy a person is until they're a corpse. There's no way I am going to be able to lug her into the stairwell by myself, and certainly not unnoticed. The kitchen bin is only big enough to put a part of her into, and I feel sick as I realise what I have to do. I throw a load of sheets over the body and take a long look in the mirror before I leave.

Bitch had it coming.

You killed her.

She deserved it.

You'll never get away with this.

You will get away with this.

The voices argue with one another as I put my head in my hands and shake both of them out. This is no time for debate. I have to think practically. The knives in the kitchen aren't enough to cut through flesh and bone. I need a saw. A chainsaw would be best, but I can't afford that kind of noise. It'll have to be a regular saw, the old-fashioned, hard-labour kind.

I take the number 17 bus to town. There is a shop which sells random items, bric-a-brac and kitchen appliances, tools, you name it. They're bound to sell a sturdy saw, and I'm unlikely to be asked for ID.

A bell rings above me as I push open the door to Gilbert & Son. The shop owner is too engrossed in *The Sun* newspaper to look up. It smells of must and damp, and the items are priced with old stickers, not barcoded. This is the right place. I'll pay in cash and there'll be no trace. I grab a basket and head to the kitchen aisle first. I load it with two industrial-sized bleach bottles, a couple of packs of yellow marigolds, Brillo pads, sponges, and heavy-duty garden sacks; the really thick kind, not the type that will split down the side as soon as you take it out of the bin. The last thing I need is Lizzy's insides spilling out onto the kerb.

I try to act normal, but my heart is pounding in my chest. I don't feel very well and it occurs to me it has been hours since I've eaten or drank anything. I think about Lizzy's body lying still and lifeless on the kitchen floor, her glassy eyes like fish on refrigerated slabs in the supermarket. My heart skips a beat when I reach the hardware section. There are two choices: an Irwin junior hacksaw or an Eclipse junior hacksaw. I hold both of them in my hands. The blades look similar, like the jagged teeth of a piranha, but the handle on the Irwin looks easier to grip and hold tension. I decide to buy both, just in case one breaks. I need to get the job done in one sitting. I can't go back and forth.

I load the contents of the basket onto the counter. The register is covered in a film of dust and the numbers on the raised keyboard have faded. The old man behind the counter rings through the items by punching the buttons and a paper receipt begins to roll through; just numbers, no item description. Just good, basic numbers. He double bags a white carrier and packs the contents for me.

'Cash only,' he says.

No problem...

I hand over £32.90 in exact change. When I leave the store, I let out a shaky breath.

That was easy. Now comes the hard part.

When I get home, I set to work straight away. I start by cleaning the pool of blood and the splatter on the walls, feeling annoyed it tarnished my paintwork. It's a struggle, but I manage to pull Lizzy's body up on the kitchen counter. I place a pillowcase on the top of her head, and leave her pale neck exposed. Lizzy's head flops into the sink like it would in a hairdresser's basin.

I take the saw out of its plastic packaging and hold it in my hands. Bile rises from the back of my throat and the voices come back.

You are evil... you will burn in hell for what you've done.

If it wasn't for her, he would have never been in your life. You were a child, an innocent child and look at what he did to you. Look at what they all did to you!

The words echo over and over: *what he did to you... what he did to you...*

The first cut is the deepest, and the blood has changed substance. It's thicker now, darker. I turn the tap on and let it drain away as I slowly gain a rhythm and try to convince myself I'm sawing a piece of plywood. Her insides feel sticky and slimy, I soon grow used to the smell and it isn't that different from standing in the butcher's; flesh is flesh. As I push the blade back and forth I make more progress until finally it thuds against the stainless-steel basin. Strands of her fire-red hair stick out, I gently swipe them back into the blood-stained pillowcase ready to bag her up properly. I wipe my brow with my forearm and congratulate myself on a job well done.

I look out in the distance at the glitter of lights along the mainland. Getting rid of Lizzy's body had been difficult; I didn't have the time to take her out piece by piece. I used an old suitcase with a hard plastic shell to conceal any bodily fluids that may leak out and withhold the stench of decaying flesh. I placed her arms and legs along the edge of the suitcase and then placed her torso and head in the middle; her body fit perfectly, like a jigsaw. I reached the secluded caves which met the gaping mouth of the sea; the waves towered above the rocks and hungrily devoured anything close by. Bracing myself, I unzipped the suitcase and tossed the body into the sea, imagining a frenzy of sharks eager to gobble her up, and waited patiently as it plunged into the depths of the ocean, then I jumped up and down on the suitcase until the shell was crushed enough for the sea to pull it deep beneath the surface to prevent it rising again.

Bitch got what she deserved.

The wind assaults me like a screaming rush threatening to hurl me in the sea. I steady my hands over a rock and remain frozen while trying to gather strength to regain my balance. The adrenaline courses through my veins at the severity of what I've just done, of what I was now capable of. I move forward slowly until my feet are on a flat piece of ground. The suitcase is gone, the body is gone, the sea churns and grows turbulent. Is it angry with me?

Or is it satisfied?

The next morning, my body feels heavy. I try to move, but I feel like I've been nailed to the bed. I'm due to be at the café today, but I'm not sure I can face it. I imagine more cleaning, and grease clinging to my clothes. I've dealt with enough putrid disgust in the last twenty-four hours to last a lifetime – I don't think I can stomach much more. I try to lift my head off my pillow, but the weight of my head is too much so I flop back down, stirring memories of the night before. The darkness of it all.

Lizzy's acidic words were not lost.

Somehow, even though she's gone, I can still hear her raspy voice, *'You ain't never been right in the head, can see it, see it right in your eyes.'*

CHAPTER FIFTEEN

JENNIFER MACK

It's Saturday and I decide to go to the beach to cleanse my head of all the twisted thoughts and bad dreams that have plagued me since reporting on this murder case. Carne Beach is sheltered by Nare Head. It's a year-round dog-friendly beach and as I arrive, I see two spaniels frolicking in and out of the water, carefree, happy and wild. The sun casts light over the ocean making it appear like a sheet of glass. The air is starting to grow cooler, but it isn't coat weather yet. Still, I find myself wrapping my arms round my body when the wind picks up, whipping my hair around my face. I gather the long curly mass of it and tie it back with the hairband placed on my wrist. I remember coming to this beach as a teenager, longingly looking out to the big ocean with big plans of who I was going to be, where I was going to go... I feel disappointed. So many people dream of moving to Cornwall for the idyllic life, but I dreamed of moving as far away as possible. Something stirs inside me, it's in my gut, and I wonder if I'm here for a reason – the story – was this mine to tell, the making of my career? The thought empowers me, a quiet knowing that this is why.

Lost in my thoughts I'm interrupted by a dog jumping on me, dragging his sodden sandy paws down my jeans.

The man yells at the dog. 'Down, Max! Down!'

He grabs the dog by the collar and clips a lead round his neck.

'I am so sorry. He's never done that before. He's still learning, still a pup. My fault. Are you okay?'

'It's fine,' I say, brushing the grains of sand from my jeans with the back of my hand. 'How old is he?'

Through a curtain of thick, dark hair he pushes the excitable black Labrador down and holds his hand up to him to stop.

'Seven months. He's not my dog... well, I guess he sort of is in a way.'

I look at him quizzically. 'So, he's your dog but not your dog?'

He smiles and shakes his head. He has a nice smile, one that softens his chiselled features and reveals a deep-set dimple on his chin.

'He belongs to my sister, but she can't look after him, so I guess he's mine by proxy for now. He has a lot of bad habits, I came here to meet a dog trainer today, but she's had a family emergency and can't make it.'

He looks to be in his early thirties – the first light lines setting in around his brown eyes. He has a London accent, but it's less West End and more East End, it suits him.

'Are you holidaying here?' I ask.

'Nope. Just moved here actually. From London originally.'

I knew it!

'I just got back from London... beautiful city.' My heart sinks when I think of Lilith Grain and the fact that she still hasn't called me. I wonder if I should swallow my pride and call her again – beg maybe?

'Yeah... I miss it. I mean Cornwall is beautiful, but the pace is so much slower here, takes some getting used to,' the man says.

'Why did you move, if you don't mind me asking?'

'Well, Katie isn't well and my brother-in-law is in the army, so she needs somebody to take her to hospital appointments and help with my niece; the school run, that kind of thing. I work from home, so it doesn't matter where I live.'

I imagine his sister is extremely sick; you don't uproot your entire life if it's just the flu. His kindness isn't lost on me and basic humanity is the perfect dose of medicine I needed today after all the evil and crap I've been dealing with.

'You sound like a good brother.'

'Ah, she'd do it for me too.' He pauses. 'She probably wouldn't, but it's just the two of us in the family and I'm the big brother, so that's the long and short of it, I guess.'

'I'm Jennifer, by the way.'

'Pete... and in case you want to stalk me on Facebook later, it's Pete Flannigan,' he says, before giving me that same dimpled smile.

I look at Max who is now lying at Pete's feet like a hairy rug. I'm kind of glad he decided to jump on me.

'I won't stalk you,' I say pointedly. *Oh, but I will.*

Pete holds his palm over his chest and lets out an exaggerated sigh. 'I'm not worthy of being stalked then? Ouch. You know how to hit a guy where it hurts.'

I laugh out loud and the dog jumps on me again with his long tongue centimetres from my lips.

'Max! Down!' Pete demands. And almost to his own surprise, the dog obeys.

'I don't like social media. I don't really find it all that *social* actually.'

'Ah, so you would stalk me if you *had* social media then?'

'Maybe... but stalking is kind of my profession anyway.'

'Clue number one. Okay, okay, I like this game. You work for the council?'

I laugh. 'Guess again.'

'You're a copper?'

'Try again.'

Pete holds his hands up and says, 'Give up.'

'Reporter.'

He raises his thick eyebrows and nods his head, downturning his mouth that looks a little like De Niro's.

'I knew there was something a bit Nancy Drew about you.'

I laugh again. 'Oh yeah? Tell me, Sherlock, what gave me away?'

'Well, you've got that look in your eyes, absorbing all the information you can. Meanwhile, I bet you can tell me who is walking on this beach right now.'

My heart skips a beat because he's right. He's worked me out quickly and although I know it's just banter, he's read me like a book and my stomach churns. *I don't want him to go.*

'So, we've talked about me, what is it you do from home?'

'Not telling. How about we go for a drink and a bite to eat and if you guess correctly, you get to see me again. If not, we will bid one another farewell and send you for some reporter training or whatever it is you call it.'

'Deal!' I say faster than I wanted to.

We find a café with outside seating for Max.

I order a hot chocolate and Pete orders a pot of tea and scones. My mouth salivates when the scones arrive with cream and jam. He offers me one, but I politely decline.

'Just take half, you know you want to,' Pete says.

He's right, I do, but I can just imagine the jam running down the side of my mouth and a dollop of cream spilling on my top. I'm not very graceful when it comes to pastries; not that I think Pete would care, but I want to make a good impression.

'So judging by your smooth and well-maintained hands, you don't work with them, at least not in the labour sense. You told me you work from home, which means you work on a computer, but doing what, I wonder.'

Pete leans in and rests his chin on his hand. He's close enough now that I feel his warm breath touch my cheek. My stomach does that flip again, and I'm not sure if I like the feeling or not.

'Give up yet?'

'I'm just getting warmed up. You have connections in London but even there you worked from home, so your job is about making a network online and not in person.'

'She's onto something.'

'Judging by the way you're dressed just to walk the dog, you care about appearance, you care about the image you portray to the world – so that tells me your job may entail design of sorts.'

Pete's mouth widens and he gently bangs the table with his fist, egging me on to probe further.

'Wild guess... graphic designer,' I say, uncertain.

'Fuckin' A...' He whoops and punches the air with his fist. 'That was crazy clever, or else you are just really lucky.'

I feel a little smug. Being observant has always been one of my strongest attributes and I love it when I have a chance to let that part of me shine. It reminds me of all the reasons I am a good reporter, even if the right story hasn't come along yet.

Pete's watch vibrates on his wrist. As he reads the message on his watch, his happy-go-lucky mood transforms into something darker, like a thin film of cloud layering over the sun, dimming its light. I avert my gaze and look at the scenery as I shift in my chair uncomfortably.

'I'm sorry, Jennifer, I really am, but I have to go.'

'No problem, hope everything is okay.' I offer him the bait, the reporter in me craving information, but he doesn't bite.

There is a pause before he reaches into his pocket and pulls out his phone. He stares at the screen and unlocks it with face ID.

'I'd like to see you again, so if you'd like, add your number and I'll call you. If not, that's okay too. It's been a really great Saturday morning, and I think Max agrees.'

Flustered, I take the phone from his soft, *non-laboured* hands and try to recall my own number which has escaped my memory. I can't remember the last time a guy asked for my number, but there is something about Pete that gives me a warm feeling, like when you walk out of the cold into a house and the warmth wraps around you with a soothing hug.

He holds his phone in his palm and suddenly my pocket vibrates.

He gently leans in, smelling of fresh air and deodorant, and gives me a kiss on the cheek. When he and Max walk away down the craggily uneven path, I realise I'm still holding my cheek from where his lips just touched it. I memorise the feel of his sandpaper stubble, the softness of his lips. I play it over and over in my head on a loop because I don't want to forget.

The sky is charcoal and I'm huddled up on the sofa, cradling a cup of tea, and my favourite sage-green blanket hangs loosely over my legs. The sky falters and the rain falls. I consider working but I'm not sure I should fill my Saturday afternoon with unpleasant stories of killers and their darkened souls. But it will certainly match the atmosphere of the gloomy weather. I love the sound of wind-driven rain and the beads of water forming on the window, I especially love being at home in my cocoon and watching puddles form on the pavement; it makes me feel cosy – and in a strange way, *secure*.

My phone buzzes a little after 4pm.

My heart jumps out of my chest.

If he was going to make contact at all, I certainly didn't expect it to be so soon. Isn't there some rule somewhere to keep a potential date waiting, at least for a couple of days? I move my finger across the screen to open the message.

> Are you free for dinner tonight? I'm a great chef, I could cook for you!

I stop for a moment. Think.

There is a serial killer out there and I wonder if I should be going out to a man I don't know's house.

That's crazy, right? Saying yes would be absolutely ludicrous. The thought of entering into his house, a stranger, after all. I don't know him at all. And why did he leave so suddenly? Was he scared that I was a reporter? That I was reporting on him if he was indeed a serial killer?

I think of his hands, smooth and gentle, surely not the hands of a man who butchers bodies.

But I want to see him again and if I suggest a restaurant will he just think I'm overcautious? Surely he'd understand that one can't be too careful though.

I imagine him opening his front door, his dark gaze luring me into a spell and then what? I'd go in and he could be a lovely, perfectly normal guy. Or not!

CHAPTER SIXTEEN

THEN

I wince as I walk barefoot on the pebbles. I put mind over matter, convincing myself that the jagged stones piercing through my skin don't hurt.

It's been six months since Mum's passing and almost just as long since ridding the world of Aunt Lizzy. It feels like a bad dream, the kind where you only remember snippets and eventually everything fades. Social services have been round a couple of times, but it's nothing more than a tick-box exercise to say they've done their jobs and that's that. It's also been six months since I last saw Grace.

The aroma of fish and chips from the food van hangs in the air, and a burst of a memory takes me back to when I had fish and chips on the beach with a girl named Becky and her mum. They were kind to me. Becky knew I didn't have much to eat because most days Mum forgot to give me a packed lunch, leaving me at the mercy of the school for free meals. But as I got older, I began skipping lunch altogether because I didn't want to see my name scribbled on that list: the free school meals list. It was harder to swallow my pride than fill my belly.

I'm ready to dip my toes in the water again. I thought of Grace often, and we still texted one another, but I had to take my time before seeing her again. It was necessary to be reborn, to let the stigma of my council roots wash away from my skin. I needed to become the person I wanted *her* to see.

It had been a process, like a caterpillar entering the chrysalis and emerging as a butterfly. My time had finally come; I had completed my transformation, and I was ready for her. We agreed to meet at the beach, away from the distractions of other people.

I see her in the distance. Her butter-blonde hair and her signature effortless style – a leather jacket teamed with a short dress, black tights and ankle boots – are unmistakable. She treads cautiously down the weathered steps, holding the rusted rail for extra support.

'It's really you!' she says as she approaches me.

My heart is caught up in my throat as her gaze travels down my body, over my dark jeans and carefully styled scarf before settling on my bare feet.

I hug my arms to my chest, protecting myself from the wind that has ramped up a notch and try to shield my nerves from pouring out of me, convinced she'll be able to sense my unease, my feelings for her.

'In the flesh,' I reply.

She leans in for a hug, but I remain stone still. I take a second to take her in; her smell reminds me of a department store, when you walk in and take in the mix of expensive perfumes, new clothes, the tang of leather and money.

'How have you been?' she asks.

I wait a beat to find my voice. The voice I had practised.

'Very well, thank you.' I mentally berate myself for sounding like a pompous twat.

'It's so great to see you! All this time we've been texting, it's nice that we have finally met up.' Grace pauses for a moment. 'But I know you've had so much to deal with.'

'I've managed.'

'You certainly have. You're amazing, living on your own, making it all work. Even though my parents drive me up the wall, I'm not sure I'd be able to fly solo, not like you.' She smiles. It's warm and lights up her whole face. Her eyes are bluer than I remember.

We take a moment and look at one another before Grace breaks the silence.

'Do you want to stay here or go get a tea... coffee?'

'I don't mind.' Again, I scold myself, my limited vocabulary is jarring and not the person I want to portray. I'm being the old me – weak.

'Actually, let's stay here for a bit. There's a bench over there and it's been a while since I spent time at the beach. It'll be nice to reconnect with you and the sea.' *There, that's better. Confident. Decisive. Go me!*

We walk in silence to the bench; the waves are starting to dance in a frantic rhythm. Grace folds her arms tightly around her slender frame as her shoulders hunch up to her ears and she pulls her knees up to her chest.

'Bit chilly?' I ask.

'Just a bit, but I'll be fine. I always have the heating on high in my car, so it'll just take me a minute to get used to it.'

'How's life at the nursery?'

'I'm enjoying it. I've started helping out at the florist's in the centre too and I'm loving the creative process of it all.' Grace reaches into her back pocket and takes out her phone. 'These are some of the designs I've been working on.'

I take her phone from her hand and swipe through photos of seasonal blooms, wreaths with small artificial pumpkins, berries and pine cones with a mix of yellow and brown maple leaves.

'Grace... these are exquisite.'

Her cheeks flush as she gently takes her phone back into her hands. 'I love it. I think... no... I know this is what I want to do.'

'Be a florist?'

'I love growing the plants and tending to them, but there is so much more to floristry. It's an art. And there are so many big occasions I'll be a part of. Births, weddings, anniversaries.'

'Funerals,' I say, deadpan.

'Yes... but giving flowers as a final farewell gift to a loved one is a beautiful thing. It's a celebration of their life.'

I think back to Mum's funeral and the few bunches of wilted supermarket flowers wrapped in cellophane I tossed on her grave.

'So,' Grace continues, her eyes wide with enthusiasm as she talks about her passion for flowers. 'I've been offered an apprenticeship at Stalks.'

'That's great! I'm really happy for you.' Somewhere deep inside my gut is a pang of something I can't quite place... jealousy, maybe?

My days at the café are coming to an end. I can't handle the endless piles of greasy plates and the stench of fried onions clinging to my clothes. But I have no other prospects. With my final results I can probably get a shitty admin job working minimum wage and spend my days making some fat bloke rich. With my earnings and when the benefits stop, I'll barely have enough to get by and I'll become one of them. A product of Grahame Warner Park locked within its miserable fortress of imprisoning walls.

I will myself to be better. Do better. Just like Grace.

'Shall we go get that tea? And cake? I can't ignore the cold anymore.' Grace stands and takes my hand. It feels like an electric current is surging up my arm through my veins, and my heart begins to thud.

Thud thud thud...

I feel warmth spread over my skin; she wants to spend more time with me. She hasn't called our meet-up to an end with a perfectly plausible excuse of the chilling winds and the rain that is starting to fall.

We cross the beach, and she loops her arm through mine. A triumphant symphony plays in my head, trumpets bellowing, *tra-la-la-la.*

The warmth of the café is inviting, the smell of freshly brewed coffee hitting us as soon as the bell chimes above the door. On the counter is a selection of home-made cakes in domed stands and delicious scones begging to be smothered in cream and a hefty dollop of strawberry jam. We take a table by the window, a thick mist engulfing the view of the sea and making the boats look like distant dark shapes out on the water. An older woman with a thick Cornish accent and a bright yellow apron with daisies printed all over it approaches us.

'Shielding from the weather?' She has a hearty laugh and tells us the specials. 'Butternut squash soup. Made fresh this morning, perfect on a day like this, warms your insides right up.'

'Actually, I think I'll go straight for dessert.' Grace looks up, her blue eyes sparkling, and there is some pink in her cheeks from the heating, which must be set to 100 degrees.

We talk for ages. Covering all kinds of topics and I am surprised I've been able to maintain a flow of conversation. We are from different walks of life, Grace and I. It's either she is very down-to-earth or my desire not to be council scum has driven me far away mentally. Maybe it's both.

I glance out the window and think about where we will go from here. Should I ask to see her again, or should I wait for her to ask? The conversation between us is coming to a natural halt, but it isn't uncomfortable. I don't feel the need to fill the silence. I can't think back on a time I've felt so at ease. I haven't ever been able to speak to anyone the way I have with Grace today, not anyone. I don't know what it is about her, nor do I know why she seems to like me too, the odd one out.

The café owner comes over and asks if we'd like anything else. I politely decline and ask for the bill. It's a bit of a risk, since neither of us has mentioned the next time we will meet up again, if at all. The thought of not seeing Grace again makes me feel off-balance, dizzy, and even a little ill. But I've made up my mind. I can't just leave this up to her, I have to dive in and stop being such a fucking pussy.

My heart feels like it's moved into my throat again. I try to find my voice, but I can barely swallow.

Is this how hard it is to ask somebody out, ask to see them again?

'This has been so lovely. I know we've been texting, but you never know how things will be when you meet up, even if it is just with a potential friend and not a date.' Grace runs her hand through her hair and laughs. 'This has been so, so lovely and I am really pleased to see you looking so well. Absolutely gorgeous, I might add.'

Her words hang in the air and I pick them out, pick them apart: 'Friend and not a date', 'Absolutely gorgeous, I might add'. What do I do with this? Where do we go from here? So we are just friends? *Not a date. Gorgeous.* I mentally dissect each word and try so very hard to smile. Does she not feel the same? My heart sinks into a pit. But I have to keep it together.

'Are you okay? You look a little ill?' Grace rests her hand on my forearm.

'What? Oh, no. I'm fine. Just dozed off for a second!' But she's seen the disappointment on my face I couldn't conceal.

'Let's do this again. My parents are away this weekend, so you should come over if you're not busy. You can stay if you like. We can order a Chinese and watch a movie.' There is that faint sound of the orchestra in my head again, but it isn't quite as bold, not nearly as joyful.

'That sounds great!'

I am already counting down the hours to the weekend.

CHAPTER SEVENTEEN

I never go to Padstow, the people there look down on me, like I'm the piece that doesn't fit the jigsaw. Here, the struggle is a long way off; gleaming Range Rovers and Jags choke the winding lanes and the shift of wealth moves up a hundred notches. But I'm here for Grace. It was supposed to be a night in, but she changed her mind and wanted to go out for a meal instead. At least it wasn't a bar, where people chase shots – there is nothing fun about being sober and being around drunken idiots where everybody hugs one another or tries to jam their fucking tongue down your throat. But I'm invested in spending time with her, so I go with what she wants and wait patiently for her to arrive at the not-too-pretentious Italian restaurant. I bag my entertainment as I wait by watching a jealous girlfriend burn her beady eyes into her boyfriend's back as he leans in too closely and chats up the waitress pouring a cocktail. The waitress has over-defined eyebrows and outlandishly false eyelashes; she simply oozes with too much unwarranted self-confidence. The girlfriend plays with her phone, scrolling with vacant, unseeing eyes. When the boyfriend finally comes back, she keeps her gaze fixed on her phone. He reaches for her hand, but she snatches it away. He really has no clue.

'I'm sorry I'm late,' Grace says, breathless. It doesn't matter that she's late; she's rushed, which means she cares.

'Imogen broke up with her boyfriend. She was a bit upset and she's never upset, so I felt I needed to be there.'

Imogen... fucking Imogen with her critical gaze and fucked-up posh voice. The very mention of her name gets my hackles up and I feel heat rise to my cheeks. I take a gulp of water, trying to wash her name out of my head, but Grace carries on.

'I mean, it's not the longest relationship she's ever had, but I guess Ben got under her skin.'

'That's a shame.' I sigh, hoping I don't sound uncaring.

'Well, this is what happens when you fall for a sociopathic player.'

Grace's mobile vibrates on the table, a photo of Imogen and Grace with pouty lips lights up the screen and I want to pick up the butter knife and stab the phone. I imagine the cracked screen and jagged fragments of Imogen's face. It feels satisfying.

'I'm so sorry,' Grace huffs. 'She's needy when she's upset. I did say I was going out. I'll just take this call quickly and I promise we can get on with our evening.'

'It's fine,' I lie. I wonder if Imogen knows Grace is seeing me and that's why she has suddenly succumbed to heartbreak. My insides churn. I scratch the underside of the table with my fingernails, all the while keeping a fake fucking smile on my face and waving Grace away while I whisper, 'It's no problem, not to worry,' and point to the menu asking her if she wants me to order anything.

Grace leaves the table and I look back over at the couple and hear the guy say something about being *oversensitive* and that 'possessiveness isn't a good quality to have'. What a joke. I see how he's twisting it, but she's not backing down and tells him there's a difference between possessiveness and loyalty. I kinda like her.

Finally, after what is a borderline rude amount of time to be away, Grace returns to the table.

'So, so sorry.'

'Is she okay?' The words feel sticky in my mouth.

Grace grunts. 'He's a dick. He posted nudes of her on some site and is asking her for money to get them taken down. It just goes from bad to worse.'

I want to find this Ben and high-five him. People like Imogen think they own the world, that it revolves around them. It's about fucking time somebody taught her a lesson.

'May I take your order?' the waiter asks.

'I'm thinking of a cocktail.' Grace eyes the menu and taps her red-polished fingertip on her chosen drink and motions to me to have the same.

I shake my head and tell her, 'Not for me thanks, I'm on antibiotics.' My excuse works a treat and Grace tells the waiter we'll need a little longer to decide on food.

'I'm starving and everything looks so good. What are you going to have?' Grace stares at me. I mean I've had plenty of time to settle on my order, with all the Imogen drama saturating my time. But I was so pissed, I didn't bother looking at the menu.

The phone buzzes again.

She takes a deep breath. 'I am just going to let it go to voicemail.'

But I can tell she is waiting for me to give her my blessing: *Go on... answer it... she's your friend... she needs you.*

Finally, the phone stops and soon it lights up with one missed call. She looks at me, gives me a weak smile and shifts uncomfortably, and I can't push away the wave of annoyance. This is my night, not Imogen's. So she whored in front of the camera and now the vengeful party-boy ex is taking advantage of it. Maybe if she were smart, she could pull a Kim Kardashian and make it work to her advantage. But Imogen, as much as Imogen might think, is just not that special.

The waiter returns and places a coupe glass with an illuminous cocktail cherry to garnish. It looks like a sophisticated drink sitting on the rustic wooden table, the tea light flickering against the glass making it look seductive and mysterious.

'Actually...' I say, 'I want what she has.'

If there is going to be anything to exorcise Imogen out of this night, it will be alcohol.

Grace puts her hand on my arm. 'You can't. You're on antibiotics, remember?'

I gently pull my arm away and stroke her fingertips. 'One won't hurt.'

And that's how the night started.

The moon casts a diluted glow over the water. There's a breeze with a slight chill to it making us both shiver. I pull my jacket tighter, my shoulders hunched towards my ears. There's silence between us, a comfortable silence, like a spell has been cast and we're just two souls intertwined and happy in each other's presence. It's enough. The sea sprays against the jagged dark rocks, and for a split second I can hear a whisper; '*I'm here.*' It's ghostly and faint. I shake my head, tell myself I've had too much to drink but it was only a couple of miles from here that the sea swallowed her to the depths of her burial ground. Then, in the distance, a light flickers.

'You look like you've seen a ghost,' Grace says.

I don't want to ruin this moment between us. It's the booze, this is why I don't like to drink because I lose control of my mind and that's not a good thing for me. I have to be in control one hundred per cent of the time or else it leads to stupid hallucinations like this one. When I was little, before it all happened, I always had this feeling that I was being watched, a looming feeling of dread. Of course, I never saw anything, but I wondered if it was a premonition of what was to come. Perhaps the watchful feeling wasn't there to hurt me but to warn me.

'I think it's just the fresh air hitting me. The restaurant was boiling, we had a lot to drink. Perhaps I'm just sobering up a little.'

Grace laughs. 'I'm far from sober. I've not drank that much since my last school dance, but then I felt worse because it was vodka, and vodka and I, let me tell you, do not mix.'

The wind is starting to pick up. Grace cuddles into me, and my thoughts of ghostly voices drift away as I close my arm around her small frame like a protective shield buffering her body from the sting of the salty air. Her body melts into mine, I'm not sure where I start and she finishes. My feet are bare, but I no longer notice the cold sand.

'We should go, but I love being here,' Grace murmurs. Her voice is dozy and relaxed, as if it's drenched with sleep. I could listen to that version of her all day every day. It's mesmerising, like that of a snake charmer. I'm the snake, helpless at her command, dancing to the rhythm of her plush tone.

'Have you heard that the best way to warm up is to go into freezing water?' Grace says, her eyes glinting. 'Fancy a swim?'

I wait for her to start laughing and tell me she's joking, but she pulls away from me and tugs my jacket while she unzips her jeans and pulls them off, revealing her long milky-white legs. She's wearing a lace thong, and even in the darkness I can see her skin is dotted with goose pimples.

'Sounds like the best way to get hyperthermia. I'm not going in that water.'

Grace strips to her underwear, her body slender and soft. I'm taken in by her beauty and the way the moonlight shines on her pale skin, making her look otherworldly. She walks away from me in the clear direction of the sea. I wait for her toes to meet the water and for her to run back into my arms, but she keeps moving forward until the water meets her waist and she pushes off, submerging her entire body into the sea. I run to the shore, fearful of her drowning, but her head bobs up and her smile is euphoric.

'Get in.'

Hesitantly, I begin taking my clothes off, every blast of wind stealing my confidence to carry on, but I resist. I feel nervous. I've never done anything like this before, I've never let myself be seen and my relationship with my body is just a functional one, not sexual. Sex is something that represents pain, advantage, and shame. I always cover up, even in the blistering hot summers. Winter is my favourite season for that very reason, but it's Grace, and she wants me to be with her. I want to lose my inhibitions, allow myself to just live. I'm down to my underwear and try not to focus on the cold biting my exposed skin. I work to steady my breath as my heart thuds in my chest. Finally, I allow my body to be swallowed by the bitterness of the sea. My skin feels like it's been stung with tiny needles, but it isn't unpleasant. It's a painful pleasure and the further I move into the water and kick my legs, the more pleasure I feel.

Grace swims towards me. Her hair is the colour of the moon; yellow and bright. She looks like an angel. I long to reach out to her and kiss the salt off her lips. We both tread water and say nothing, with only the sound of the waves crashing against the rocks and the quickened pace of our breathing. I love how blissfully peaceful it is here. No buzzing of phones. Nobody else. Just us.

Soon, Grace is at my side and slowly circles her palm over the curve of my back.

This isn't what friends do, is it?

I've never had a friend. Not a real friend. I dare not move and misinterpret what I think she wants. I didn't want to ruin this entire, wonderful, best night of my fucking life!

CHAPTER EIGHTEEN

JENNIFER MACK

I 've tried on fifteen different outfits and none of them look right, feel right. I've never been one of those girls who enjoy 'getting ready'. The girls at uni treated it like a rite of passage, a deeply empowering ceremonious occasion displaying all the best parts of modern femininity. But that's not me. I apply what I think is enough make-up to look somewhat presentable and not too much to make him think I'm a circus clown. I remind myself he met me on a blustery beach, jeans drenched with sandy dog paws and he still called. My hair will not sit right; it's always been an issue, those thick untamed curls. So I opt for a headband that's black, plain. I have a flower one but I don't want to turn up like a burnt-out hippy child who drinks wheatgrass and drones on about Chomsky. Before I can change again, I pick up my new bag, the one with a gold chain strap. It looks alien hanging from my shoulder; I'm used to lugging around tattered rucksacks and practical totes, nothing at all like this statement piece. I feel like an imposter.

I walk to the living room. The TV is still on and the sofa looks crumpled from where I'd spent the afternoon lazing around. A cup of cold tea sits on the coffee table. I start to fluff the cushions and make the place look just a tiny bit tidier. There's nothing worse than coming home to a mess. In a few minutes I'll make my way to the car and take the short journey to Nonna's Pizza. Somehow, I couldn't shift my cautious side and agreed to go out on a date. Going to his house felt claustrophobic, and as much as I like him (really, really like him) it wasn't smart. I arrive at the pizzeria a little after eight. The tables are set close together, the smell of fresh dough and garlic swims in the air and laughter and chatter makes the atmosphere burst with a weekend vibe. I scan the restaurant and try to pick out Pete from the sea of people, and out of the corner of my eye I see him stand up waving his arms. I feel a small kernel of nerves pop in my stomach. Meeting Pete this morning was by chance and now it's intentional. I can't help shake the feeling that this is all going to go horribly wrong and that the flow of conversation we had earlier is going to run dry.

'Jen. Good to see you.' He comes out from behind the table and kisses me on both cheeks, a perfect complement to our Italian surroundings.

He clears his throat and pulls out a chair. Top points for being a gentleman.

'So glad you could make it.' There's a sincerity attached to his tone, like he is genuinely pleased I'm here, his eyes are engaged, and his smile is as I remember; warm and easy.

'How's Max?' I ask, surprised my voice hadn't come out broken and unsure.

'Oh, fine. He was a bit pissed I left without him. Soon as he hears the door open, he races to where I hang his lead and paces by the door expecting to come out with me.'

'He was your sister's dog?'

'That's right.'

I know before it crosses my lips that I should not ask the next question, but I can't help myself.

'You mentioned your sister is unwell.' I pause, willing myself to shut up. This isn't an interview. I don't know why I can't let the need-to-know details progress organically.

'She has breast cancer and is recovering from a double mastectomy.'

'I'm so sorry.'

'She's responding well to the treatment but hates the constant bed rest. She's practically crawling out of her skin trying to get out of the hospital.'

My shoulders start to relax as I realise, I haven't offended him, and he is open to talking about his sister.

'Simon, her husband, is in the military. He's a good guy but he's not cut out for this kind of shit. He can't stay in one place for too long. He loves Kate and Emily but...' He locks his gaze on me and shrugs his shoulders and lets out a long breath.

'Emily's your niece?'

'An absolute firecracker, that one.'

It's nice to hear about family but it's so far removed from how I grew up, so foreign. There was only me and Mum.

'Like I said, Katie's a royal pain in the arse but she's my sister and much as I hate to admit it, she's my best friend.'

I smile, but there is an emptiness in my gut, a want for a family of my own, a sister to call to talk about nothing of particular importance. Because of the death of my mum, there is a hole in my heart that I don't think will ever heal. The drinks arrive and break our conversation. Pete picks up the bottle of beer which sits sweating on the table and carefully pours it into a glass. He takes a long, satisfying sip and places his elbows on the table.

'So what's it like being a reporter? Is there anything happening I should know about? You know, any crazies lurking about?'

'I'm working on something pretty big right now, actually, but I can't say too much about it.'

'Oh, mysterious. So you haven't broken the story yet?' His eyebrows furrow together and in the dim lighting of the restaurant his eyes look even darker than they did on the beach.

'I have, actually,' I say, realising where he is going with this.

'Then you should be able to share what is already public knowledge.'

'Yes...' I reply hesitantly, but this conversation won't stop. The writing was on the wall. There isn't a single person who isn't fascinated by serial killers, which is why the world has so many crime shows, books and documentaries on the worst people mankind has to offer. We all hate the crimes, but we can't get enough of the hows and whys.

Happy stories don't make the front cover.

Tragedy does.

There is a market for happy ever after, but crime and injustice top the ratings.

Every. Damn. Time.

'I'm writing about the Grace murders.'

His eyes widen and his jaw drops like an animated Disney character. 'Christ.'

I stare at him. I think if I hold his gaze, he will know how seriously I take the story and hopefully realise that I'm not sharing the information to impress him.

'That's some fucked-up shit. It's crazy because it's all Katie has been talking about lately. She almost called Emily Grace because it was Simon's grandmother's name, but she chose Emily because she has a major fangirl crush on Emily Blunt. Wow. That blew my mind.'

'So, she picked an actress over a family name?' I ask.

'She didn't like Simon's grandmother; said she was a bitter old hag with twisted fingers like gnarly old tree branches.'

'I see why she picked Blunt then.'

We both laugh.

I rest my head on my hand and stay silent while I look at the menu. I already know what I'm having, but I want Pete to ask more questions without me offering information.

'Doesn't it blow your mind that the killer could be in this restaurant right now, stalking his next victim?' Pete's eyes are wide with interest.

It's as if he's read my mind. 'I think of it all the time,' I say.

I think of the research I've carried out so far. One particular killer has caught my attention: Bundy.

Of course, there are dozens of serial killers out there, the ones that don't make celebrity status but heinous just the same, cut from the same cloth, because it takes a certain kind of person to end a life just for kicks. The thing about Bundy is that he was considered charming and good-looking. When you ask most people what they think of serial killers they will probably tell you they live in a dark basement and have pictures of their victims plastered to the walls and keep body parts in jars. They will imagine the likes of Leatherhead from *The Texas Chainsaw Massacre*, or a shifty dark figure, the town weirdo, the skinny awkward guy with thick glasses but cold, calculating eyes. No one thinks of the handsome, charming man you go out on a date with.

'Any clue as to who or why?' Pete asks.

'The why is in the name. All of the victims are young, blonde women named Grace.'

'Perhaps a scorned lover?'

'Perhaps, but doubtful. These things usually involve issues with their upbringing, not romantic partners. We're trying to work with the police, but they're just as clueless. They aren't being very co-operative in giving information.'

'How many Graces do you reckon are changing their names?'

He has a point. If I was named Grace and had blonde hair, then keeping yourself safe would be an easy fix: change your name and hair colour. If only it was that simple.

'Can I tell you something?' Pete asks.

I don't say no, so he goes on.

'You know how I joked about social media and stalking this morning?'

'Yeah.'

'Well, I suppose you've already thought about this, but if you haven't it's where you need to look. You can learn so much about a person by what they post online, the things they share, what they like.'

Our waiter arrives and takes our order. Suddenly I'm not that hungry. My mind has been transported into work zone and the Grace murders, and I can't help but wonder if there will be another killing and what poor girl awaits her grisly fate. This is supposed to be a date, and this is the problem. I can't draw a definitive line between my work life and my personal life. Every aspect of my life spills into the other and I'm left with a diluted soup of dysfunction. Or maybe it's simply because I have no personal life? When the food arrives, Pete's eyes widen as he leans back in his chair in preparation to dive into his very juicy-looking steak.

'You know, I just thought...' he says, as he takes his steak knife to make the first cut. 'Do you think killers have to practise before they kill or do they just dive right in?'

'From what I've read,' I pause, 'and I'm no expert, but a lot of killers show disturbing tendencies from a young age and it often starts with animal cruelty, pulling off insects' legs and watching them wither and suffer till they die, stuff like that.'

'Stop!' Pete raises his hand in protest. 'Can't deal with

hearing about some sick bastard hurting animals. Can't tell you what it does to my insides.' His voice is urgent, he takes a long gulp of beer and sighs.

'I understand. I don't know how you could intentionally inflict pain on another living thing.'

'I guess you must think I'm a right hypocrite!'

'Why?' I ask.

'I'm eating a cow. There is a cow on my plate, and I am slicing through its flesh.'

'But that's different... we are all part of the food chain, we all gotta eat. Animals eat animals,' I say.

'That's true, but I still try not to think about it.'

'Suppose you're camping in Canada and a bear attacks you, you'd do anything to defend yourself. We all have it in us. One way or another.'

I have always doubted people, especially relationships, and with good reason, but there is something about Pete that draws me to him. Maybe it's his acts of kindness, caring for his sister, and his clear compassion for animals; it tells me he's a good egg.

'Tell me about your work,' I ask.

'Well, I'm a graphic designer, so all of my work is based on visual content. I'm also a trained photographer so I combine the two together. I used to take photos of architecture, but lately it's been beaches. Cornwall has such a stunning coastline, sometimes I have to remind myself I'm in England.'

'It truly is beautiful, but because I've lived here my whole life, it becomes a blur and I just don't stop to really see it anymore. When I went to London, I felt excited. I was taken in by the buzz of the city, the pace in which people purposely moved. I think I'd love to experience living there even if it was for a year or so.'

'It's funny because you can still be isolated in a big city and it can feel even more isolating when there is so much happening around you and you are just standing on the sidelines, not really a part of it at all.'

That struck me deep, perhaps deeper than it should have. I've been around people my entire life, but I'm always on the sidelines, always alone.

'Here is some of my work.' Pete hands me his mobile and a screen filled with photos. 'This is the Instagram account where I post the work I'm most proud of. Should give you a clear idea of my style.'

I scroll through the photos of Pete and am drawn in by the side profile photo of him. His hair is longer in the photo and touches the collar of his denim shirt. A pair of headphones hug his head and sit over his ears. There's a view of buildings beneath him. With his beard he looks like the true poster child of adventure.

'Where was this taken?'

'This was on a chopper over Sydney. I got some fantastic shots that day. Amazing what you can take from a height.'

There are other photos of the view and they are breathtaking, but I cannot draw my eyes away from the one of Pete in the chopper. He's right, you can tell a lot about somebody by the content they post. In just these few moments I have absorbed so much information: Pete is creative, adventurous, and talented, with a clear hunger for life.

'Will you take a break for now?' I ask.

'I can still do what I love. Cornwall has a lot to offer.'

I nod. He's right. And I have spent so long trying to get away I've taken for granted what is right in front of me. Sometimes it takes seeing things through someone else's eyes, and I like the way things look through Pete's eyes.

'You should come with me this Sunday. I'm planning on taking some beach shots.'

'I'd like that,' I say. And I mean it.

After dinner we go for a walk, the air is cool, and I hug my arms tightly round my chest trying to tame the chatter of my teeth. Without warning I feel Pete pull me in against his warm body. I stiffen. The atmosphere between us since the restaurant has shifted. It has been so long since I've had a hug, it feels alien to me. It's not that I don't want Pete to touch me, I just don't know how to behave. I think I had a few too many beers at the restaurant and I feel strange, trepidatious.

'Are you all right?' Pete asks.

'I'm fine,' I reply and rearrange my expression into a happy-to-be-here smile and I am. *I think.*

CHAPTER NINETEEN

THEN

I twist onto my side. I listen to the slow and steady rhythm of her breathing. I study the shape of her head and want to crack it open and make her dreams spill out. Her unconscious thoughts. The house is asleep. Everything is silent and still. Only the glow of the moon casts a shimmer of light through the crack of the curtain. My thoughts are not silent. They are wide awake and dancing. They jump around my head and refuse to calm. Every so often my heart thuds harder as I think about the moment her lips pressed against mine. Even under the warmth of the duvet, I can still feel the chill of the water stabbing though my skin. Eyes open and my senses raised, I don't know where this will go from here. I fear regret. Rejection. But she came to me, pressed her body up against mine. I let her because I want her. I want her so much there is an ache in the pit of my stomach that will not switch off. I have never worried about losing anything before, and I realise it's because I never cared about anything as much as this before.

My eyes sting as I open them. I don't remember falling asleep. The side where she laid now lies empty and cold. There is a depleted feeling that washes over me. I glance at the red digits on the clock: 7:45. Does that mean she's escaped, hoping not to wake up next to me? This is her house. Who escapes from their own house? I remember all that time ago, waking up in this very room but now everything is different, the shift between us has moved miles – nothing is as it was before. A few minutes later, the bedroom door opens. She stands silently, wearing a pale-pink nightdress, her blonde hair hanging loosely over her bare arms. Her gaze locks onto mine and finally she breaks the silence between us – the air feels like it's been sliced with a knife.

'Before you say anything, I need to tell you how I'm feeling.' She sits on the edge of the bed and looks ahead, pausing, making sure the words she uses are the right words and that they are delivered exactly how she intends to deliver them. I feel my heart leap into my throat, and my air supply feels paper thin.

'I have only been interested in having simple relationships. But this feels different because it is different, and I don't know what it all means...' She takes another deep breath at the same time I cannot find mine.

'I...' she starts to say, but pauses.

Is she crying?

Is this where the night has taken us? The cold, hard light of day has changed everything.

'I have had two one-night stands and a few longish relationships. I don't know what this means... and I would be lying if I told you I am at ease with this transition or whatever it is. All my life, I was sure of who I was and what I wanted and then you came along. The first time we met, at the party, I was interested. Because you were different. I liked how genuine you seemed. I am so used to fakery. I love my friends, but it is always a competition, a contest I feel like I can never win. Sometimes I don't want to be this perfect version of myself. It's so tiring. But with you, I don't feel tired.'

She sets her hands on her lap. 'Let me tell you, I *loved* last night. I got lost in the moment. Or should I say *moments*? I'd have never gone into the sea like that. I actually hate feeling cold.' She lets out a laugh and I am not sure if I should laugh along with her. My stomach starts to flutter with excitement. What I feared is nothing to fear at all. I am afraid of a 'but', willing it not to come. For the first time ever, I need faith.

'I am not ready to call us a couple. But I like you, I know I like you and I don't want to let the feelings I felt last night, and this morning, go. But...'

There's the 'but'. I hang on to it, wanting to expel it out of the air, make it go away.

'Grace.' My voice is still fused with sleep. With fear. It wobbles and is uncertain.

'Wait, please let me finish and then you can say or do whatever you need to do. I've been up since the early hours thinking about what I needed to say to you and if I stop–'

'Say it!'

Her gaze meets mine in the mirror.

I have a strong sense my whole life is about to change.

'It's you. I've never been hurt enough by a man to feel put off for life.'

It's hard not to respond and give her the stage.

'I want to see where this goes. I hope you do too. But because of my mixed feelings, I am not ready to reveal this side of myself to my family, my friends.'

'So, what you're saying is, you want me to be a secret?'

'No! I mean yes. For now. I don't know.' Her eyes are wide with confusion and her forehead is beaded with sweat.

'I shouldn't feel close to you. We hardly know one

another, but I do. I know how screwed up I must sound. I don't want you to go but I can't be open about us. If that is what you want, I can't give you that… but if you want more of the conversations on the beach, the chemistry we shared last night, that I can give you. If I've made an absolute twat of myself and you didn't or don't feel like I do, and it was just one fun night out, then I'll understand that too. We never have to talk again.'

'Don't say that.' My answer is short and direct.

'So, it wasn't a meaningless night of fun?' Her eyes dart back and forth searching for reassurance.

I rest my hand on hers and shift toward her. Her body presses into me and she rests her head on my shoulder. I watch her chest rise and fall with every cry she tries to suppress. I run my fingers through her hair, and for a minute I just let us be.

'I don't want to let any of whatever this is go, Grace. If it means it's a secret then it's our secret.'

We both stop short at the sound of footsteps. A door closing.

'My parents must be home early. They weren't supposed to be back until tonight.'

'Oh, so it's my fault, Annie. It's always my fucking fault,' a male voice booms, followed by a loud thump.

Grace jumps off the bed and presses her ear to the door.

'No, Harold. It's not your fault that slut calls you while we are on a weekend away trying to fix our fucked-up marriage. How could it possibly be your fault?'

The voices become louder. Closer.

I pull my knees up to my chest and wait for Grace to tell me what to do but she does not look at me. Her ear is firmly fixed against the door and she is still.

'For the fiftieth fucking time, Annie. It. Is. Over. I am sorry but I cannot control whether she calls or not.'

'See, here's the rub, Harold. If you hadn't have fucked her in the first place and cheated on our marriage, she wouldn't be calling you.'

'I know. I don't know what else I can do to tell you I'm sorry. This weekend was supposed to be about that and if I had known she'd call I would have changed my number, thrown the fucking phone on the motorway.'

The voices are now muffled, but the tone is still very much hostile. I feel like I'm watching a drama on the BBC, waiting for the music to leave this moment on a cliffhanger. Grace's body is pushed so tight against the door that she looks as if she has melted into it.

I gently place my hand on her shoulder, she looks back to me, her eyes pooled with tears.

'I hate to leave things like this, but I need you to leave. I'll call you later.' Her words sting. It's started already; do not be seen, do not be heard. I just didn't count on it being this soon.

'Why don't we get ready and leave together?' *Breathe*, I remind myself. *Smile.*

'I need to find out what's going on with my parents, and I need to do it alone. I will call you later.'

I snap my gaze away. I don't want her to see the ripple of pain needling itself through my body. *Aren't couples supposed to be together in everything? Isn't that how it's supposed to work?*

'I'll get out of your hair,' I say.

Grace furrows her eyebrows together and folds her arms around her. A swell of panic rises when I realise I've said the wrong thing and it could cost me.

'I meant that in a nice way. I realise how it came across. Sorry.' I hope my words will put to bed any misunderstanding and she will come back to me.

'Sure.' She puts her ear to the door again. 'I think they are probably out back. If you leave now, they won't see you.' She then picks up my clothes and thrusts them into my arms.

I sit on the edge of the bed, pulling on my clothes. My legs seem to be shaking and I can't get my leg into the leg holes without having to rebalance myself again.

I never grew up with parents. Let alone in a setting where I've been well provided for. I don't know what to say. What should I say?

'I don't know what to say.' It's the most honest I have ever been.

'I don't expect you to say anything. It's a bit awkward, isn't it? I mean, having the conversation and then my parents... bad timing, I guess.'

She opens her palms and I place my hand in hers. The atmosphere in the bedroom feels heavy and oppressed. Truth is, I need fresh air. It all feels too overwhelming.

'I'll call you later.' She propels forward and gives me a long, meaningful kiss on the lips. My insides feel like they are fusing back together again.

I leave the house and step out into the cool air. I take a deep breath. I'm not ready to return home, but I don't want to walk into the bleak concrete jungle either. Last night feels like eons ago, so far removed from where I am standing right now. I take a slow walk, past the Range Rovers, the perfectly manicured lawns, the blinking alarm systems and I wonder about the people inside those houses. Suddenly, it becomes obvious to me that money does not create happiness. I've lived my life always short of money and yet Grace's parents have money, a nice house, nice cars, and her father still had an affair, they are still at a breaking point. It's a realisation. No matter how much money is in the bank, it does not make a happy home. Just a snippet of the argument revealed so much – we are all breakable. When is enough truly enough?

CHAPTER TWENTY

THEN

The person in the seat behind keeps jolting me forward with their careless leg movements. The bus crawls along, past the affluent shops. People dressed in expensive casual wear gather outside cafés to sip on their lattes, and the women wear oversized, almost comical, sunglasses with their wrists dripping in gold jewellery; an outfit that costs more than my salary, I'm sure. My head leans against the bus window; I have been looking at strangers' lives all day and drawing my own conclusions on how they live. The happy families who gather together on Sunday for lunch look fanciful, but it's all a sham. The truth is much more bleak: the husband fucks anyone who's willing to spread their legs for him, the wife has an addiction to online gambling and opioids, and their seemingly well-mannered 'little angels' are nothing more than a bunch of rich, spoiled brats who have no concept of real life or the true meaning of hard graft. *Grace.* My Grace is the pinnacle of those sorts of families, but I don't see her in the same light as I do the others. The bus lurches forward and turns a corner, the landscape changes, I try not to look up. I try to ignore the idiot behind me and restrain myself from grabbing them by the throat. I play with my phone, willing it to buzz, hoping it will be a message that will end the journey on the 157 and I'll jump off and run back to the place where there aren't drunken tramps stinking of piss in abandoned shop fronts. I'll take the ostentatious, high-and-mighty arseholes in exchange for my life in the grime any day of the fucking week.

The text message doesn't come, and the bus growls as it moves, like it needs to defend itself from the plagued neighbourhood it's entering. I get back to the flat a little after midday with a bottle of wine in a white plastic bag I picked up on the way home. As I open the door, misery pours over me and my stomach tightens, paint doesn't cover the scars and stains of the memories this place holds. I could never bring Grace here. Not ever. I'm too embarrassed to call this place my home, but before her it didn't matter. I sit the bottle on the kitchen counter, strangle it on the neck to twist open the screw cap, and pour it into a coffee mug that I don't even think is clean. I bring the wine to my mouth and sip. Tangy and cold, the aftertaste settles on my tongue, which isn't unpleasant. I've never been much of a drinker, but I need to lull myself out of my present state and unconsciousness is the key. Soon the room starts to sway as the effects of the alcohol begin to swirl in my empty stomach – it's a relief, it's working. I love the sensation of my senses closing up shop for the day, the memories falling to the back of my mind and being safely tucked away. Silenced.

The canvas picture of a rose in a vase begins to distort as the redness of the petals begins to drip like blood. I reach to hold a chair, to steady myself as the ground beneath me is on unsteady plates.

Then. Nothing.

There is a pile of clothes on the floor. It looks angry, crumpled up, discarded. It takes a few moments before my vision is fully restored. It's dark outside, which means I have

113

slept through the entire day. It gives me hope that I will reach for my phone and my clouded thoughts will clear. The room is so cold it slices through me, the curtains are wide open and outside the night-time activity is already starting to heat up by the bin store as I watch a man hold a woman's hand in too tight jeans and sky-high stilettos. They slink behind a graffitied wall and I watch her sink to her knees as he places his hands on her head.

My eyes and throat itch, I turn on the tap and drink straight from it. I search the room for my phone, but I can't see it. I wipe my mouth with the back of my hand and go into the bathroom where I catch sight of myself in the mirror. My face is puffy from the wine and my skin looks grey. I grimace as I remind myself of my mother before she passed away and it freaks the hell out of me. I reach for the basin and splash cold water on my face to wash the remnants of the image away. I still can't find my fucking phone. Did I lose it on the bus? I don't know Grace's number by heart... I don't think, 07957 *no wait... 07956...*

I try to wrack my brain and then it comes back to me. The pile of clothes. I almost run to it and shake the pile until I am greeted with the sound of a clunk. There it is. I bend down to pick it up. I have only one per cent of battery left and just as the phone is about to die, it's there. True to her word.

I plug the phone in and wait eagerly for it to come back to life.

When it finally does, I punch my code in but when I do the phone freezes. It can't cope with the demand of speed I am putting on it. 'For fuck's sake!' I shout. I close my eyes and take a deep breath.

This is only the beginning. The very start and already I feel like this. I need to gain control. I can't go through my days feeling so dependent and desperate but no matter what I tell myself, I cannot remove the overwhelming urge of wanting Grace.

> I am so sorry about this morning and what you had to see.

> My head is a bit of a mess after talking to my parents... they're talking divorce.

> Not sure where that leaves everything... so confused!

I feel irritated that her parents should choose this time to announce they are divorcing, and I am also equally confused by the message: *Not sure where that leaves everything?*

Does she mean with her home life? Or with us?

I start to type a reply and then pause and delete. Type and delete.

I can't tell her what I am really thinking. I have to be seen as supportive. Kind. Caring. Not anger her and scare her away.

> Sorry to hear things are tough. Want to go out and forget about things for a bit?

Her response is delayed and when it finally comes through it isn't worth the wait.

> I've got plans tonight. Maybe Wednesday if you're free? Xx

Plans. She has plans. I'm *not* happy. This morning she gave me a big emotional speech and hours later I'm already at the bottom of her list. Is this where her rich girl persona is going to trickle through? So long as she has what she wants then that's all that matters?

I want to ask her what is more important than picking up where we left off this morning, but I don't. I know if I do, I'll be left humiliated and sounding desperate. It's not as if she is leaving me to...

> Promised Imogen drinks, she's still feeling a bit crap after the whole Ben thing. X

I know now how I will spend the rest of the evening. Wallowing in my own self-pity. Waves of happy memories and flurries of frustration. I need to keep my destructive self at bay, but I don't know how far I'll get with that. Aunt Lizzy had been an irritation, but the easy thing about her was nobody came looking. I imagine with somebody like Imogen people would send the bloodhounds. She'd have a well-to-do family who would spend thousands to find her. Is that a risk I could... *should* take?

I stop. Think. The thought of making Imogen void fills me with excitement.

Does the world really need people like Imogen in it?

Would it be the worst thing I could ever do?

I have been thinking about Grace all the time, unable to focus on anything and picking out every single word in her texts, looking for hidden meanings. Our night together feels like something I have imagined; none of it feels true anymore because since then, none of the good stuff has been topped up. If I were with her, I would be able to see her expression, have a clearer reading of where we both are. Perhaps this is what relationships are like and this is why there are so many songs about broken hearts and why people are driven to craziness. I feel exhausted this evening. I am stone-cold sober and not ready to revisit the feeling. But what the hard, sober reality leaves me with is other demons; the challenge of pushing the jealous undercurrent of Imogen away, the way my heart lurches out of my chest when a new message buzzes through on my phone. If I had a life, I wouldn't be sitting in this miserable little flat stuck with toxic feelings. If I had a life, maybe Grace wouldn't be at the forefront of my fucking mind. The reality of my own loneliness hits me like an anvil. Usually, people cry when they are unhappy or sad, but I have no recollection of ever having shed a tear. At school, when I was pulled into the headmistress's office for pushing Debbie Foster off the slide, I was asked why I felt no remorse.

'Debbie has broken her arm and you show no emotion. Not an ounce of compassion. Why?'

I remember Mrs Henley's cold blue eyes fixed on me. So, I did what was expected of me and tried to cry but nothing came, so I slumped my shoulders, let my head drop, and wiped a finger under each eye. It was enough to satisfy her that I wasn't the monster she believed I was.

I'm still awake at midnight, staring at the ceiling. A dragonfly catches my eye, it gravitates toward the yellow lamp, repeatedly bashing its body against the shade. It doesn't learn, it doesn't fly off into another direction. I can relate to that. Lying flat on my back just thinking isn't going to change anything. I think about Imogen, taking up Grace's time with her pathetic self-deprecated tale of victimisation. The dragonfly lifts its body above the lamp and lands on the light bulb. I hear a fizzing sound followed by the smell of burnt hair. It is then I decide I will not be scorned.

Imogen needs to go.

CHAPTER TWENTY-ONE

JENNIFER MACK

I sit in the office waiting for the rain to come. The sky is patchy with dark clouds and the leaves on the trees rattle like a chorus of maracas. Three photographs stare up at me from my desk. I wish the photos would come to life and speak, tell me who it was that took their life.

Each young woman bears a striking resemblance; they could be sisters. I imagine them sitting next to each other, posing, smiling, happy. Their blonde hair is both similar in hue as it is in texture. I delicately touch each picture as if I will get something from it, a hunch, a feeling... something.

Grace Matthews has left behind a trail of broken hearts. A family who will never be able to fill the gaping hole in their lives. The family has kept in close contact with the police, but beyond that they remain silent. Grief does not play out the same song for every person; it doesn't act uniformly. I exhale hard and pinch the bridge of my nose. Everything feels so hopeless. I've been watching *Britain's Most Evil Killers* and listening to criminal psychologists, trying to learn. Serial killers back in the seventies and eighties were like kids in sweet shops, where everything was for the taking. Back then there was no advanced

CCTV or sophisticated forensics. The police relied on hunches more than physical evidence. Here we are in the twenty-first century and still no further along with this killer. I don't understand how the UK, the most watched country in Europe, has come up with fuck all. A lot of the blame, I feel, lies with me. My lack of experience is shining through and this is my one chance, the only chance to prove myself as a reputable investigative reporter. The pressure mounts each day; tension sits at the back of my neck knotting and kneading its way through my body – I feel like I am out of my depth, being eaten alive. There are bigger reporters making their way to Cornwall, hoping to take a fat piece of the action.

Social media has gone crazy; women are changing their natural blonde hair to brunette and red and #overtothedarkside is trending. It never fails to amaze me how young girls will do anything to grab five minutes of internet fame. Sometimes I wonder if social media were to disappear, would the world go back to a more forgiving and kinder place?

I leave the building in need of fresh air to clear my foggy mind. As I head to the back of the building and push open the fire exit door, the cool breeze washes over my skin and instantly offers relief. I lean against the brick wall and let my head rotate in small circular motions.

I lean my head on my hands, lost in thought. Victims' families and the public have a right to know what's going on, but the words aren't coming easy to me. My mind feels frozen. There haven't been any fresh leads and the truth is the police know as much as we do. The results from the lab following the Earth Rabbit murder haven't brought back any significant evidence – whoever this killer is, they have planned each killing with perfection. There isn't a speck of information we have to go on. It's as if the killer is a phantom. Unheard and unseen.

There will be more. It isn't a matter of if, but when. And I feel responsible, because if I don't do my job and catch the scent, blood will be on my hands.

The mobile phone buzzes on my desk: number unknown.

'Jennifer Mack?'

'Lilith Grain.' My heart stops. 'Lilith... how are you?'

'I have been speaking with my colleagues and it seems the Cornish police are a bit shit... pardon my French. So, I'm coming to Cornwall.'

'When?' I try to contain my excitement. This case needs Grain. The police have been useless during this entire investigation, but I don't let my professional guard down by agreeing with her.

'This Monday. I have a few loose ends to tie up here. I'm staying at Barnaby Lodge, an Airbnb just outside Truro. After I've met with the superintendent, we can meet. Make arrangements for dinner, and send me the information when you have it.'

She hangs up.

I was almost certain I'd never hear from Lilith again, and I wonder what's changed her mind. Not that it matters. The point is, she is coming to Cornwall to put pressure on the investigation. This is such a triumphant moment for me. I immediately go online and look for a decent but quiet restaurant. I feel an obligation to pick the right venue but tell myself it isn't my job to worry about the food.

Lilith is intimidating. Her brutal honesty and no-nonsense tolerance for ignorance sets her apart from almost everyone I know in authority. Cornwall has always been known for its slower pace. I guess it is not used to grisly serial killers and unimaginable crimes; it's used to glossy holiday brochures, coastal second homes, tranquillity. It doesn't know how to handle the incredulous debacle it has been thrown. Looking back on the archives of *The Chronicle*, the biggest story the paper has ever covered was a high-profile chef who opened a Michelin-star restaurant and used the upstairs premises for high-class prostitution and selling crystal meth. This story is bigger than that. I have a strong feeling Lilith will be the key to opening the door and catching this killer.

When I return home, it feels unusually cold, as if a window has been left open, but I am sure I closed everything before I left this morning. I move through the long, narrow hallway and notice my rain jacket lying on the floor; I was sure I'd hung it in the airing cupboard. I mentally run through the last time I wore it and can't ever remember leaving it out. I shake it off and put it down to my crowded mind. I pause outside the kitchen door; there's a photo of me and Mum in the middle of the kitchen table, it wasn't there when I left this morning. It lives in my bedside drawer under my journal. I don't look at it often because it's painful. Because it's the last photo we were ever in together. The kitchen window is gaping open and there is a chilly breeze making its way round my shoulders. I shiver. Not just from the cold.

I pause and slowly cast my eyes over the kitchen, taking in my surroundings. I always unplug the kettle, but the plug is firmly in the wall. My coffee cup sits on the draining board. I am meticulous and never leave any item out. The cup is always returned to the cupboard next to the microwave... always.

I inhale and exhale and then reach into the drawer to remove a bread knife. It's the first thing I lay my hands on. It may not be the sharpest, but it is sharp enough to really hurt.

I walk through the rest of my flat with caution. Blood rushes through my body and my nerves are on fire. I tell myself there must be a logical explanation. My hand shakes as I point the knife out in front of me before I enter each room.

There is nothing else untoward. Nothing except the overwhelming feeling that the air has changed and I feel like a pair of eyes are watching me. Perhaps I need to sleep more. Perhaps I should install a camera just to settle my nerves.

When I'm satisfied I have searched all the possible areas somebody could be hiding in, I return to the kitchen and decide tea isn't going to detain the fear rushing through my veins, so wine it is. I take a sip and let the tang of alcohol rest on my tongue. I squeeze my eyes tight, and then a sharp breeze travels through the window and picks up the photograph of Mum and me.

It flips to the back, and blood rushes through my body again.

It takes my eyes seconds to process the information, but my logic is having a very hard time catching up.

I finally find the strength to launch myself across the table. The ink is blood red, thick and angry. Join *her*...

My breathing feels shallow, like I have just come out of the deep end of a swimming pool and I'm trying to steady myself from a time spent underwater.

Someone has been here. There is no doubt.

I don't touch the photo. Instead, I reach into my pocket for my mobile and dial 999.

My voice is unsteady.

'Police,' I say.

It feels longer than it should for the police operator to answer.

'An intruder... an intruder has been in my flat. Please send somebody.'

'Do you think they are still in the flat with you?' the operator says.

'No... I've searched.' My throat feels clogged up.

'We are going to send officers to your home now. Can I please take your address?'

After I finish giving my address, I lean against the kitchen counter gripping the edges. My breath is hard. Heavy.

'I know it's hard but try to stay calm. Help is on the way. I'll stay on the line with you until the police arrive.'

'Thank you. How long until they get here?'

'It won't be long. Hang tight.' The operator's accent is Welsh, there is something soothing and comforting in its rhythmic inflection.

Finally, there is a knock at the door, I open it and tell the operator two police officers have arrived. She wishes me well and the call ends.

I wrap my arms around my body. A male and female officer stand on my *welcome* mat.

'We received a call regarding a possible intruder in these premises,' the female officer says. Her complexion is pale, blue eyes bright, skin clear and smooth, she holds herself upright, maintains eye contact. Her professionalism isn't fractured by her young age, the opposite. She continues to maintain eye contact with me which alleviates a little of the judgemental doubt I had when I first laid eyes on her.

'I did... My name is Jennifer Mack. I am the lead reporter for the Grace murders. I think the killer has been in my flat.' My voice is breathy and fast, but I can't help it. It is unnerving to think somebody has been in my home, touching my things, breathing in my personal space, and analysing such an intimate photograph; it makes me feel violated. The officers enter the property and start to look around.

'I didn't leave my rain jacket out. I put it away and when I got home it was on the floor. Here.' I point to where the caramel-coloured jacket had lain.

'Where is it now?' the male officer asks. I take an instant dislike to him. He reminds me of my old geography teacher, small beady eyes, receding hairline and a tone that is laced with accusation and disbelief.

'I put it back... in my airing cupboard.'

'Why?' he says curtly.

I feel my cheeks flush. Surely, I must be turning the colour of a strawberry.

'Because I thought I may have left it out by mistake. But since seeing the photograph, I know somebody has been here, there isn't a doubt in my mind.'

'But you doubted whether or not you left your jacket out.' He cocks his head to the side.

'I didn't write a message to myself on the back of a very personal photograph, of that I am certain,' I retort.

He shrugs his shoulders and turns his back. He walks upright with a swagger and moves into the living room to the corner next to the sash windows where my writing desk sits, one of the very few pieces I took from my mum's house after she died. I like the heavy oak and water-stained top, its clunky legs make it stand out against the contemporary oatmeal-coloured sofa and flat-screen TV hanging from the wall. It looks like an out-of-place guest. But I love it because it belonged to Mum. It came with fond memories of her writing *actual* letters in her beautiful swirly handwriting, she kept a wad of airmail envelopes and packets of stamps in the water-swelled, hard-to-close drawers.

The female officer removed her hat; her fine blonde hair was cut into some sort of deliberate mess.

'Has anything been moved in this room?'

'Nothing that I've noticed,' I say with caution.

We finally enter the kitchen. I feel myself stiffen. The window was still open.

The female officer eyes the open window. 'It's not big enough for a person to slip through.'

My heart drops, there's no sign of forced entry, *so how did they get in?* I make a mental note to call a locksmith, change the locks, and get a security system installed. Most of the neighbours work so it's doubtful anybody would have seen anything, but it is absolutely worth an ask. Loretta Woodgrave lives above me and is a nurse, she works shifts so it is possible she could have seen something, and I hope she has.

The intercom has been broken for the better part of three months despite my efforts tasking the management company to fix it. Robert Epsom, at number 76, withheld his service charge but was soon met with a stern letter and a copy of the leasehold agreement reminding him of his obligation not to withhold his service charge under any circumstance or he would be taken to court.

The male officer, PC Hinch, looks at the kitchen cupboards, the windows, and finally at the untouched photo on my kitchen table. He's like an irritating itch that I can't reach to scratch, and he has not shown an ounce of warmth or registered that I am scared shitless. He's too wrapped up in his own self-importance.

PC Hinch leans over the table and is silent, his eyes taking in the words. I feel so exposed, my personal possessions have been tampered with and will be forever tainted. Now I won't look at that picture and think of my mum, I will look at it and think of the violating hands that manhandled it, drifting in and out of each room, sucking in the very air I breathe. *My* air. In *my* flat.

How much has this intruder learned about me?

How will I ever feel safe within these walls again?

'There isn't anything we can find that suggests there was

forced entry. Does anybody else have a key to the property?' PC Hinch asks.

'No, just me.' I pause. 'The estate agents told me they gave me the only key they had for the property on the day I moved in.'

'How long ago was that?'

'Just under a year.'

'And you didn't change the locks when you moved in?'

I take a deep breath and sigh. 'No.'

I remember the day I received a phone call from my solicitor advising me I was now the legal owner of 70 Bluebell House. I loved how whimsical my new address sounded, and how proud I felt to be able to buy my own bricks and mortar. I fell in love with the large sash windows and the exposed floorboards. The flats used to be the wing of a hospital. Its exterior was solid, the interior begged to be transitioned as the previous owners had done little with the place. It was a second home barren of items and fabrics that make a house feel homely, as many flats are in Cornwall. In the summer months, families pile in with buckets and spades, surfboards and wetsuits a plenty, but out of holiday season many properties are void of holiday chatter, excitable children. In the winter, Cornwall falls into hibernation, and the locals enjoy the reprieve from the pesky tourists.

'I think it would be a wise idea for you to get those locks changed now, don't you?'

The lid I've been trying to contain pops. 'I am sure you are well aware there is a serial killer out there, and I guess they are getting away with these evil crimes because, well, what are you lot doing to find them?' I place my hands out on the table and don't stop, I'm on a roll and I am fed up with victim blame and PC Hinch's incredulous gaze.

'We will take the photograph and check it for prints.'

'That's it?' I yell.

'That's all we can do for now. As I said, if we had some CCTV footage, we'd be looking at it. We'll look around all the flats, see if there is anything that will help, but beyond that there isn't a lot we can do besides file a report and advise you to change your locks.'

'What if it is the killer?' I say.

'We will do our best to run prints, if something comes up, we'll let you know.'

A statement is taken, my precious photo bagged up and taken away, and then they are gone, just me and the silent walls that I wish could talk.

This is my first home, I saved and worked so hard to get it and it has always been a safe haven, but now I feel as though the walls around me are made of glass and I am on show. Every move I take, I feel I am being watched. I comb every square inch of the surfaces, reaching high up onto cupboards and shaking out the curtains and blinds making sure there aren't any cameras. I spend over two hours doing this until I am sure there is no trace of surveillance. Later that evening, my stomach begins to protest and growl, it's then I remember I haven't eaten anything all day. I can't face going out to the supermarket and I'm hesitant to call a delivery in because I don't want another stranger peering into my property; I feel exposed enough as it is. I remind myself a delivery guy is just doing their job and I am already allowing the killer to take up my headspace. He intended to scare me, and I'm letting him do just that. But thinking about his hands touching my belongings, the same pair of hands he has used to savagely rob 'The Graces' of their lives makes me feel physically sick. I pull open the sash window in the lounge and allow the cool breeze to flow through as if the salty sea air is cleansing my flat of the intruder's lingering presence even though he is no longer here. Everything feels different, like a bad dream I cannot wake up from. I read somewhere that it is important to open your windows often, that a change of air makes for a healthy mind and body. Right now, I can only handle leaving the window open for a few moments before I slam it down so hard it makes the cracked paint on the ledge chip away. I remain motionless, a mix of frustration and anger mixes up in my stomach. I can't ignore my hunger pangs anymore, so I decide to order food. I tell the pizza place to call me when they're outside so I can meet them at the main door and I pay over the phone to make contact as minimal as possible. I don't want another living soul crossing my threshold.

CHAPTER TWENTY-TWO

REDBRICK ROW

The room is dark and her eyes strain to adjust. Her body shivers as an icy chill creeps over her like crawling insects trapped beneath her clothes. She sees the outline of a doorway. She tries to move but can't. Her hands are bound behind her back. She screams but only a muffled moan escapes her mouth. Tears leak down her temples and the feeling of helplessness washes over her, fear unlike any she has ever known.

Will I die here? she thinks.

The hopelessness is malignant, she feels it cramping in her stomach as waves of nausea flow through her like a violent river, virulent and infectious. She lies still, trying to remember how she got here. She remembers Rob offering her a lift, she can recall going to the library. Then she remembers coming over hot and clammy so she went to the loo to splash cold water on her face and after that, everything went black.

She has no concept of time, whether it's day or night, or how long she's been here for. She is in a suspended time lapse. The smell of damp tells her she might be in a basement, and above her there is a dripping sound, the constant *drip drip drip* assaulting her ears. She drifts in and out of sleep; her body is in flight mode, trying to protect her from the horror in which she finds herself.

The sound of a door creaking open jolts her out of a light slumber followed by the sound of footsteps. She feels her body stiffen. The footsteps come closer and she draws a breath.

'You're a tough one.' The voice isn't what she expects; it's velvety soft, breathy, and seductively sinister.

'Please... let me go.' Her voice is fractured and bounces off the walls.

'Afraid I can't do that.'

'Please. I'll give you money. I won't tell anyone, I promise.'

'If only it was that simple.' As the abductor moves closer, she recognises the scent. Chanel No. 5. She knows this because it's the perfume her sister Charlotte wears. She thinks of Charlotte, living in New York, making her mark in the fashion world. She's missed her since she left last year, the long evenings watching films and chatting on the sofa with mugs of tea in hand. A pang of emotion hits her. Will she ever see Charlotte or any of her family and friends again?

'Who are you?' The 'who' doesn't matter nearly as much as the 'why' does, because only with the 'why' can she work out a solution. She can't think of any enemies, she's always been such a homely girl, so nice to everyone. She isn't the type of person who deliberately seeks out trouble, and she can't think of any altercation that would bring her to this dire point in time.

Here's what she knows.

She is tied up in some sort of underground basement. She thinks her captor may have killed somebody else before her, why else would he have the scent of a woman's perfume clinging to his skin?

CHAPTER TWENTY-THREE

JENNIFER MACK

The sun bounces off the rain-slicked pavement making my eyes squint. The camera crew has arrived; this is national news now. They are hungry with their long black snaky cables trailing round their feet. A sea of North Face jackets, large eyes, sweaty faces, and bodies poised waiting to pounce on the action.

The other journalists push past me, banging into my shoulders in their scramble to the front of the queue. I am so out of my depth, and I feel like I won't ever rise to the surface. I want to scream, tell them all to 'fuck off' this is *my* story, how dare they trespass, how dare they try to steal *my* words.

This is fast becoming a celebrity serial killer. Netflix is already rubbing its hands together eagerly waiting to green-light the inevitable docudrama.

'They got there just in time,' Phillip Underwood says, complete with his silver-fox hair and chiselled features. He is always camera ready.

Just in time...

Before she became one of them.

The police have cordoned off the red-brick building, several PCs stand in front of the yellow tape, arms crossed, expressionless. An ambulance sits waiting with its blue and red lights still flashing. A stretcher clatters as it comes out of the ambulance.

I scramble to get to the front, but all of the other hyenas make it near-on impossible. We are all after the same prey, ready to scavenge what there is to take. But if I want to survive them in this jungle, I'll have to outsmart them all.

Sirens shatter the cool air; their piercing wail a declaration of survival. Nobody knows what state the victim is in; all we know is she's alive and she's the only person who will be able to talk. I look around and the circus is still in full swing. The chaos is focused on the red-brick building, there is a forensics team already inside and I wonder if they will find anything this time. To my left I see a man with his gaze fixed on me. He's about my age, early thirties with dark hair and a five o'clock shadow. His eyes are sunken, tired but restless. He's wearing a suit that doesn't hang right on him; it looks like he borrowed it just to be here and look the part. He holds a camera in his hand, he must be a reporter. There are so many faces I don't recognise today. When I catch him staring at me, I expect him to quickly look away but he doesn't.

What do you want?

He keeps a distance, but he shifts his footing, looking nervous, but his uncertainty doesn't deter him from me being his prime focus. I'm not good in these situations, my head is telling me to ask him what he wants, but I also don't want him to know he's getting to me. What if... No, he can't be. Would he be that brazen?

Why focus on me?

The flat. The photo. Thoughts rush through my mind thick and fast. There's enough people here. There isn't anything he can do. That's not how he works, is it?

The murders were all premeditated. Planned. This is not

how it will end, right here out in the open, none of it makes sense.

I've been on edge ever since the break-in, even if the police won't call it that because there was no sign of forced entry. Apparently, items being moved around my flat is not admissible evidence that somebody was there. I decide not to show I am afraid; I keep my eyes fixed on him. His gaze travels over me, he makes no pretence he isn't looking at me, no mistake. Something about the way he looks at me tells me he's judging me. His dark eyes don't boast admiration; if anything, it's distaste. He doesn't take me in the way Pete took me in; he looks like he's chewing me up and wants to spit me out. So, what the fuck does he want?

It starts to rain and a sea of umbrellas start to pop up one by one. He doesn't move. Nor do I. We are two wild dogs, neither willing to give in. No matter how hard my heart thuds in my chest that makes me feel like my ribcage is rattling, I will not be the one to turn away.

If he is the reason I was too scared to get up the other night to get myself a glass of water, then I must face the beast head-on. I won't be the victim. There are enough of those right now. Before my thoughts have caught up with my movements, I put one foot in front of the other and make my way cleanly in his direction. My mouth is dry and I'm craving a drink, a proper drink, to help me deal with this situation with a little more gumption.

'Do I know you?' My voice is cutting, harsh.

He says nothing. His previous nervousness seems to have dissolved and is replaced with a new-found arrogance. His thin mouth curls into a slight smile and it unnerves me. I imagine him walking through my flat, his hands on my personal belongings.

'I asked you a question,' I repeat.

The crowd around me has blurred around the edges and all I can see is him. A nagging feeling tells me he's dangerous and I need to be careful. It feels like a tight ball is kneading together in my stomach, my limbs frozen, my spine rigid. His head falls forward. Is he laughing?

Is this actually happening?

I can't take my gaze off him. Like a lion stalking deer, it will take just one second of a lapse of concentration for something bad to happen. My heart is beating so fast I wonder if he can hear it.

Without thinking, I jab my finger into his shoulder.

'Who are you and what do you want?'

He looks at my hand and I quickly snatch it away. His calmness is more frightening than if he were to yell at me. Whether he is the one who came to my flat or not, whether he is the killer or not, none of this is okay.

'There are police over there. All I have to do is scream and they will rush right over. You have been watching me and I want to know what the hell you want!'

He shakes his head before turning away to disperse into the crowd.

I close my eyes and try to regain the steady rhythm of my breathing, try to stop the feeling of dread and darkness swallowing me. I haven't had an attack in a while, when my breath is so short, intense fear morphs through my body and a surging sensation of losing control results in the overwhelming feeling I am going to die. I move away from the crowd, the loud voices around me drift away and I can only hear muffled sounds. I walk and walk until I reach a park, and slowly the feeling starts to pass. I sit on a park bench, rest my head in my hands, and take deep, slow breaths, counting: one-two-three... one-two-three – there, that's better.

The panic attacks began a week after I moved to Oxford.

The reality of being away from home had hit and although beautiful, the stark contrast of my surroundings had shocked me in a way I didn't expect. I'd spent so long planning my great escape from Cornwall that I didn't expect to feel so... homesick. The first couple of weeks were all about making friends and navigating your way through an urban labyrinth to find your place. The next couple of weeks were about shaking off some of those people that you didn't feel a connection with; for me that was most of them. But I couldn't break away from all of the other students because I ran the risk of isolation. It is entirely possible to be lonely even when you're surrounded by hundreds of people. At first, I thought something was really wrong with me, but I was too afraid to go to a doctor. It wasn't until somebody called an ambulance after a particularly bad episode that I found out I was suffering from panic attacks. To relax, I began having a glass of wine at night, but before I knew it a glass turned into a bottle, then wine turned into liquor. I have always seen it as medicinal; people take antidepressants and you have to do what you need to do to get by, so as long as it's under control, I know I can stop anytime I want to. My phone starts to buzz. It's Jacob.

'Where are you?' he asks. I can tell he isn't happy.

'I...' I pause. 'I was at Redbrick Row.'

'And what did you get?'

Nothing. I got fuck all.

'The police have taken the victim to hospital.'

'For fuck's sake, Jen!'

I swallow back the words I want to say. *My name is JEN-NIF-ER!*

'Our paper is a sinking ship,' Jacob hisses. 'We aren't getting the headlines we should be. I know we're not *The Daily Mail*, *The Times*, but we are still journalists and we still need to report what is happening on our doorstep. Maybe... maybe this isn't working out.'

When people say something isn't working out, they mean *you* aren't working out. It never means anything else. I am hanging by a thread. My education and all of those big dreams I have/had are slipping away from me. It suddenly occurs to me that if I can't handle a small paper then how the hell will I ever reach greater heights?

'There was a man... he was acting strange and I think he might know something about the Graces. Jacob, I know this sounds insane, but I have a hunch.'

'Find out more and bring back something useful. This is your last chance, Jennifer. If you can't close this out, the case will go back to Hayley. Find something and write the goddamn story.'

He hangs up.

I reach into my backpack and pull out my flask. I give it a little shake and a wave of relief washes over me; it's not enough but it's something. The only problem is it's going to leave me wanting more.

———

Padstow is not a place that I come to often, but when I do visit, I wonder why I don't come here more. It seems a little odd that Lilith Grain chose to stay here instead of Truro, but I suspect she's mixing business with pleasure and making this into a mini holiday – maybe. The torrential rainfall from the past few days has finally waned and the clouds have broken up to uncover a brilliant azure sky. I sit outside a waterfront café perched high above Padstow harbour and sip Diet Coke from my glass. It tastes sickly sweet and flat. I crave an extra zest, that little extra something to cut through the sugar. A Range Rover snakes round the narrow bend in the road a little too fast. Somehow the car navigates its way into a space on the road that looks impossible for it to fit into, but with tiny slow movements it slips in. The door opens wide and a woman slides her body out rather than steps out. The woman wears a Barbour jacket that swamps her small frame and Hunter wellies. Dressed head to toe in dark colours, she looks polished and prepared for a long country hike. It takes me a few moments to realise it's Lilith. I should've known, but out of her business attire she looks different. The car dwarfs her, she looks like a child standing next to it – I wonder if she has a booster seat installed so she can see over the steering wheel. She straightens up and makes her way toward the café. She recognises me straight away but skips the pleasantries.

'Have you got a table for us?' she asks.

'Yep. I was just waiting here for you, getting a bit of fresh air.'

'Hmmm. Hmm. It's a nice day, not that cold either, quite pleasant actually.' Her voice is as authoritative and loud as I remember it from London.

The menus are placed on our table, the choices are better suited to a restaurant than a café, with dishes like market fish of the day, beetroot-cured salmon, and home-made curried gnocchi. I'm not sure how good the food will taste without a glass of wine to accompany it, maybe I'll just have a tipple, a small glass... yeah, that'll be fine.

'Another victim... but this one got away!' Lilith says as she scans her eyes over the menu.

'Do you know anything about her?' I ask.

Lilith is wearing reading glasses which slide down her nose, but this only makes her look even more intimidating, like a stern head teacher or a barrister.

'I'll work with you, Jennifer. But only if you promise to follow the rules I set. Let me be clear, I don't like reporters because what I've learned is they write junk to grab headlines. A serial killer is headline enough, wouldn't you say? So, there is no need to make this into a gripping Hollywood drama… Reporting facts is your only job and if you deviate from that, this is over, *kaput*. We clear?'

I admire her honesty. It's somewhat comforting to know where I stand with her and since she will get all the inside information, I'll play this any damn way she wants.

'Deal.' I set my hands on the table and look directly into her eyes. 'What changed your mind?'

'About what?'

'Working with me.'

'You need this. There is a hunger in your eyes, I can see it. But this can go one of two ways; this will be the making of you or the breaking of you. Nobody ever challenges me like you did, so you clearly have passion. That's why I decided to help. That and the police in this part of the country need somebody like me.'

'I want to solve this case, give people the truth,' I say with a surprising amount of conviction.

'If I'm being honest, even from the time you walked into my office I was curious about you. Perhaps I was intrigued as to why you'd travel all the way to London to speak to me. You've clearly done your research and stalked my profile, haven't you?'

'Whatever's published on social media becomes public knowledge.'

We are like two actors, each playing a role, but at the same time there is a raw honesty between us. I am confident our relationship won't be plain sailing, but we both have the same drive, the same end goal.

'Murder is fascinating, isn't it?' Lilith says.

I'm not sure if this is a test. I swallow a sip of water and lean back in the chair.

'I want to know the whys and hows. Don't we all?'

'I read that they are no more intelligent than the average person,' I say.

'The fact is we all have primal instincts to kill. If our lives are in danger we would not hesitate to kill. We all have something that makes us tick; be it gambling, alcohol...'

I feel my cheeks burn. She can't know. I'm just being paranoid.

'But serial killers...' I say. 'They have to have a different drive.'

'Sure, sure.' Lilith's gaze is fixed on me and for a moment I'm paralysed, taken in by her.

'In my line of work, I've seen it all, but serial killers are quite rare. That's why they always make such waves in the media. People are morbidly drawn to the violence of serial killers because for most of us, we don't understand it. We are both appalled and curious, when you mix these two opposites together, they create the perfect recipe for fascination. As humans, we are naturally curious, and most of us have compassion, but serial killers...'

There is a faraway look in Lilith's eyes. She, too, is fascinated. Or maybe there is something more that I've not quite caught onto.

'Did you know some people are attracted to serial killers?' Lilith's voice is hushed, carefully orchestrated so other patrons of the café can't hear her. 'It's known as hybristophilia, the thrill of being with a partner who is known to have committed an outrageous crime, such as rape or murder... or both!'

'Like Fred and Rosemary West?' I say.

'Funny you should mention them as a comparison.'

'Why?' I look at Lilith, all those years of experience so telling in her tired eyes.

'Because I think there are two killers working together.'

CHAPTER TWENTY-FOUR

THEN

It's just before midday, my jacket isn't thick enough and I hug my arms around my body, walking faster. The sea churns back and forth as if it cannot decide its mood, the sway of the waves unrhythmic and unpredictable. I've been up for hours, waiting for the first dribs of daylight to penetrate through the curtains and as it did, I headed to the beach. I haven't had a proper sleep in days. I hate this, hate all the waiting. Insomnia first introduced itself to me when he came into my room, after he first touched me. I knew even then his gentleness was just an act, and I knew he was crossing over to a forbidden place where he had no right to be. This is likely why I don't like men. Their brains are wired wrong, I'm sure of it. I don't believe their primitive instincts have differed much from Palaeolithic times: what they want, they take. This is what confuses me about Grace. She is acting like a man and it's fucking with my head. The build-up, the sex, the admiration, and then silence. Women aren't supposed to act this way, they are supposed to be more linear, softer creatures. It has been one whole week since the last message – seven whole days, 168 hours filled with conflicting thoughts, insomnia, and doubt. I hate living this opaque existence. Is this why there are a gazillion love songs dedicated to confused broken hearts?

I left the flat with a fully charged phone battery, but further along my walk I have also lost the signal. There is something welcoming about this, blaming the signal for lack of contact rather than Grace just not bothering. Somehow, it gives me an opportunity to breathe. After a mile or so, I pause, feeling hot and clammy. My skin is damp from the sea and fine mist. I take a deep breath and focus my gaze on a seagull dive-bombing into the water for fish, taking what it needs, what it wants with no apology. Nature is black and white: eat or be eaten. It's humans who have made things so complex. Animals hunt to survive, humans hunt for sport. Knowing I have taken a life goes beyond mere power, it was a necessary intoxicant. In one of my recent reads I came across a statement made by Carl Panzram: *'I believe the only way to reform people is to kill them.'*

This quote resonated with me. Let's forget about his actual crimes for a moment, because I am no rapist, nor am I an arsonist (although I once started a school fire) but there is so much truth in these words. Take Imogen, for example. She was brought up in a place of privilege and walks through life with an offensive air of superiority that is the only thing holding her upright. *Could she be reformed?* Well... no. Even if you took away the wealth, the big house, and suddenly she was poor and destitute, she would simply play the victim. 'Poor me,' she'd cry as the passers-by dropped their change. She would never once resort to thinking about the way she has treated people in the same circumstance before her. Never once would she consider her place in the karmic wheel. Her social status would certainly change, but who she is, who she *really* is, won't ever change. So, if you want to void such a personality, then the life tied to that personality must be voided as well. And let's face it, some people are just better off dead. We euthanise animals who show aggression, yet the same cannot be said for people: such as grown men who sneak into little girls' and boys' bedrooms and put their goddamn hands where they don't belong to steal their innocence. Somehow, they still live but we all know, deep down, that those people are better off dead.

In a world that has given me so little and has taken so much, I did the world a fucking favour when I put down Lizzy. I think of her face right before I killed her, still and ashen, yet so completely unexpectant, as if she was too privileged to die. If she knew what a bad person she was, she should have *begged* me to kill her. But people like Lizzy, like Imogen, and so many before and after them can never reform. What about Grace? Hmm... she is a problem for me, but the fact that she has left it this long makes my insides tangle, but if Imogen were out of the picture, she wouldn't cloud her mind. I believe Grace is too easily led and it pains me. I don't know. The rush of the feelings swooshing through me makes me feel nauseous. I don't know if this is really about Grace or whether it's about the lack of control I seem to have. All I know is, the only thing that gave me a sense of control and put me in the driver's seat was draining the life out of another wretched human being. The thrill of it, feeling a body begin to stiffen. I can barely even think of that time without my heart racing, the pure adrenaline pulsating rapidly through my veins. Everything's been a bit of an anticlimax since. I must do something, at least a small piece of action, to make me feel alive again, the good cause of removing yet another venomous snake from the world.

I stay at the beach long enough to gather my thoughts. My body can't seem to climatise to the bitter chill. In a lot of ways, being alone has major advantages; and I keep reminding myself of this. As the wind picks up, I move behind some tall rocks to offer a break from the cold, it's here I feel a slight vibration in my pocket. I remove it with my ice-cold fingertips, my hand feeling like a hundred needles are piercing through my skin. My fingertips move across the screen rigidly when I see her name. The block of ice that is my body begins to rapidly thaw, a surge of adrenaline gives me unexpected energy.

Hey... how are you? X

I leave it a few seconds before I reply.

Yup... good 😊

The smiley face I just typed looks alien on the screen. I've never typed a smiley face on a text before. I'm left with a slight distaste for myself.

If you're free, do you want to meet up later?
Perhaps go for a drink?

I look out to the ocean, waves rising, white-capped. The sea is becoming rougher and the thought of warmth and Grace is so welcoming, but there is a part of me that's still angry with her for making me play second fiddle.

Later as in today?

If you're free that would be great! Xx

Two kisses this time. I stare at them, decoding the true meaning: *Please?*

I glance at the time: 14:30. I need to freshen up, certain as of now I look like a bedraggled animal. I agree to meet her at 18:00. That's enough time to get back to the flat and fix myself up. I place the phone back in my pocket and begin the long walk to the bus stop. I walk too close to the shoreline and a wave sprays over me in a huge arc.

'Fuck's sake,' I shout. I'm soaked through and the cold I'd felt before has now penetrated deeper into my flesh. A man walking a scruffy rat-dog comes toward me.

'Oh... poor thing.'

My teeth are chattering and my body is shaking.

'My car is just up there. I've got a blanket in the car...' the man says.

I blink salt water from my eyes and stare at the man before me. He speaks quickly and I can't take in half of what he's saying. My hands are bloodless, pale, and stiff. For a split second, I look at the man and see Lizzy's face. In the whisper of the howling wind, I hear her strangled voice: *You ain't never been right in the head, can see it, see it right in your eyes.* As the man places his heavy hand on my shoulder, I lash out. A sound escapes my mouth; a scream (I think) but I am not sure if it's my own voice or that of a child. Suddenly I am transported back to my bedroom in the flat and he walks in. I smell the stale beer on his breath, the tobacco clinging to his clothes. The dog reacts to my outburst and begins growling and snapping at my heels. I kick it and it squeals; the man yells at me and tends to his dog. I want to run, back off. There's a pulling sensation through my legs as if the sand is trying to swallow me.

Eventually, I fall backwards. My whole body shakes.

'Jesus Christ!' the man shouts. His voice sounds distant, like a faraway echo bouncing through the emptiness of my head.

I don't answer. My gaze focuses on the sea and I try to reset my mind, tell myself I'm safe. There's the sound of a woman's voice. Urgent and worried. My head snaps up to see her hurtling toward the man. My fingers dig into the sand and I notice a group of dog walkers huddled close together, watching. The empty beach suddenly seems crowded with too many pairs of eyes focused on me. The woman, in her late fifties and bundled up in layers tends to the small dog, pressing his small body, checking for signs of injury.

'He's okay,' I hear her say. 'But... you... you could've killed him!' A green vein pulsates on her forehead.

'Love... I think we need to call an ambulance.'

'Don't need a bloody ambulance, we need the police to take this crazy person away,' the woman snaps.

Slowly, I begin to rise and the flashbacks fade. I'm in the present again.

'The least you could do is say sorry.' The woman is relentless, hell-bent on coming at me, whereas the man looks like he wants to help, but I don't want or need any of them close to me. I'm not apologising for shit.

I finally stand, still shivering, and dust the sand away from my soaked clothes. I begin to walk away as the man calls after me. I look over my shoulder, smile, and wave them goodbye.

The clock on the kitchen wall ticks, piercing the otherwise unusual silence in the flat. I cradle a cup of hot tea, letting the heat permeate through my hands. I close my eyes and try to recall the events of the afternoon; an uneasy feeling knots up in my stomach. I cross the kitchen through to the living room and lay on the old tattered sofa, inhaling the scent of mothballs. Decay. Oldness – my mother. My phone comes to life with a buzz, dancing across the coffee table. A flutter of panic beats in my chest: Grace. Cancellation. I push myself upright, my hand shaking as I go to reach for the phone. I stare at the message, scanning it at lightning speed. When I see the key critical words I straighten, bolt upright and fully alert. Imogen... sorry... another day!

From cold. I burn hot.

From calm. There is rage.

I can hear the sound of my heart thudding in my chest like a hammer against a nail through hardwood. I stand up. Pace. Back and forth, back and forth.

I don't know why I am letting this happen, leaving myself open, so out of control.

I went too far with Grace. I let her in too quickly. This only proves people cannot be trusted. I take myself to the window and squeeze my eyes shut and swear under my breath. My blood feels like it is simmering within my skin, like soup on a stove, bubbling and ready to boil over the top of the pan. I fall back onto the sofa, feeling the full weight of a headache kicking in.

She is the core of this problem. I pick up a cushion, an old, frayed and worn replica of how I feel inside. Holding it in my hands, I feel my fingers begin to curl into tight balls of fury, ignited with a physical rage I cannot contain. The soup has well and truly boiled over and I am punching my fists into the cushion over and over. Suddenly the faded pattern of circles on the cushion begins to move, like a kaleidoscope, only it's forming a face. A face I long to punch until the dark pools of brown eyes roll to the back of her head and there is no longer movement. No longer life.

This is what you need to do... it's the only way...

Stop. Think. Did killing Lizzy bring you the vindication you were searching for?

She must die. She must pay. She must die. She must pay.

My head is in my hands as I rock back and forth. Both voices becoming so loud, I am sure the walls will shake.

This is what she's done to you...

The phone comes to life once more, and my head quiets. The room sits perfectly still.

Why is this happening to me?

It was so close to being something special.

That night, just the two of us.

The possibility was right there in front of us. She wanted to see how it went and since that bitter feud between her parents and the abhorrent Imogen, outer influences have snatched away what could have been.

But... Grace... Grace... Grace. You let it happen. If you were the girl you portrayed yourself to be that night when your bare skin pressed up against mine – the cold bite of the sea in contrast to the hungry needful kisses – so passionate, desperate, how could you let others get between us?

Should it be Imogen who pays? The parents? Grace?

They all played a part. One way or another, something's gotta give.

I see her face flash in my mind once more and now I know what needs to be done.

CHAPTER TWENTY-FIVE

JENNIFER MACK

The atmosphere is brimming with an institutionalised, oppressive tone. The modern medical equipment looks space-aged and incongruous against the 1960s backdrop of putrid yellow walls. Nurses are known as heroes, angels, but they look anything but angelic under the harsh strip lighting. They operate like robots, following regimented procedures and completing charts, smiles vacant from their weary faces. You could create a life, a beautiful life, but this is the place where it could all end, the stagnant air where you will draw your last breath. Death lies in the shadows, waiting to extend its clawed hand to snatch the next soul. You can almost see the blackness of it, hear it through the hum of the machines and hissing oxygen tanks. When we walk into the ward, the first thing I notice is a curtain pulled back and a person sniffing to suppress sounds of crying. I don't like being here. But this is where she is, and she's awake. A senior nurse approaches Lilith and I; authority oozes from her pores, her hairstyle is severe and stiff, cut into a jet-black box-dyed bob. Her facial features are as sharp as her frame, there are no curves to soften the edges. She wears a dark navy dress with red piping, a plastic white apron clings to her svelte figure. She wouldn't look out of place wearing a longer dress, a cotton apron with frills and a cap from the Victorian era, her stony face would be well suited to it.

'Can you show me some identification?' the nurse asks without any pleasantries. Her directness doesn't seem to faze Lilith who co-operates without further challenge or comment.

The nurse, who is named Lucy according to her fluorescent yellow name badge, casts her eyes over Lilith's police ID and hands it back.

'The family has agreed you can speak to the patient with the understanding if the patient becomes unable for whatever reason you must cease your inquiry. Understood?' Lucy says.

'Yes,' Lilith responds.

'The patient's mother and father will both be present but they are not here yet, so I must ask you to wait in the family room until somebody notifies you of their arrival.'

We walk into a windowless room, its walls weary from surely having witnessed many tears over the decades. The grey carpet tiles have worn into what looks like chewing gum patches and the mismatched chairs have seen far better days; they should be burned rather than used. Lilith and I remain silent until we hear the door push open. The parents are much younger than I expected; the mother, her blonde hair tied into a topknot, wearing tight jeans and an oversized cashmere jumper with a designer handbag dangling from her arm, walks in proudly displaying the large diamond stone ring that sparkles on her left manicured finger. The father, also wearing jeans with a fitted shirt, fills the room with his expensive aftershave, he's clean-shaven and a Rolex watch wraps around his smaller than average wrist.

Lilith is the first to stand and extend her hand. 'I appreciate you allowing us to see Grace today. I know how difficult this must be for you both.'

The mother gives a weary smile, beyond the façade of make-up, her dull eyes still portray fear, an uncertainty and shock that she has not yet fully absorbed and processed.

The father, however, is harder to read. Passing him in the street, you'd never guess he had the weight of worry on his shoulders, that his daughter was a victim of attempted murder; he steps forward, extending his hand as if this were a business meeting to discuss the disappointing fiscal quarter.

'Larry Phelps, and this is my wife Danielle.' He's got a plummy accent, I can visualise him as a child in a boy's upper-crust boarding school.

'Shall we?' Larry holds the door open and the rest of us follow.

We come to a door where a bored security guard sits holding his phone in his hands, which he quickly shoves in his pocket as we approach. He stands and gives a nod to Larry and Danielle and steps aside.

The room is filled with an array of get-well-soon cards and bright balloons. Grace Phelps stares ahead at the blank wall until her mother puts her hand on her arm and she jolts like a scared cat about to dart away.

'It's just us, Gracie. Daddy and the inspectors we told you about.'

I do not correct her, but I feel like an imposter in the room without the correct credentials to be here. Lilith picks up on this and gives me a reassuring nod.

'Hello, Grace.' Lilith moves to the foot of the bed so Grace can see her clearly. 'I'm Detective Inspector Lilith Grain and this is Jennifer Mack, she works for *The Cornwall Chronicle* and is working as hard as I am to find out who hurt you.'

Grace looks at me for a fleeting second but then turns her attention to her mother and pulls her toward her to whisper something in her ear. Danielle sits next to her daughter and puts her hands on Grace's, gripping her fingertips tightly around hers. I start to reach for my bag and pull out my notepad. I'm mindful not to appear too eager... heartless.

'Grace... we're going to ask you a few questions. Simple things about who you are. Your interests, things like that, and then we will move on to other questions.'

'Like what happened to me?' Grace's eyes are wild and feral, like a fox caught in a snare, and suddenly I find myself with my back to the wall. The room becomes instantly silent with red-hot wrath rising in the too-small space. Heart thudding, I look at Grace, fear etched on her otherwise beautiful face.

Lilith clears her throat and adopts a softer voice; I admit, I didn't realise she had it in her, but it's here when I finally see the true professional that she is.

Larry stands with one arm across his body and rests his knuckles on his lower lip, then he turns to draw back the blind and opens the window. A blast of cool air cuts through the room, offering much needed refreshment for us all.

'I'm from London originally. I came down to Cornwall specifically for this case,' Lilith says to Grace.

Grace seems to perk up a little. 'Where in London?'

'Richmond.'

'I always wanted to go to London. I was supposed to go for Winter Wonderland in Hyde Park with my friend this Christmas.'

'Supposed to?'

'Yeah, well... it's less than two months to go and I don't know if I'll be fit enough. Everything hurts. And what if he's still looking for me?'

Grace looks to her mother for reassurance. Danielle lightly strokes her arm and whispers, 'It's okay, Gracie.'

'Can you smell that?' Larry says. 'Ugh... it's like old people and death in this place. We need to get you moved, darling. Now you're out of the woods we have to go private.'

Lilith's head snaps up, her face reverting to the cast-iron lady I met that day in London.

'Mr Phelps, let's hear from Grace.' Her tone is clipped.

'I don't remember much, but I do remember the perfume. Chanel No. 5. I know it because it's what my sister wears.'

'Have you spoken to your sister since the ordeal?' I ask.

'No.' The word is firm. She offers no further information.

'Charlotte lives in New York in the West Village,' Larry says.

I look closely at Grace; her eyes stare vacantly ahead. She switches on and off, as if she has a mechanism attached to her back that winds her up and down.

'Okay, so... besides wearing perfume, is there anything else that you can remember?'

'I want to remember but everything is blurry...'

'Any tiny detail. Even something you think might not matter?'

'If I knew, I would tell you.' Grace's eyes are wide.

'Are you okay to carry on?' Danielle asks, her gaze resting directly on Lilith.

Grace nods. 'I don't know what's real and what isn't. This is the problem. I can still feel hands around my throat squeezing so tight the air escapes my body, but then I wake up and realise it was all just a dream.'

Grace's neck is swollen, with faint blue and red markings on the surface of her otherwise pale skin, evidence of fingertips pressing hard with a furious grip.

'Before the attack. Do you know what you did that day?'

'I went for a run along the beach and then I met my friend for a coffee. We were together for about an hour but then she had an appointment at the GP. Her boyfriend Robert picked her up. He offered me a lift home, but I needed to go to the library at Redbrick Row to pick up some books for college.'

'What are you studying?' I ask. I want to see if there are any connections to the other victims.

'Beauty,' Danielle answers on her daughter's behalf. 'They have to learn about the anatomy of the human body. It's a lot more involved than people give it credit for.'

'The library has a café. I was thirsty, so I went to buy a bottle of water. I picked up my books, left, and after that I had plans that evening to meet with a couple of friends I hadn't seen in a while, we just went for a few drinks, I felt stressed and just wanted to... I don't know. It was like the dream I was just telling you about. I don't know what's real and what isn't. I woke up... I think. It was dark. I couldn't move my hands. They were tied up, and the perfume, it instantly reminded me of my sister. There was a dripping sound, like a tap leaking and then a voice, husky... and so creepy.'

Lilith's expression is flat, poker-faced. 'Did you see anything?'

'No. It was too dark. I told the police and you everything I know.'

'How did you get away?'

'Somehow I got out of the rope and pretended to be tied up and then I kicked them, screamed, then I woke up at the hospital.'

Her answer doesn't satisfy me, but then again, not many of hers have so far. How can she not know how she got away?

'It is very common after such an ordeal to block things out. Memory loss is a natural survival mechanism. It's not my field but with the help of a trained trauma specialist, you can be helped to remember events in a safe environment. Lucy Beckwith has worked with me in many of my cases and can help patients with PTSD,' Lilith says.

'Oh, come on! Everybody who has been through something seems to be labelled with PTSD,' Larry intervenes.

'Is she in London?' Danielle asks.

I notice how Danielle ignores Larry. I see his chest rise and fall, anger he's trying to bottle up.

'Yes, but we can work to what suits Grace best. We have options. You could go to London, or if Lucy's schedule allows, she could visit you here in Cornwall. She does video calls, but I would suggest you need somebody you can build a trustful relationship with, and I'm sure Lucy would agree. She's a brilliant psychologist, I wouldn't ever recommend somebody any less than that. I know what you, Grace, and you, Mr and Mrs Phelps, must be facing right now.'

'Can I think about it?' Grace's voice sounds childlike and small.

'Of course. Talk it over. Take your time.'

Why is Lilith acting like less of the ballbuster I know she is and more like the kind therapist she's not? I have the strongest desire to shake Grace and tell her she must remember, but my better judgement stays my hand.

'Is there anything else you need?' Larry asks.

'Not unless you have anything else you want to share with us at this time.' Lilith fixes her gaze on Grace.

'No,' she says tightly.

'If you're sure.'

Grace sighs, exasperated now. 'Look, I told you I don't remember. If I did, I'd tell you. Do you know what it's like knowing this evil monster has me on their list? I'm unfinished business and that scares me more than anything.'

The room falls silent once more. Larry's gaze does not leave Danielle. Eventually she meets his cold, hard stare and I see her eyes widen, her calm demeanour melting away. I see genuine fear.

'We will do everything we can to protect you, Grace.'

The comment delivered so compassionately by Lilith doesn't hold any weight for Grace.

'Yeah, well... there's a number on my back that says otherwise.'

CHAPTER TWENTY-SIX

JENNIFER MACK

I hear footsteps hurrying against the pavement.

'Jennifer! Wait!' she calls when she's almost at my shoulder. I turn to see Danielle Phelps.

'Mrs Phelps! Is everything okay?'

She rests her hands on her knees and tries to catch her breath.

'Been ages since... since I've been to the gym. I'm dreadfully out of shape!' She looks anything but out of shape; she's the type of woman who complains how 'she's let herself go' when most women would kill to look half as good as her. Myself included. Danielle looks anxious, her disposition jittery and unsure. She looks over her shoulder a couple of times and I look behind her, wondering who it is she's expecting to see.

'Can we talk?'

'Sure,' I say.

'This is awkward, but I have to ask.'

I wait for her to continue and she averts her gaze. Her long, slender fingers lace together as she asks, 'How well do you know Lilith?'

Her question takes me by surprise. I pause.

'Is something wrong?' I ask.

Her eyes are bloodshot, and in the harsh light of day her expensive make-up does not conceal the grief and tiredness consuming her.

'I know she seems intimidating, but Lilith Grain is the best person you can have on this case. I sought her out in London, she's consulted on BBC documentaries, she's co-authored several books on criminology.'

'So, she's the best there is?'

'The very best.' I want to reassure her that we all want to catch the killer, which is true, but I think better of it and try to apply more sensitivity to the situation. After all, I'm not a mother with a daughter who was almost murdered.

We stand in seconds of silence, then flecks of rain begin to fall from a brooding sky, droplets growing larger and falling harder as the pavement turns slick and the roads build up furious streams and rivers flowing into the drains. We hurry for cover under a shop canopy and listen to car tyres sluicing through the roadside puddles.

'Want a drink?' Danielle offers.

My mouth is begging for a drink. It's been a long day and I feel emotionally charged to the point I want to have a drink and go home to shut my mind down for a few hours. I feel like a computer with too many tabs open.

'There's a coffee shop down the road. I need a break from the hospital.'

Costa no doubt, nothing stronger on offer than a double espresso.

'Unless you fancy a proper drink, there's a taxi rank over there, we could go to the Axe and Compass. It's not far.' Usually in company I'd opt for the safety of black coffee but the burning thirst at the back of my throat needs to be quenched and coffee just won't do it.

Danielle's face lights up. It looks like she needs this as much as I do. 'Why not!'

We hail a taxi and make our way to the Axe and Compass. I pretend to check emails on my phone when a WhatsApp message pings through from Pete. My heart skips a beat; he's such a welcome distraction from my otherwise dark thoughts. His name offers a brief moment of escapism and I tell myself I cannot be constantly immersed in my work, everybody needs an out and there's a tug within telling me Pete is it.

Dinner at 8. Fish and chips... my place?

I type back without hesitation:

See you then!

Once we move away from the main roads, we navigate toward the fishing quay, and the downpour begins to ease. The air is cool and refreshing as we step out of the stuffy taxi.

'Have you always lived in Cornwall?' I ask.

'No,' Danielle says, deadpan.

I didn't think so. She's not the type who'd hailed from salty air and the slower pace of life. She's a city girl who, judging by her body, does yoga on a regular basis and is never more than twenty-five feet from a cup of coffee.

We finally make it to the pub. It used to be an old fisherman's hang-out, grimy round the edges, drab walnut-brown furniture dominates the interior from the tables and chairs to the framed pictures on the smoke-stained walls, but it's had a makeover since I was last here. The old carpet has been replaced with vinyl flooring and freshly painted walls; neater, cleaner. I haven't been to this pub in years, it holds memories of my mother, she worked behind the bar for a short time and I smile at the memory of her laughing her way through the many orders she messed up. The old boys she served mocked her in a playful way and slipped her a fiver when she actually served the correct drink to the correct customer. She didn't work behind the bar for long; it was just a stop gap, a temporary fix.

'What can I get you?' I ask.

'You know, I'd kill for a glass of red. Château Mouton if they have it,' Danielle replies.

Yup, city girl. A bar for her means 'wine bar' and that's about it. She's not the weekly Friday night goer at the local, that's for sure.

I nod and make my way to the bar. I eye the spirits but go for a safe option, vodka and Coke; dull, boring, predictable, but enough to satisfy the burn and still keep me sober.

I return to the table, set down the drinks. Danielle looks at me with intent.

'After you left the hospital, I followed you and Lilith and I overheard the conversation.' Danielle pauses, waiting for me to offer more detail, but I don't, so she probes further.

'A serial killer... how?' she asks.

'*How* what?' I say.

'My daughter's attacker. What information have you gathered?'

'The police are carrying out their investigations. I'm sure they've shared what they can.'

'Bollocks they are! They are hiding something, I know it.'

An enormous pressure is building in my chest. I start to feel uneasy, and deeply afraid I am going to have another panic attack. Now is not the time. Not the place. I excuse myself and dash to the toilet. I push the door with such force it makes a loud bang, I set my hands on the sink and turn the tap, I let the water run until it turns cold and cup my hands to fill a pool of water and splash it on my reddened cheeks. The contrast in temperature offers a welcome reprieve. I carefully breathe through my nose and out through my mouth... counting to ten.

I focus on the dripping tap. *Drip drip drip.*

I close my eyes, take another deep breath, and open them again and focus once more on the tap.

Soon the intense wave of worry and fear eases. The rhythm of my breathing steadies and my heartbeat slows so I no longer feel the heavy vibration against my chest. I begin to feel reattached to my body.

I whisper, 'I am okay... I am okay.'

I wait a few moments before I go back out. I see Danielle sitting at the table with an unreadable expression on her face.

'Sorry about that,' I say. 'Felt a bit off-colour. I haven't eaten all day, so it might be that.'

'Do you want some food?'

'It's okay, I'll just get some water. I've got dinner plans tonight.'

Danielle's face looks ashen, and she wraps her arms around her body as though she is cold.

'Are you okay?' There's genuine concern in my voice.

'I can't stop thinking about my Grace. Locked up with that monster... I can't eat, can't sleep. The irony is, we're the lucky ones. The other families have lost their daughters to this crazy psychopath. Something has to be done. How can people like this be allowed to breathe the same air? Prison isn't enough. Not enough by a long shot. If there was a wild dog on the rampage it would be destroyed. Surely the same should be done for crazy lunatics with a thirst for pain and blood?'

I can't disagree with what Danielle is saying, so I just nod and listen – listen and nod.

'The other families. What are they doing about this?'

'I can't talk to you about the other victims. I can only share public knowledge. We can't take things out of context and blow the case up, there's too much at stake. I can only imagine how it feels but–'

'Do you have children, Jennifer? I suspect you don't.' She brings her eyebrows down momentarily and sharply.

'No. I–'

'Then you can't possibly imagine how it feels. To love a child is to protect a child from any harm. She may not be a child in the eyes of the world, but she is my child and I failed her.'

'You couldn't have known.'

'But I did know. Letting her out, not having somebody with her to protect her.'

I feel like no matter what I say, it won't give Danielle any reassurance. I don't know what I can do in this moment.

'I'm going to keep on top of this story. Make sure it makes headlines, that this killer is brought to justice.'

'You need to give me more than that.' Tears prick her eyes.

'I promise to do everything I can to get Grace's attacker. The media can be a very powerful tool.'

'I need to find my daughter's attacker.' Her voice is clipped, like a possession is taking place.

'Lilith is the detective. She's the one who can give you more information. What we know so far, we've told you. My job is to report the facts and findings.' I am mindful of my words as well as the fact that I am here alone with Danielle, which will likely piss Lilith off.

'I'm willing to pay you!' The comment, so carefully delivered, a mother so desperate to find her daughter's attacker.

It's as if the fog has lifted and I can see the horizon ahead: *crystal fucking clear*. She thinks I'm an easy target and that's why we're here, it has nothing to do with not trusting Lilith, quite the contrary. I have one of those faces, I've always been told that. It comes with being the plain one in the crowd.

Danielle takes a sip of wine and lifts her chin, looking up at me through her long lashes.

Heat builds up in my cheeks; I'm angry with myself for my inexperience. I knock back my drink and it helps.

'I want to find the killer too,' I say in an attempt to blanket the flames rising between us.

I am about to rise to my feet and get another drink when Danielle places her hand on my arm. I look at her hand, knowing a line of sorts has been well and truly crossed.

'Have you ever heard the expression "Mama Bear"? I'm sure you have. Well, I would do anything to protect my babies, and I mean anything. It's my job to seek out redemption for them. Are you following?'

I absolutely am and I don't like it. This case is becoming so much bigger than who I am. What I know.

'Danielle... the pain and fear you feel must be huge. I get it. But you have to let the police do their job. You have to be there for Grace. Does your husband know how you feel?'

'What do you think?'

Danielle's barbed question sits with me and it suddenly occurs to me that Larry Phelps must be in on this too, that using Danielle as a prop to get to me was a plan the two of them made together. They are used to getting what they want by throwing money at it.

It really is a case of an eye for an eye, a tooth for a tooth.

'One million pounds!' Danielle says.

A life for a life.

CHAPTER TWENTY-SEVEN

Grace Murderer Strikes Again

Wednesday 24 October 2018
Jennifer Mack

The Learning Centre of Redbrick Row was rocked by news about the attempted murder of a 17-year-old girl; the killer, believed to be the 'Grace Murderer', attacked the victim, leaving her hospitalised. The victim, 'Grace', who cannot be formally identified for legal reasons, is being supported by her family and specialist care team. Reports are emerging that the killer is believed to be someone with a personal vendetta against young blonde women named Grace.

Detective Lilith Grain, transferred from a London Unit to lead the case, has refused to comment, except to say that 'these attacks are an act of pure evil and a full investigation is underway.'

Our sympathies are with the family and friends of the victims who did not survive the heinous attacks at the hands of the Grace Killer.

Night-club owner Rocco Patterson found the body of Grace Martin, 18, in the Earth Rabbit's basement two months ago and has been outspoken regarding the handling of the police investigation; 'You'd think they'd have some sort of a clue by now. My heart is with the families of these poor young girls whose lives have been savagely taken. The killer needs to be brought to justice.'

This year, Cornwall has been marked with fear, people are living on a knife edge, wondering when the attacker will strike again. While we know the killer appears mission-oriented, it is impossible to know at this stage if they may take a different direction for their own thrill-seeking satisfaction.

Police are appealing for witnesses or anyone who might have information regarding this case.

I keep my eyes focused on the screen, ignoring the lingering presence of Hayley behind me and her eyes peering over my shoulder. The piece is due to print shortly and her spying ahead of the article being published will have no bearing.

'Even for you, that's dull.' Hayley throws the comment at me, fully expecting me to react, like I always have, but I can't let her get inside my head. Not today, there's too much on the line. Plus, my mind is already filled with so many conflicting thoughts, there's no space for her. So I pull my desk drawer open and reach for my earbuds. I pull back my hair, giving her a visual of inserting the earbuds, and then let Bullet for My Valentine and the sound of the thunderous beat of the drums drown out her constant bitching. The music helps pull me away from my current reality. Now, if only my flask was full too.

CHAPTER TWENTY-EIGHT

THEN

I t is 2.45pm. Outside the window the sky is flat and grey, unwelcoming and miserable; perfectly matching my mood up to the point of my decision. The voice is loud inside my head, and I can't shut it out. When I leave the flat, the voice whispers into my ear as though it is a person perched on my shoulder, directing me, guiding me.

Take back control.

Hurt the one who has hurt you.

The lift is out of service yet again, forcing me to walk the dark, narrow stairwell. The stench of piss and damp permeates my nostrils. As I take the final step toward the main door, the ground falls away and I instinctively hold out my hands before my body hits the concrete floor. A surge of pain runs up my arm, I look down and slowly try to move it, praying it's not broken. I can move my fingers; it hurts like a bitch, but slowly I rise to my feet and reach down for my bag with my good hand. It's just past 3.15pm by the time I make it outside the door. I have no idea if he will still be waiting, but I go anyway.

Garsmouth House is framed by agitated clouds that seemed especially dark against its baleful reputation, the centre stage of

Grahame Warner Park. As I approach, Little Ron stands by the bin store eyeing me up and down. I'm swimming in the big shark's habitat. I should be afraid, but I'm not. The thing is, I don't give a shit if I live or die. If coming here today brings me to my end, there is not a single thing I can do about it, as shit as that is. I am being driven by a bigger force than the disease festering in the walls of the estate. We are just as dangerous as each other. All of us are capable of unbelievably bad things.

The first thing I notice about Little Ron is the size of his dilated pupils, like bulging black marbles, and then his bone-thin arms showing a long trail of needle marks.

'Got the cash?' His voice is rough as sandpaper and I find myself wanting to clear my throat when he speaks.

'Got the supply?' I reply.

Little Ron (who by height is not actually all that little) reaches into his large coat pocket. Two syringed vials emerge with contents that could knock out a horse.

I smile.

The exchange of money is made; he carefully counts it as I delicately place the vials into my bag. I get back to the flat and let out a long, shaky breath. My arm is aching with pain and there is visible swelling. I remember the strength it took with Lizzy and that was with two arms!

'Shit!' I say as I slam the front door shut.

I don't need this.

In the cupboard is a mix of Mum's old medicines. I take two paracetamol and down it with flat lemonade which leaves me with a bitter taste in my mouth and makes my insides churn.

It's just after 7pm. When I wake up from a fitful nap, I check my phone. No messages.

I take a deep breath and find the energy to text Ian; tell him I've badly hurt my arm and I can't do my shift tomorrow. I cross the room to take more pills to dull the pain when my phone rings.

'Hello?'

'I need the cover tomorrow. You need to come in.'

'I can't. I've broken my arm.'

'Then don't bother coming back at all.'

'You're joking, right, Ian? That's... illegal.'

And so is murder!

'Look,' Ian says quickly, 'I've got a business to run, and if you can't turn up for work then I'm afraid I have to let you go.' Then he hangs up.

I stare at the screen willing for Ian to call me back, tell me it was a joke, and hear his fag-fumed laugh.

The job at the café was ticking me over, and now I've just paid a shitload to Little Ron. I doubt I'll even be able to afford a hot meal.

Fuck!

There is a whisper in my head, quiet but forthcoming.

You know what you have to do.

Make it worthwhile. Go now... before it's too late.

The voice has commanded me, taken over. I try to put my jacket on, but my arm is so sore I scream out in pain, a swoop of nausea washing over me. I just make it to the toilet.

I take my backpack and set off. It's time to take back what's mine.

CHAPTER TWENTY-NINE

JENNIFER MACK

The weather is perfect today. The rain has finally departed, and the sun is shimmering off the waves. It's Sunday and an element of peace has descended upon the beach; everybody looks comfortable walking along the shoreline arm in arm as dogs dart in and out of the sea fetching soaking wet tennis balls. Somehow, the weight of the week is temporarily lifted from my shoulders and I feel a bit lighter, but it's somehow impossible to push the impending dread of the Monday morning meeting with my editor aside and allow myself to just breathe. Bounding toward me, Max leaps onto my knees, leaving wet sandy streaks down my jeans. It's becoming our thing, Max and I. It's his way of saying: 'Hey, I'm so pleased you could make it.'

I walk toward Pete and he leans in for a kiss on the lips, long enough to descend my heart into my stomach.

'Look at us,' he says as our eyes meet. He takes me into the warmth of his body and holds me tight. 'Like an old married couple walking our dog on the beach.'

We don't talk about anything substantial, it's just an easy Sunday afternoon walk, the being-together-after-being-together. He asks me if I enjoyed our fish and chips and I laugh, knowing what he is actually talking about. What he doesn't know is how absolutely screwed up my head was that night. I pushed myself onto him to dull the weight of the crushing decision hammering my brain. Today, I have left the torment of my overactive mind at home, not to be interrupted by the shrill of a message ruining my *perfect* afternoon. I'm holding it together until the conversation turns to work and suddenly I'm a jittery mess in a desperate need to get back. What if I missed something?

'Was it something I said?' Pete picks up on the starkness of my mood change.

I zone out momentarily. I imagine Jacob firing me and Hayley parking directly in my spot. I imagine the feeling of defeat as I am cast out of my safety net. I'm overcome with the surging urgency to call Lilith to make sure I'm not missing a damn thing.

Pete calls my name (twice, I think) before I am pulled back in the present and back to the man who usually takes me away from it all.

I wish I could explain what this is doing to me.

How I long to be at the forefront of the action.

How jealous I feel when other reporters break huge stories and become household names, how the ache in the pit of my stomach swells if I can't be the one to break the story.

I wish I could tell him how I feel. I'm just not the right person to tell this story, but I can't even say it to myself because I don't want to admit it.

I look down at my empty palms, wishing I had my phone. Maybe then I'd be able to enjoy my afternoon.

'I'm feeling a bit sick.' It's not a lie.

'Want me to drive you home?' He leans forward and puts his arm around me, like any caring partner would do. I don't meet his gaze because I am scared he will see straight through me and know it's not sickness driving me away but my inability to detach myself from a faceless killer. Max circles my feet as we head back to the car park.

'Do you want me to come back with you?' Pete asks.

'I don't want you to see me unwell...' But what I mean is, I won't be able to be on a wild rampage with him there, typing the buttons furiously on the laptop trying to weave another story together to stop Jacob from giving me the axe.

'I'm pretty used to being around sick people.'

The guilt floods through me but it's still not enough to ignore the pull to get back to work.

We get back to the car and he kisses me gently on the forehead before opening the car door for me. He's smitten, and not doing a great job of hiding it. I have never experienced this kind of loving attention before. He slides into the driver's seat, the breath of Max's heavy panting steaming the windows up and giving the car a pungent fishy stench. I quickly put down the window and let the sea air banish the aroma of wet dog and kippers.

We turn onto Hillview Avenue, my flat is just past the park, and there's a group of mothers gathered together holding coffee cups and watching as their children play in the playground. The first person I think of is Andrea Matthews. I bet she was the mum who had regular playdates, friends with the other mums, a happy little community, but now she is set apart from the other mothers, she is in her own elite group, the kind where she will find the rare breeds at self-help groups for grieving parents.

'How are you feeling?'

'I think I need a nap,' I say. His hand reaches for mine, it feels right to be there.

My flat has an access balcony on a low-rise development which means I can see my door from the car park, and I'm certain I just saw my front door close. I squeeze my eyes closed and open them again.

I bite my nails. I have a feeling of dread building up inside me, like the impending drop of a rollercoaster. Suddenly my mouth feels dry, and I am not quite in the present moment. I look at the flat again. Did I imagine it?

My skin flares hot. I tell myself, I'm tired, it's easy to hallucinate when you're tired, it's something that happened to me during my exams, stress manifests itself in strange ways.

There it is again, the absence of light by the window, a shadow, like somebody is there.

I pause, drawing back my arm, my head telling me something isn't right. I put my hand on his shoulder.

'Pete...' My voice trembles. 'I think somebody just went into my flat.'

Thoughts whirl. The killer could be back, is she planning to find me, kill me?

'What are you talking about?'

'I just saw the door open.' My answer is sharp, eyes fixed on my front door.

'Give me your keys.'

Pete stands at the front door with a brick that he picked up from the car park clasped in his hands. I told him to wait, but he just tossed his phone onto my lap and was up the flight of stairs and at my door before I had a chance to pull him back. He demanded I stay in the car and I did as I was told, rooted to the seat, heart thudding in my ears. Pete's phone is a Samsung, not an iPhone, its unfamiliar profile builds frustration in my chest, wishing he were still next to me and not running into harm's way. A simple 999 call looks like an impossible task. I feel like I'm in one of those horror films where you scream at the screen, *'That person is such a moron! No way would I do that!'*

I make the call to the police. My legs won't stop shaking. I open the car door and place my feet on the ground, taking a long, deep breath, when I hear a scream so primal it pierces through the air like shattered glass. Two doors open, and the neighbours spill out wondering what the commotion is about. I run toward my home and bark at my neighbours, 'The intruder is back... call the police... tell them... tell them to get here faster!' I'm breathless, like somebody has sucked the air from my lungs and I have nothing left.

Robert Epsom gingerly walks from his front door to my window. His eyes wide, he looks at the gathering crowd and puts a finger to his lips. There is no more noise. We wait. Silent and still. I don't know what to think, there is a tangent of scenarios playing out in my head and none of them end well. It's my fault. If I had grabbed Pete and stopped him, he wouldn't be in there. He'd still be with me.

Two police cars pull in. No wailing sirens, no flashing lights. When they come to a complete stop, an officer opens the car door and then the two other officers in the car follow suit. Robert grabs their attention by waving his hands and pointing at my flat. I can't find my voice. I'm like a lifeless puppet. I watch, waiting for someone to tell me what to do. A voice comes from within my flat, muffled and low. The officers proceed, the wait is driving the fear into my skull, my head is pounding. My legs start to regain strength and I make my way to my front door. My space is filled with intrusion, violation. I imagine hands on my personal belongings that will now forever be tarnished, never clean again. The officers are inside. I push open the door and am met with the familiar scent of perfume. I know it, but I cannot place it.

I try to keep calm and not unearth the storm raging from within.

An officer stomps toward the door and uses his shoulder to push me out.

'This is my home.'

The officer sighs. Taking a step away from the door, I look at him, pleading with my eyes for answers: Is Pete okay? Where is he? Who broke in? What have they done?

What were they planning to do?

CHAPTER THIRTY

JENNIFER MACK

Shock runs through my body like an electric current. None of this makes any sense. I knew she couldn't be trusted. I knew I had to watch my back, but this, this is insane. I watch a police officer guide Pete out and I let out a loud sigh of relief. I am not a religious person, but I thanked God. Her face was pink when she saw me. I could barely look away. She'd shed her superiority and I could see the vulnerability shrouding her. It never once occurred to me that she was capable of doing something like this. I remember the way she was, the way she's always been. Confident. The type of woman who would walk into a room and demand attention if it weren't already aimed at her. But... she hid it well, underneath the expensive clothing and haircuts, the two-tone voice hovering between pompous and patronising.

'Are you okay?' I thrust myself into Pete's arms. He's got a scratch mark under his eye that looks like he's been at war with the talons of a wild jungle cat.

'That was fucking insane!' He laughs it off, like it was no big deal, but I can tell he is a bit shaken.

'Pete... I know who she is.'

He stares at me, waiting for me to elaborate.

My chest swells as she looks directly at me. She smiles lightly, and then throws her head back. As if invading my home wasn't enough, she goes that one step further. I want to run up to her and hit her so hard, yell, scream, but I remain motionless.

I take a deep breath as I watch an officer place her hands on top of her head and put her in the back of the police car.

'Her name is Hayley Woolley; she works for the paper.'

'What the hell?' He runs his hand through his hair and lets out a shaky breath.

'Why the hell was she in your flat? What does she want?'

'That's what I want to know.'

The gathered crowd begins to disperse, and people return to their homes, nothing more to see here, they've had their slice of community drama for the afternoon.

'Excuse me, are you the owner of this property?' The officer is polite, young, skin as smooth as a baby's backside, but not unconfident.

'Yes, I am,' I say to him. I lean back against a wall and cross my arms around my body. 'The woman who broke into my flat, I know her. She's my colleague.'

'And where is it you both work?' The officer has been joined by an older policeman, his presence seems to unnerve him as he stands straighter and squares his shoulders, voice deepened.

'At *The Cornwall Chronicle*. We've both been battling for the lead on the Grace murders. We don't get on but...' I pause, catching the look from the older officer, a quiet knowing written on his face means he thinks this is likely to be some feud and nothing more. But people don't just go around breaking into people's homes, it isn't normal. Once I go through the on-the-spot questioning, Pete is asked to go to the police station to make a formal statement, and I can go into my flat accompanied by an officer to see if anything has been taken. Pete kisses me on the forehead as we part ways. I walk up the steps that lead me to the second floor. I have walked this path a million times, but today it feels different.

The last time I knew somebody had been in my flat, the air felt different, but now it feels even thicker. To the naked eye nothing is disturbed, it's pretty tidy, as I'd left it, so what was she looking for? What does she want?

'Anything missing?' the officer asks.

I laugh awkwardly, not sure how to react. 'Not that I can see.'

I cross the hallway and enter my bedroom; my duvet has been pulled away from the bed. I point to it. I never ever leave the flat with my bed unmade, I saw a clip on Facebook once about the importance of making your bed and how it sets the tone for the day, and it's true. The thought of Hayley's skin cells embedded into the fabric makes me want to hurl. I imagine her lying there, in my personal space, discovering more of me than I ever cared to share. I go to my bedside table; the drawer is slightly ajar. I open it and my heart sinks, there is an empty space where my journal usually sits. I swallow hard.

'Did she have anything on her when you arrested her?' I ask.

'Not that I am aware of.'

So where is it? Who has it?

Thoughts of my journal sitting in the hands of Hayley, or anybody else fills me with panic. I imagine my handwritten words being read for the first time by someone other than me, a possession so gravely personal, my every thought exposed and examined. What will they think?

What parts of me will they uncover?

CHAPTER THIRTY-ONE

THEN

The day has come when we are finally together. Over time, so much has built up in my head that I've transformed her into this mystical creature. Being with her in the physical sense feels surreal, as if I would wake from a dream and then *poof!* she'd be gone, like a puff of smoke. The house feels too warm with the artificial heat pumping out from the radiators. We sit in the living room, photos of her as a child adorn the pale ivory walls. On a heavy oak bookshelf is a photo of her much younger parents. She catches me looking at it, but I don't avert my gaze, why would I? If a photo is on display, it is there to be admired.

'That was the day they found out they were having me.' She laughs awkwardly.

'How are things?' I want this time together to be about us, and not talking about her father fucking another woman, but that's the normal thing to do, I suppose. People want to know you're invested in them, even if you don't actually give a shit.

There is something stifling about this house today and it isn't just the heat. On the surface it sits in its beautiful glory; the wall art and furnishings look like they could easily have jumped out of the pages of a glossy *Town & Country* brochure. It is all I could have wanted, but the atmosphere feels clipped.

'My mum cries all the time. At first, she was angry, now she's sad. She throws the word *divorce* around, but it no longer holds any weight.'

'What is it she wants?'

'For him to grovel for forgiveness, to swear she is the only woman he truly loves, I guess.'

She takes a sip of water and places it on a coaster on the elongated glass coffee table which holds a large spray of lilies delicately perfuming the room.

'Is your dad willing to—'

'My dad is an arsehole. This isn't the first time he's cheated, but it's the only time he's not put an end to it, which says a lot.'

I pause, thinking of *his* hand climbing further and further up my leg, his hot stale breath upon my cheek.

'Most men are primitive. They want what they want no matter who it hurts.'

She looks at me quizzically, her blue eyes searching for elaboration, but I don't give it to her. I can't go there because by going there I will remember the life I lived and the time that followed. I don't want that to spill over into my time with her.

My eyes shift back to the bookshelf, looking for a distraction. It's not long before I find it: *To Kill a Mockingbird* by Harper Lee.

'Have you read it?' she asks.

'No, but I know what it's about.'

'Oh, you must!' Her voice is infused with breathy enthusiasm. 'There is so much in this book which transcends a deeper message of how we haven't really evolved that much since that era.'

She has my attention.

'There are so many book covers given to the novel, but this is the one that I connect to most.' A tree set against a blood-red background. The fonts look somewhat amateurish, but I guess for its time may have been looked at as forward-thinking with a hidden meaning, perhaps this is where the saying comes from: 'you can't judge a book by its cover.'

'You love books, don't you?'

I've pushed a button that makes her face light up, the sullen face from earlier disperses. Her brightness is quite literally beaming.

I like that she has an interest away from other people. A book is a physical object that I don't need to compete with; if anything, it's something we can share.

'I like horror. I recently finished *A Good Marriage*. I read it years ago, but I wanted to read it again. I saw things from a different perspective this time.'

I wait for her to burst, leap across and shake my shoulders!

Me too... me too...

But she nods, and I'm not sure if it's registered.

'Have you read it?' I ask, remembering the photo I have stored in my phone, the reason for my afternoon visit to the bookshop, and the feeling I had flicking through the pages immersed in the thousands of words I believed I was reading at the same time as she was.

'Funnily enough, I bought it a while ago for my friend Betts. She's a huge horror fan, I've seen a couple of his movies but I haven't read it.'

My heart sinks.

We spend the rest of the afternoon talking about books and films. We sit close to one another but not close enough. The whole time I'm with her, the nagging voice interrupts and shakes me out of my otherwise enjoyable afternoon.

Just friends...

Two words are enough to send my head into a tailspin, trying to keep a lid on the wave of uncertainty and doubt.

If I lean forward, will she lean in for a kiss or will she push me away?

As it approaches six, headlights beam into the living room.

'That's my mum. Listen, if it's okay, I'll just introduce you as my friend.'

It's the first time that day she is suggesting we are anything else. It gives me something to hold on to, as pathetic as that is. I take it.

An attractive woman opens the door. She shares her daughter's wide blue eyes, but there is a heaviness behind them that makes them a hue darker. Her clothes are casual but expensive, they hang from her svelte frame, swamping her, but she can pull it off.

'Hey, darling.' Her voice is strained and her face looks as though it might crack, but I admire her for trying at least. Each and every break-up my mother experienced meant I had to experience it with her. Pain was the only thing that woman was ever willing to share.

Her mother stays for only a moment. When she leaves, the conversation flows and we eventually reach a point where I can barely restrain myself from pressing my lips against hers. As the room grows darker, she lights a scented candle and curls her legs on the sofa. It would have been a perfect moment until her mobile buzzes.

'It's Imogen.'

The mention of her name churns my insides, but I, of course, pretend to be unperturbed.

Grace takes the call out of the room.

She returns, saying, 'Sorry about that.' She sits back down and places her phone closely next to her.

'Everything all right?' I ask.

'Oh yeah, fine.' She pauses. 'Well actually, Imogen is still upset. She wanted me to go out with her for a few drinks... but I told her I was busy.'

'Busy doing what?'

'I... I just...'

'You didn't tell her I was here, did you?'

'No. I know I should've, but she'd complain that I was putting her last or she'd say we should all go out.'

The room fills with silence.

'So, let's go then!' I say.

'What? No.'

'Let's go. Come on.'

'But your arm?'

'My arm is fine, look.' I wave my arm around, pretending there is no pain.

'A drink sounds good, and I know Imogen doesn't like me, but–'

'Oh no, it's nothing like that. She's just a complex person.'

I laugh. 'I'm not stupid.'

CHAPTER THIRTY-TWO

THEN

The cab driver's mirror is angled at Grace's legs. He catches me looking and begins to fiddle with the plastic football air freshener dangling from the mirror.

'Are you sure about this?' Grace asks.

'Yeah. I'm looking forward to it.'

'Imogen can be pretty abrasive. I can handle her when it's just the two of us, or with Steph with the really lovely long red hair.' I know who she means, the ugly one of the three, the clinger, but what Steph lacks in looks she makes up for with a loud mouth and massive tits.

'It will be a good night,' I say, doing my best happy enactment.

She sighs and I find it sweet how nervous she is, how careful she is to mind my feelings. We both know Imogen is a grade A bitch.

'Well, don't say I didn't warn you.'

'I won't.' She is convinced this is all going to go horribly wrong.

I shrug and she examines me, and I feel her taking me in, it feels intense.

We arrive at New Wave just after midnight. We pay the cab driver and step out of the cab. Outside the club, girls line up in too-short dresses as the sound of over-excited voices fused with alcohol drift along the street.

The truth is, I hate this. Opportunities don't come along all too often, and sometimes you just have to seize the fucking day and go with a golden opportunity.

A hefty bouncer with a face like a bulldog and oversized jowls stands at the entrance. He thinks that because he's dressed in a suit he has some class about him, but he's just a brute with a mere sliver of authority. He looks past me, all eyes on Grace. But that's okay. The less of me he remembers the better. He only looks at her ID and we go in. The music (if you want to call it that) thuds loudly and I think my head will explode. Strobes of light angle across the dance floor, the room is filled with coked-out twenty-somethings, dancing in unrhythmic, awkward movements, their eyes glassy and hungry.

She pulls me in and shouts into my ear. 'Let's move to somewhere quieter.'

I nod and let her lead the way.

We stand outside the toilet, door wide open, and I see an uninterested bathroom attendant scrolling on her phone, a basket for tips next to a pile of disposable towels. Most of the women ignore her, but there is a couple who toss in a crisp note to show their charity and all that bullshit.

Away from the thudding music I can finally hear myself think.

'So where are we meeting Imogen?'

'She said to meet her by the bar, she came with Jemma.'

Great, so there are two of them to contend with tonight. This makes things harder.

'Ah,' I say. 'Well, it will be nice to see both of your friends.'

'You must really want to get out of this place, right?'

'No. Why would you say that?'

'You look like a fish out of water.' She laughs. She is so beautiful when she laughs. The way her nose crinkles up and her mouth expands to reveal her perfect white smile.

'God, no.'

'You sure?'

'I can't wait for things to get messy.' I clap my hands together and then take her hand as she leads me into the lion's den.

Imogen is wearing a tight black dress; it clings to her every curve. Her long dark hair hangs wild and free. For somebody worried about a sex tape, she's sure not shying away from any unwanted attention.

She greets me with a cold stare, like she wants to lift me over the table to crack me in half.

'Hi,' I say, but the simple greeting gets caught up in my throat.

Within seconds, Imogen and Jemma have their backs to me, and flirt with the guy behind the bar. Grace gives me a sorrowful look and mouths, 'I'm sorry.'

Other people may run off to the bathroom with tears rolling down their faces, but not me. My feelings toward these two are indifferent, and I am not going to let their bitchiness seep into my bones. I've had my fair share of poison, the venom that still lurks under my skin, never to be completely drained of the violation. I promised myself never again. No matter who. No matter what.

Imogen turns her attention to Grace, her back acting like a gateway between us. Jemma at this point is spilling her enormous cleavage right onto the bar. I reach into my pocket and clasp my fingers around the small vial from Little Ron. Carefully, I pop the lid off and empty the contents into Imogen's drink.

Now the party is really getting started.

CHAPTER THIRTY-THREE

JENNIFER MACK

I wait outside Jacob's office, the rest of the staff walking past me with curious expressions. My stomach cramping, a mix of nerves and an impending period, accompanied by a heavy head from the night before. Overall, I'm not functioning at top capacity today, and things are only set to get worse: the end of my career. The job I feel is beneath me is kicking back, and now I'm forced to confront the arrogant person I've allowed myself to become. This job offer was my absolute last resort; but it took a chance on me when I'd been rejected from all the big papers. I've worked hard, but it's only a matter of time before your team realises you don't really want to be a part of it all in a beautiful twist of irony.

'Jen,' Jacob calls. There it is. Jen, the name he knows I hate, but he still calls me by it anyway. I swallow back the words that are fighting to spill out and correct him – but now is not the time; if he wants to call me Gloria, Beryl, Frankie, well, he can, because my future sits right in the palm of his hands.

Suddenly, the room I have sat in a thousand times before feels incredibly small; the clutter worse than usual; empty, unwashed coffee cups; piles of paper just waiting for a fire to come along and eat it up. Now I sit up straight, my hands resting on my legs. I feel my skin grow hot, certain he sees the redness of my cheeks glowing. Jacob smiles lightly – for a moment I think he is taking pity on me. My chest constricts as I focus on him. I'm sure he can hear my thundering heart in the quiet of the room.

I take a breath.

'I'm not quite sure how to say this,' Jacob starts.

He's never been one to hold back on coming forward, he's the type of man who speaks without a second thought. All the time I've known him, he has barked orders and when he says jump, he expects his team to do as they are told and ask, 'How high?'

The phone on his desk rings. He answers it and gestures with his hand that he'll be a couple of minutes. The wait makes my anxiety bubble up and I start to feel my air supply shorten, my pulse quickening. I cannot fall down the rabbit hole, because once I do there is no way I'm coming out of this office with even a shred of self-respect.

The call finishes and Jacob looks at me.

'Sorry about that,' he says. 'Now the reason I called you in here today is because of the Grace murders. Well, that was the main reason, but during the weekend I was made aware of the break-in. Fuck. This is all very complicated.'

'Jacob, I just want to–'

He stops me talking by moving his hand up and down like he's dribbling a basketball.

'We had a complaint from another member of the team claiming that you have an issue with alcohol, and this causes you to have blackouts. I didn't believe it at first, but that day at Redrow, well, it made me think differently. To be perfectly frank, so long as you do your job I couldn't care less what you do in your own time – but I do care about what happens when you're on the clock. You follow?'

'Jacob, I do have the occasional drink but...' I keep telling myself that; sometimes I even believe my own lies.

'Look, you've got talent, you've got what it takes to be a really *great* journalist but drinking to get you through the day will ruin you.'

He doesn't believe me.

'Your work on this case needs to be better.'

'So, I'm getting fired?' I'm surprised at myself, how I just lay it right on the table.

'Until the break-in, that was the plan.' Jacob pinches the bridge of his nose. 'Jennifer, listen to me. As I said, you've got talent, but right now your work is mediocre at best. It doesn't make sense because I can see how gripped you are by this story. I also see how much Hayley wanted to drag you down. Mike and I, we've talked and we're willing to give you one opportunity to be the bona fide journalist we know you are.'

A few tears spring to my eyes. I try to swallow them back, but I can't.

'Do whatever it takes,' he says.

'I promise I won't let you down.' *I won't let myself down.*

CHAPTER THIRTY-FOUR

JENNIFER MACK

Letter to the Graces' Killer

She must have hurt you, and now you seek revenge.

I wish I could understand, get inside your head. The rest of the world probably don't care, they just want you to stop. Does anybody commit such heinous crimes without a history?

What happened to you?

Take us to the beginning, where it all started.

There are so many unanswered questions. Reaching out could rid you of these demons that live within you.

How many is the perfect number?

The scars they bear on their backs, you want us to know it's you, a number staking your callous claim. Does it make you feel better?

Does it offer redemption to your unhappy heart?

I take the short piece into Jacob's office and let the draft float onto his desk. His glasses are halfway down his nose. He looks older today. His dark hair showing winter-white strands, his eyes heavy but still dourly handsome.

'An open letter. This is what I want to print, along with photos of each of the victims.'

'Have you spoken to Lilith about this?'

'No. I'm following my gut.' I sit down and rest my hands on my lap. 'As reporters, we have to report facts and I also know that it's our job to tell the public factual findings. But you and I both know that feeling you get in the pit of your stomach, that knowing, the true punch that lets you know what you need to do.'

'What makes you think the killer will even read this?'

'I don't know. But you said to me I have one shot. This is the way I need to report the story, by getting them to tell theirs.'

He leans back in his chair, fiddles with a pen in his hands and lets out a long, heavy sigh.

'This is crazy, you know that don't you?'

I smile.

Jacob shakes his head. 'You're bonkers, but it *could* work.'

My heart leaps from my chest and a huge smile breaks across my face. I'd been following the rules for so long, carefully treading a fine line, and now I could write what I wanted to. I don't know why Jacob has taken this chance on me, but I don't want to look a gift horse in the mouth. I'm just grateful.

I settle back at my desk, hearing a few hushed whispers around me from my colleagues.

I decide to embrace the moment and talk about the big, fucking fat elephant in the room. I perch on the side of my desk in clear view of the whole team.

'I don't know why Hayley broke into my house.' All the attention is on me, eyes wide, jaws dropped, and phones being placed on the desk.

'I don't know who said what about me, but I don't care. We all have our secrets.' I look across at Yasmin Happier, a newlywed who is having an affair with Dennis Smith who writes the sports column. Her sweet husband runs after her like a smitten lapdog, unaware of her big secret.

'We've got the chance to put this paper on the map, and I intend to do so. If you've got questions, ask me.'

'I've got one.' Barry Gorman stands up. I watch as he runs the pad of his thumb across his lower lip.

'Let's hear it.' I place my hands on the desk, I'm wide open, with my let-me-at-'em expression.

'What's really in the flask?'

His question takes me by surprise. But I've put myself up on stage. My palms feel sweaty, I reach to rub my neck and take in a deep breath, like I'm going to jump into an icy lake with no clothes on. I brace myself.

Only the hum of the computers can be heard. They know the truth, the hard, cold stare of their judging faces now impossible to avoid.

CHAPTER THIRTY-FIVE

JENNIFER MACK

A splash of cold water to my face takes away the hot sweat and offers a temporary reprieve. I feel as if I have taken two steps forward and one step back. They say that admitting you have a problem is the first step you take to sobriety. That may be true, but why do I still have a burning sensation at the back of my throat, a thirst so intense, I want to down a bottle in one go? One day at a time. One hour at a time. I can't quite remember when it became a dependency. My mind is a huge mix of thoughts, the break-in, Hayley. I have too many pairs of eyes watching me now, all waiting for me to slip and fall. My job depends on me.

How do people get past the constant craving?

The thing I depend on to block out the darkness has been exposed.

It's always been the thing that I turn to, always there to pick me up. I know there are support groups, but I'm not sure if I am ready to sit in a circle with strangers every week and share parts of myself I'm not ready to face, a story I have never told. I know I need to take back parts of my life, the pain that remains under the surface, the devil within. I've searched high and low for my journal. The police said nothing was found on Hayley. Does that mean somebody else has been here?

That is partly why I admitted to the office I had a problem. Better they hear it from me than very personal words I have scribbled on clean white paper.

But the other things... I don't know what to do.

I leave the flat in my running gear, ready to let the sea air whip through my hair and hopefully clear my head of all the thoughts floating around like rubbish in a polluted river. The sun is blinding, my head feels like it is weighing too heavy on my neck, and, weirdly, everything hurts. It is as if my body is protesting that it hasn't got its fix. For a long time, I stopped feeling hungover in the mornings. I guess my body was tolerating the position, learning that it's normal, but today isn't normal.

I put in my earbuds and begin to pound the pavement, pushing past the pain raging through every cell within me.

When I get to the beach I stop and look out to the sea. I soon find myself wading in till the water is up to my waist. The cold bites through my legs. It hurts, but in a good way. In a way it feels like a baptism, being born again and given a second chance.

CHAPTER THIRTY-SIX

THEN

'She's not going to pull through.' Her voice is strained, coarse through the phone.

I refill my glass of wine and sink back into the sofa.

'I'm so sorry.' These are the words that are expected of me and I dutifully recite them in a rehearsed sadness.

'I just can't believe it.' The pending doom of death, waiting, the finality of it all. She doesn't see it now, but she will. The world is better without her.

'I can't believe she will never wake up. The hospital found something in her system, I had to give them a statement, and I feel so guilty but...' Her voice turns into a whisper, barely audible. 'It's not the first time she—'

'Drugs?' I say.

'Yeah. She fell into a terrible habit, got to thinking she needed to get high to have a good time. Her mum said before she fell into the coma, she... she tried to tell her something – a name.'

I set my glass on the table and panic rises, rattling my ribcage and squeezing my heart.

'But she couldn't hear her. Only the machines keeping her alive know now, I guess. Her family isn't going to prolong the process.'

I imagine her funeral. The fanfare.

'Grace, I wish I knew what to say.' My tone is off-kilter, but she doesn't notice.

I was the last person Imogen saw before she exited consciousness. Her last words were filled with abhorrence toward me. I left her alone in the cubicle, watching her shut down. A public setting was risky, and I recalled how my stomach twisted, how badly I wanted to wring the nerves out of my insides. But there was also a thrill attached to it. I guess this is how people feel when they have sex in a public place. It's not the act itself, but the *wrongfulness* of it.

All night, Imogen had set her gaze on me with quiet, loathing eyes and the more hatred she shot in my direction the more I wanted to make her suffer. The acid itself acted quickly. But there was a part of me that wanted her blood to boil under her skin. I wanted ungodly pain to surge through her body until she begged for death.

'I'm going to go to bed,' Grace says softly, interrupting my thoughts. It's a relief though. I don't want to spend the evening talking about what a *wonderful* person Imogen is/was.

I set the phone on the table. I'm tempted to have another glass of wine, but I resist. Sometimes it's good to allow the organic thoughts to flow through my mind; I like the process of it. Alcohol can cloud that process and tonight I don't want any thoughts to be fazed.

I go to bed and flick off the lights. I lie still in the darkness. I wonder what she sees in me, because Imogen and I couldn't be more different. How can one person care for two people who are such polar opposites? I never really thought of myself as good-looking, but as I approach adulthood, my reflection gives something back. To look at me, on the surface, I could be considered average (at best) but the awkwardness of childhood is falling away and what were known as creepy eyes are now an exotic icy blue; the one feature people comment on.

CHAPTER THIRTY-SEVEN

JENNIFER MACK

The Graces; young, blonde, and beautiful, take precedence on the front cover of *The Chronicle*. Underneath their pictures is my name and an open letter addressed to the killer. I can't help but feel judged by my decision. All eyes are on me. But once the idea occurred to me, I couldn't rinse it out of my mind. It's a bold move, some might even say out-and-out crazy, but what else was I going to do? I needed to take a different approach to all the attention this story was getting.

Later, after the story went to press and had been delivered to the local newsagents and online spheres, social media went crazy. Some supported it, others thought it was absolutely disgusting, but I had got what I wanted: attention and reaction. I sat at my desk, reading through the comments pouring in.

These young women are nothing but rotting corpses. They don't get to have a voice anymore. My mobile phone rang with a no-caller ID.

'Are you out of your fucking mind?' Lilith's voice is so loud I cover the receiver with my hand and skulk away from my desk into the dusty corner of redundant files. I press my forehead onto the window and watch my breath steam it up.

'Maybe. But it's got the attention this case needs,' I say sharply.

'Why didn't you talk to me about this? I promised to help you, but you do this behind my back? How can I trust you now?'

'Why can't you trust me?' I feel heat rise to my cheeks, every breath she takes seems to cut me down, little by little. I tell myself I don't need her approval but each time I try to defend myself, the words will not come out of my mouth.

'Talking directly to a killer is one thing, but this? Now any number of crazies will be responding to you just for kicks.'

'Lilith, I understand your concern, but it could also lead us to the killer. Call it a hunch. Call it whatever you want, but we have people's attention, and the more attention we have, the harder it's going to be for the killer to hide,' I say with absolute conviction.

Usually when I talk to Lilith there is a wobble in my voice I am acutely aware of, but not today.

'Have you got any leads?' I ask.

I glance across at the newsroom, convinced my colleagues can hear every word of this conversation, which is impossible, but two days without a drink has turned me into a paranoid mess, there is nothing to take off the edge of stress and my hands have decided to take on a life of their own by randomly shaking. Now is not a good time to go cold turkey.

'Meet me tonight at The Old Bull and Bush. 8pm. Don't be late.'

Before I have a chance to tell her I'll be there, she hangs up. I wander to the kitchenette and start to fill the kettle with water, I am in need of a strong cup of coffee. I place my hands on the counter and take several deep breaths. The threats of a panic attack have become far more frequent, but I am working really hard to push them away. I move to the kitchen cupboard and take out a jar of coffee, I heap two tablespoons into a cup, pour the hot water in and stir what looks like black tar before it goes onto the road. As I take a sip, hot pain bursts into my cheeks making my mouth feel like it is about to explode. I quickly run the tap and put my mouth under the water. It feels like there is a fire in my mouth. I glance down at the kitchen floor and wonder if giving up the booze is really worth it.

I push open the heavy oak doors to see Lilith already sitting at a table with a drink in front of her; nothing for me. She looks different today. She's dressed in a casual blue shirt paired with neat blue jeans and a sensible pair of loafers. Softer maybe. But her presence is anything but soft. I smile, she doesn't smile back. I remind myself I'm on a different road now and as much as I want Lilith to help me I have to go on, with or without her. I pick up a menu from the bar. My stomach has been growling at me every ten minutes, it's as if it's begging for something to fill the usual gap of gin or wine sloshing around my belly. I eye the menu, feeling her gaze and hearing a few hefty sighs of annoyance, because up until now I practically kissed her feet. But not anymore.

'I'm not sorry,' I blurt out. 'I needed a new angle.'

'And now you have one. You got the attention, but it's not the right kind of attention. I get it. Young and hungry, trying to make it up the ranks, but this is not the way.'

'Why?' I snap.

'You may think this is some brave, bold thing you're doing, but you've only made yourself look desperate.' Her words slice through me like a knife. There is a rage bubbling up inside me. The comments from social media floating around in my head, the sheer exhaustion of it all. Fuck it. I abruptly stand, the chair makes a grating sound against the floor, sending my nerves on fire.

Before I have a chance to second-guess myself, I call to the barman.

'Jack Daniels.'

There is a sliver of light piercing through the small gap in the curtains. It penetrates my eyes like a laser, intensifying the throbbing headache I've woken up with.

I'm officially off the wagon. *Way to go, me.* It didn't take much.

My brain calculates the day and I have a short burst of triumph when I realise it's Saturday and I don't have to rush to the office. I can have my pity party alone in the safety of my protective walls. But I guess that's not completely true. Since the break-in I haven't exactly felt the comfort I should in my own home.

There's a bottle of water next to the bed and I grab it by the neck and guzzle the lukewarm water like my life depends on it. I haven't had a hangover like this in years. I swing my legs out of bed and drag myself to the bathroom. I splash cold water on my face to wash away the night sweats. Then I feel a wave of nausea rise up in my stomach and I throw up in the sink. My hands rest on either side of it. It takes me a moment to catch my breath and when I do, I also catch my reflection in the mirror. I don't like the person staring back at me. Who is she? This pale woman with sunken eyes and dried-out skin. It's in that very second I wonder if I've hit that all-time low recovering alcoholics always talk about; but I'm not lying in a gutter, I'm not in a jail cell, I'm not waking up from a night of casual sex with a stranger who repulses me on sobered sight. It's just me,

Jennifer, waking up alone in my bed, being sick in the privacy of my own bathroom. But do I need to meet a certain criteria? I don't think so.

If I can't stand to look at myself, how can I expect the world to take me seriously?

We all have our weaknesses as people. Mine happens to be common, yet it is frowned upon because you have a choice whether you drink or not: life choices.

But is it? Do I actually have a choice?

Or am I about to admit to myself that I am sick and I need help.

There is a sinking feeling in the pit of my stomach. I avoid my reflection for a moment but then I force myself to slowly lift my heavy head and take a long hard look at myself.

It feels like I'm facing the demon that has been lurking in my body for years, unseen but felt. There is nobody here telling me to do this. I am not in the office with prying eyes, judging expressions. It is just me facing the ugly truth.

I remember when I'd turned fourteen. It was considered cool to meet your mates in the park, smoke cigarettes, and down bottles of Hooch and cheap beer. Then it was considered sophisticated to drink a glass of wine with a meal – a grown-up. Wine bars became the norm and getting drunk was a fun thing to do. So, I try and think back to when it became a problem, and why was it a problem? A voice in my head answered me: *Because you need it to get through the day and this makes you an addict.*

After I scrub the acidic taste out of my mouth with bouts of toothpaste and mouthwash, I step into the shower and turn the tap, which sounds like an angry hissing snake. I cry so hard that the air in my lungs escapes me so quickly I feel dizzy, but as I let the water and soap wash over me, I begin to scrub my body hard, like I am ridding myself of grime and dirt, of all I have, and all I am doing to myself. Steam fills the room and settles on the mirror. I wipe it away with the back of my hand and there is a new reflection of the one I saw twenty minutes ago. I'm not going to paint this to be some guardian angel with a halo and fluffy white wings. It's just me. Only this time the woman in the mirror knows she has a problem and knows she needs help. I don't check my phone; this is always the first thing I do when I wake up. It will no doubt be filled with tweets about the open letter and messages from work, possibly Pete and Lilith. Oh God. Lilith. My memory is so vague from last night. How much did I drink? Snippets of memory come to me like broken shards of glass, a snippet here and there, but what feels like a great fog is after I drank. I sit on the edge of the bed and reach into the bedside drawer for headache pills. I pull back the curtains. My head feels so thick, unsteady on my neck. Beyond the window the sky is a diluted saxe blue, a light film of cloud slowly disperses by the burn of the sun. I open the window and allow air to flow through, there's a little robin redbreast sitting on the car-park fence, its chest puffed out. There is a gracefulness to tiny birds I admire, how they live freely in flight and their only ambition is to survive. They have it down to a fine art, mostly.

A memory bursts through my brain of my mother. We're at a zoo, my tiny hand in the safety of hawking gloves with a beautiful falcon perched on it, its raptor claws curling round. I remember the weight of the bird, heavy and solid, how its hooked beak looked regal and how my heart thudded hard inside my chest as it spread its broad wings. It's funny how little things can ignite long-forgotten memories. I wish Mum was here. I don't think I would've struggled as much in my life with her here. After she died, my drinking became habitual. I try to think about when I last mourned her, not just thought about her. When were any of my tears about her? Or were they all about her and I just didn't know it?

I return to my flat from a walk to clear my head, and take slow steps toward my mobile phone, like it's a bomb ready to detonate at any moment. I bite down on my lower lip. Time to face the music and dance with the devil. I slide my finger across the screen and unlock the carnage, the screen goes wild with notifications.

I have four missed calls, eight WhatsApp messages, and eighteen emails.

Deep breath. Count to ten. Jump in the freezing cold water – splash.

The inevitable is waiting. The first thing I do is check my voicemail. Voicemails are somewhat more urgent, not many people I know leave them unless they are important.

Lilith. I feel my pulse begin to escalate.

'I just wanted to touch base and check if you're okay. I get it, Jennifer, I really do, but you need to be careful. Call me when you get this.' My shoulders relax from the stiffened tension built up in them like a weight of concrete. The tone of her voice was... kind, perhaps even laced with a hint of concern. It's the only message she left, and I can only hope to God that I didn't say something embarrassing, that I didn't show myself up – if only I could remember. I have to rely on Lilith to fill in the blanks.

Next are my emails. Another wave of relief whooshes through me when they are mostly advertising, a couple from Amazon, clothes companies, bill prompts. I scan each and every one of them. No gremlins. There isn't the message I was hoping to see. *Pete*. We haven't really spoken much since the day he wrestled Hayley to the ground. I guess I'd been too wrapped up in the chaos around me to notice. I quickly type him a message.

Hey! How are you? X

He instantly starts typing back but no message pings through.

Finally, a message arrives.

Not great.

There is an absence of a simple x at the end of the message which speaks volumes.

Are you okay? Want to talk? Meet up?

Just want to be alone right now. Take care.

My hands are shaky. What the hell is going on?

CHAPTER THIRTY-EIGHT

THEN

The sun bounces off the glassy waters. The ocean is calm, but underneath its surface lies a never-ending battle to win the fight for survival. Nothing is as it seems. Today is Imogen's funeral, and instead of the gratification and fulfilment I expected to feel, I am instead fuelled by envy. The sudden loss of a young life always brings about an intensified mourning amongst those who knew the deceased, but perhaps that is because the death of the young is not life's order, no matter how pitiful they were when they were alive. Her eulogy will be told like a fairy tale – make-believe. Here, we will not find the real truth of the ostentatious, spiteful, back-stabbing cretin I know she was. I offered to go with Grace, but she considered it a couple of moments too long enough for me to know my presence wasn't required. It was a blow – I think this is the moment my victory was snatched away from me only to be replaced with the toxic envy I am feeling. I wonder, just for a moment, how Grace would react if I was the one who died? Would Imogen be at my funeral?

In the near distance, a boat idles on the surface of the sea; it's close enough that I can hear the laughter of the two people on board. I force myself to laugh too, because I need to acknowledge the fact that today is a good day; Imogen Tasker will soon be six feet under with nothing but maggots and worms to keep her company. Then soon the words on her headstone will fade to nothing, the hands of time will weaken the world's memories of her and soon she'll be nothing more than a drop in a boundless ocean. *Fuck you, Imogen. I won.*

The wake was held in a forest. I imagined it would be in some upmarket pub; there was nothing real or organic about this girl, so why have her wake connected to anything but her status lifestyle?

'When Imogen was a girl, if she felt unhappy, her parents took her to the woods, and it would brighten her mood. They called it her happy place, so it seemed fitting they should go there. It was beautiful and, in a sense, joyous. I could feel her spirit as the wind blew through the trees, like she was there, approving of her final farewell.' What a lovely sentiment Grace had spoken. All I could feel was bile rising at the back of my throat. I wanted to scream, but instead I smiled. It was more like a grimace, really, like when babies are too young to smile and they're actually doing a shit. That's how I saw the situation, nothing but a pile of shit.

It is Saturday, and we sit in the warmth of Grace's conservatory overlooking the large garden.

'How big is your garden?' I ask.

'A few acres, but it has so many little nooks and crannies that, as a kid, this was my adventure playground. It's probably a bit muddy from last night's rain, but we could take a walk if you like. I've got a spare pair of wellies in the mudroom.'

'A what room?'

'It's a transition between the outdoors and the indoors. You keep things in there like coats, boots, wellies, that kind of thing.'

'They've got a name for everything.'

'My parents lived in America before I was born. That's where they got the idea from. It's always served us really well, especially when we had dogs and were living so close to the sea. Come on. Let's go.'

We enter *the mudroom* and the first thing I notice is that I live in a flat that is smaller than this 'essential' room. Everything is neatly stored; it doesn't live up to its name. The walls are painted in duck-egg blue, expensive-looking shelves are attached to the wall, and the drawers that look like they belong in a showroom are strategically placed with bushy house plants. There are even three hooks attached to the walls with names engraved in shiny silver: Annie, Charlie, Fritz. Grace catches me looking.

'Those belonged to our three Weimaraners. Mum never took them down because she was so upset when they all died.'

'They died together?'

'No, they all died at different times, old age. Except Fritz. He was only eighteen months when he died, just a puppy.'

I never had pets and I never understood why people cared for them so much. We had a neighbour who had an annoying Yorkie-terrier-whatever dog with a pathetic worm-like tail that would yap for hours on end and cock its leg up to piss every ten seconds. I wanted to wring its scrawny neck and toss it off the top floor, but I never got close enough to catch the vermin.

'He was so beautiful. Dad would say his coat was like the silver of the moon. He got bloat, which is time-sensitive in terms of life and death and passed away during surgery.'

'That's unfortunate. I've never had a pet.'

Grace opens the door and wind funnels along the side of the

house. I step back and realise my jumper isn't going to be warm enough even for a short walk.

She takes a waxy, navy-coloured coat and holds it ready for my arms to slip in. There is a weight to it that tugs on my shoulders, I try to zip it up but the zip only glides along to the underside of my chest.

'My mum is super tiny. But it will keep the chill off you.' Her nice way of saying I'm not a fat lump.

The garden is filled with shrubs and flowers that are still in full bloom even though it's out of season. At the end of the path, the garden opens up into a large clearing, there are some private steps which we walk to. It leads onto a high point in which the sea can be seen. The steps themselves don't lead onto another pathway, but the tip of a cliff, the edges pointed and treacherous. The sting of the salty air gives me a shiver, and Grace wraps her arm around my body and pulls me into her. I don't expect it. My body stiffens as we both look out onto the horizon watching pointed crests forming whitecaps, neither of us saying anything until I turn to kiss her and a voice cuts through the air like a butcher's knife, slicing right through the bone.

She quickly steps away and turns her back to the direction the voice comes from.

'It's my mum... shit, that was close.'

Reality sinks its long teeth into my skin, and I am reminded of a bitter fact.

I am a disgusting secret.

CHAPTER THIRTY-NINE

The emptiness of St George's Park was a clear indication that half term was over, absent of children at play, with a few dog walkers, joggers, and parents pushing prams, it was an ordinary day. It was hard to believe the world kept on moving when his had ended. He appreciated his sister had dragged him out for a walk, and it would have felt good to be out if he didn't feel so bilious.

'I drank too much last night, feel so bloody ropy.' Jordan didn't have the energy to fix what was broken or the headspace to analyse what went wrong for his girlfriend to leave him for another man, so whisky functioned as the anaesthetic to numb the pain.

'Fresh air will do you good.' Carly looked at him, his body trembling, his skin clammy and pale. 'Oh crap, Jordan, are you about to be sick?'

'Dunno!' Jordan leaned forward and inhaled loud breaths before his body convulsed like a sick dog and he projectile vomited onto the grass.

'Oh, for God's sake, Jordan. You can't spew up in a family park – there, look, go to the toilets.'

Jordan bolted, hands cupping his mouth. Carly walked to the swings near the toilets and waited, she heard the sounds of his retching echoing off the walls and took instant pity. Then it went quiet, and then the sound of a primal scream made her heart fall into her stomach and her legs momentarily go limp.

She ran to the entrance of the gents. Jordan appeared in the doorway gripping its frame to steady himself, panting, unable to find his voice, his face ashen, eyes crazed and bulging.

'What... what's wrong?' Her pitch was high enough to shatter glass.

Her eyes transfixed on his.

'There's a dead body in there.'

'What the hell.' Carly pushed past him. In a cubicle, the body of a female, hair matted with dried blood, spilled out on cold tiles. Both siblings were rooted to the spot, shock gripping them both as if they were watching a film and this wasn't really happening. Eyes transfixed with horror, unable to look away.

Carly threw her bag onto the floor and pressed her fingertips against the victim's neck.

'Call 999,' she shouted over her shoulder.

'Is she still alive?'

'Shut up, I'm trying to...' But Carly knew the tell-tale signs of death. She'd seen it hundreds of times on the ward. Sure, she wasn't a nurse anymore, but the nurse still lived within her and there were just some skills that never fell away.

They both crouched beside the corpse. Jordan took off his jacket and was about to place it under the victim's head.

'What the hell are you doing?' she hissed.

'I dunno... I just... it feels like the right thing to do.'

'This is a crime scene, Jordan. Don't piss about.' She looked across at her bag heaped on the floor which would now be contaminated. They slowly stood up and moved away from the body, waiting outside the entrance to the toilets, waiting for the wail of the ambulance and police cars to cut through the air.

CHAPTER FORTY

JENNIFER MACK

Just before noon, I'm standing in a park, which on any normal day would be considered pretty with its viridescent backdrop, sounds of tranquil running water from a large fountain featuring a young girl jumping over a skipping rope. But when you throw in the press, the police, ambulances, and a stretcher with a body bag on it, the scenery changes dramatically. I'm taking a witness account from a man called Jordan Fitzpatrick. He looks to be in his late thirties, maybe younger, and his withered skin indicates he's been living his own trauma, not just the one he stumbled on today. There's years of grief etched onto his face. His expression is alert when we first engage, and out of all the other journos he gravitates toward me. He is what I call a little rough around the edges, his London accent reminds me of Pete, and it makes my heart sink; but I push the thought of him out of my head and focus on the job.

'Not exactly how I planned my morning,' he mutters.

I notice his scent is really off, one that is concurrent with vomit. I take a step back which he immediately addresses.

'Sorry... I'm a bit under the weather. Nothing you can catch, mind you. Got sloshed last night.'

I nod. Been there. 'Can't have made you feel any better to find a body.'

'Bloody horrible. Is it... you know, one of them? Another Grace?'

'We're waiting on a formal identification. But in the meantime, can you tell me what happened?'

'Not much to tell. I felt ill, ran to the toilet 'cause my sister was having a go at me about throwing up in the park. Not something I could help, I might add. I pushed open the loo door and there she was. At first, I thought it was some street bum passed out or something, but then I saw the blood and the putrid smell hit me. *Fuck*. As if my life couldn't get any more fucked up.'

I think he's hinting for me to be his sounding board, but I don't bite. I don't have the time or the energy to deal with this guy's problems. And thankfully, before he can volunteer that information himself, I see a familiar figure come into view from the corner of my eye.

'Jennifer.' Lilith nods and then turns her attention to Jordan. My phone rings in my pocket. I'm irritated by the interruption; I want to hear what Lilith has to say.

I swipe the phone and snap, 'Hello?'

'Jennifer, it's me.' *Me?* I don't recognise the hurried, panic-stricken voice.

There's a pregnant pause. 'You need to get to the office immediately.' When the voice on the phone evens to a calmer tone it clicks that it's Olivia.

'I can't right now. I'm at the park where they've found another victim.'

'Yeah, I know that, but you need to get back here now. It's important. Is Grain with you?'

My head feels light, my legs unsteady.

'Yeah, why? What is this about?'

'Tell her to come with you.'

'Olivia. Just tell me what the hell is going on.'

'There's a package waiting for you, and it isn't a normal package. *Oh God*, please just come. Come now. I can't explain, you just... just get here.'

The line goes dead.

I feel dizzy. I try to steady myself but everything and everyone around me feels far away, as if I am in a goldfish bowl, a dream where I am screaming but nobody hears me. Nobody sees me.

Lilith is talking to the witness beneath a tree, her gaze is set on Jordan, absorbing every detail he is sharing with her.

I approach her with caution. Her eyes narrow at me in annoyance.

'Lilith, you mind driving me back to the office?'

'Have you lost your mind?' she says through gritted teeth.

I stare at her for a moment too long, hoping she will read my pleading eyes.

'I got a call from the team, and they asked me to come back, Olivia said it's urgent, there is a package and...'

'A package?'

'Yes, it–' I continue but Lilith breaks me off mid-sentence, sunshine breaks through the clouds and I blink into the piercing light. The seed of a headache that has been looming begins to manifest itself into the pain it has been threatening all day.

'I am at a murder scene. If you need assistance to come away from here, then I suggest you ask one of the other officers.'

Dry-mouthed, I look around and try to pick out an officer in the crowd who isn't in the thick of all the commotion.

I turn back to Lilith. I don't know where the emotion has

come from, but I am swallowing down tears, thick and lumpy in my throat.

'Lilith... I...'

'Excuse me,' Lilith says to Jordan Fitzpatrick. He holds his hand to his mouth and nods his head. He still appears dreadfully nauseated and probably grateful for the reprieve.

'What is wrong with you?' Lilith says, her tone low, talking through her teeth again.

'Call from one of my colleagues, she said there's a package at the office and to bring you with me.'

'Why couldn't she tell you what it is over the phone?'

'I don't know, but it has to be something bad.' I hate the sound of my own voice. Needy. Childish. Desperate.

'Wild wolves will not pull me away from where I am right now.' She shouts over my shoulder to an officer, and he jumps to her command like an obedient dog. He looks about eighteen, tall and slim without so much as an etching of facial hair. His police uniform looks incredulous against his slender frame, it can't be that long ago since he was in a school uniform, let alone the police uniform that makes him look like he is playing dress-up.

On the way to *The Chronicle*, we ride in near-perfect silence except for static coming from the police radio.

I take the lift with PC Hall to the second floor and we are met by a very pale Olivia. She points to a medium-sized box that sits on my desk.

I'd absolutely kill for a drink right now to take the edge off my nerves.

When I peer into the box, my heart stops.

'Holy Mary-fucking Christ,' I spurt. This feels like a

nightmare and I am waiting for the alarm to go off and take me out of this moment.

It's as if my brain cannot process what is in front of me. Or it doesn't want to.

PC Hall pulls out his phone and makes a call. I can hear the unmistakable voice of Lilith on the other end, it is distant, but I know her voice as it's embedded in my head. PC Hall ushers me back and puts the phone on speaker. 'Ma'am, this matter calls for your attention. We need you here.' He begins to explain what is in front of us, the cold, hard facts bring the sheer horror to the surface. Lilith is eerily calm. There is no surprise tangled up in her words, but then again, she is a seasoned detective.

I step forward. My eyes do not pull away from the content of the package. 'Have you called Jacob?' I ask Olivia when I finally find my voice.

'Left two voicemails.'

'And the name, it's specifically addressed to me?'

'Yeah. Here.'

'Don't touch it!' PC Hall shouts as Olivia pulls down the cardboard flap. 'Don't touch a bloody thing! Forensics need everything intact. This is now a crime scene.'

Olivia and I exchange a fearful look.

This is not a sick joke, it's personal.

CHAPTER FORTY-ONE

JENNIFER MACK

A middle-aged officer, PC Shah, takes me into a room with a red, frayed couch and pillows now stained a tobacco yellow alongside a fake house plant, its plastic leaves weighed down with dust. I feel uneasy, like I am the one in the firing line, that *I* am the criminal. With the absence of a window and natural light, the room feels closed and claustrophobic; I have nightmares of places like this where I search for a door, but there is nothing but thick concrete closing in on me. I find it hard to breathe.

'Can I please have some water?' I ask.

'Yeah of course.' Shah leaves the room and returns momentarily with a half-filled plastic cup. I gratefully take it from her and down it in one go. My mouth isn't quenched but I don't want to ask for more.

'Do you know if they've found who the... you know, who it belongs to?'

'Not that I know of, but I'm sure we'll know soon enough. Must've scared you, like something out of a horror film.'

That's exactly what it was. An absolute horror. The white, bloodless image stains my memory and every time I blink, the exposed bone from where it's been surgically cut at the radius flashes in my mind. It's one thing reading about gruesome subjects – that I'm used to – but it's quite another having a severed hand delivered to you personally.

At this moment, I cannot imagine how my life will ever feel normal again. This story has consumed me – somehow, I felt emotionally crumpled, and the reality of my loneliness has kicked in. I have nobody to call. Nobody to wrap their arms around me and tell me it is going to be all right. I keep asking myself: *Why do I take everything so seriously? When was the last time I laughed?* And then I remember it was with Pete.

Shah sits opposite me. I try to imagine what her life is like outside of work. Is she married? Does she have children? Or is she like me; lives to work and not works to live? As a female officer I'm sure the job has met with its limitations. Despite the call for equality, the force still doesn't conform in the way it does for a man.

'Do you know how much longer they'll be?' I ask.

'Not sure. The stations have never been so busy since all these murders. Most we dealt with before was drunk teens and petty theft. We're on a whole other level now. And truth be told, we just don't have the manpower or the experience, that's why Lilith Grain is here.' There is a warmth to Shah. I like her. She has a rounded face which softens her features. I don't know if it's a good thing to be liked when you are asserting authority, but I'm pleased.

Finally, the door opens and Lilith and another officer I've not seen before comes in. The atmosphere is tense, rigid. Lilith doesn't maintain eye contact with me, which unnerves me. It's like I don't know her, she's distant.

'My name's Detective Arnold. I'd like to ask you some questions.'

He has a thick moustache peppered with grey, his tone is

low but somehow still speaks volumes. He's a heavy-set man, not fat, but solid, like a rugby player.

'Can you please confirm your name?'

Lilith looks straight ahead, like she's looking through me, not at me. My skin crawls with nerves, I lean forward, my hands on the table, hair hanging over my face like a madwoman. I feel my brows knit tightly together in utter confusion.

'What's this all about? I thought I was brought here because of a hand being sent to me.'

'And now we just need to clear a few things up, that's all,' Detective Arnold says.

I take a deep breath. Think. This just feels so off.

'Am I... am I under arrest?'

Finally, Grain opens her mouth and her voice is as stern as iron. 'The body in the park today was identified as Hayley Woolley.'

'You two have quite the history.' Detective Arnold's voice almost sounds sing-song. Arrogance spilling right out of his pores.

'We didn't get on, that's all,' I say in defence.

'I'd call it more than not getting on. She broke into your home. What was she looking for, Jennifer?'

Blood rushes to my ears.

'I don't know. She's the one who broke into my home, not the other way round, she's the one who did wrong. Not me.' I'm shaking with anger now.

'If somebody broke into my home. Touched my things. I'd be pissed off. How pissed off were you, Jennifer?'

'I want a solicitor.' I'm in trouble, this is only going one way and it's fucking messed up.

'The hand has been matched with Hayley Woolley,' Detective Arnold interjects.

The room is spinning, like I'm on a merry-go-round,

thoughts whirling. Suddenly Lilith and Arnold's faces blur like a kaleidoscope, their voices becoming warped. Distortion has taken me prisoner and I can't escape.

It's too late – my breath is rapid – chest tight – *I'm going to fucking die.*

Breathe, Jennifer... Deeply and slowly as you can, through your nose and gently through your mouth.

I close my eyes and focus on my breathing.

Onetwothreefourfivesixseveneightnineten.

Onetwothreefour... five... six... seven... eight... nine... ten.

Colours begin to merge back together, and my vision comes back into focus.

'Are you okay?' I hear Detective Arnold say. His voice is clearer now and I take a sip of the water he hands me and straighten myself. I wipe away beads of sweat from my forehead with the back of my hand.

'Yes. I can continue.' My voice is cracked, low.

'Where were you the night of Friday the 15th of October?'

I look at the table and think. My head jerks up. 'With *you,* Lilith. I was with Lilith at The Old Bull and Bush.'

Detective Arnold side-glances at Lilith.

She doesn't buckle. 'Where did you go after you left, Jennifer?'

My mind draws a blank.

I have zero recollection. Not even a smidge of detail.

'I... must... I must have gone home because I woke up in my bed on Saturday morning. I had a bit too much to drink.'

'Jennifer, we recovered a journal from the victim's bag. We've had a handwriting specialist confirm it's your writing.'

Lilith's bird-like hands reach for a piece of paper. 'Do you recognise this?'

She slides the paper across the table. This cannot be real.

There is nothing that I want more than to see Hayley dead, I am tired of her torture. The way she makes me feel. People like her think they own the world, but her day will come, and her end is near. At every opportunity she belittles me. I just wish she'd finally kick the bucket and leave me in peace.

'Jennifer Mack, I am arresting you on suspicion of the murder of Hayley Frances Woolley. You do not have to say anything. But it may harm your defence if you do not mention when questioned something which you may later rely on in court. Anything you do say may be given in evidence.'

CHAPTER FORTY-TWO

THEN

I walk for miles in the downpour, rain running a rivulet down my back. I am soaked through to the very core; the too-tight waxed jacket was left behind along with my self-respect. A car slows as it passes me, part of me hopes it is Grace, apologising; the middle-aged female driver puts her window down and shouts something across at me but in a world of my own, I am unable to give a shit, so I ignore her. I can't allow myself to be that desperate again. I'd made it a thing by leaving so abruptly. My whole life was consumed with dark secrets and it isn't letting up. I finally reach the flat, ignoring the gangs gathering in close-knit groups, palms reaching out and swiftly put in pockets. I close the door, I am shivering uncontrollably, cold and exhaustion has consumed me. I start to undress at the door, peeling off jeans in several tugs.

The flat is filled with ghosts tonight. I don't know if it is the fact I am probably burning a fever or just upset, but all around me memories of the past become unearthed.

I pinch myself and squeeze my eyes shut and then they disappear and I'm back in the present moment. There's just enough hot water to have a shower, the heat of the water is a comfort. I don't want my mind to go there, but all I can think of is Grace. I think about the way she held me at the bottom of the garden – but now it feels like a cruel trick, and it bothers me how much I need her. I go to bed and before I know it, I'm falling into a deep sleep that my body has been begging for. There's a knocking on the door, but I ignore it, turn my body, and pull the covers tighter around me. But it persists and I'm slowly pulled away from sleep.

I go to the door and open it while it's still on the chain.

Behind the door I see Grace. My heart stops. Embarrassment. Panic. A mixed bag of confusion rises within me as to how she knows where I live.

'What are you doing here?' I ask. 'And how do you know where I live?'

She holds out a bill in her hand with my name and address on it. 'This must have fallen out of your bag when you left in a hurry. I knew you wouldn't take my calls, so I decided to come to you instead.' She peers into the crack of the door. 'So... can I come in?'

I slide open the lock chain and open the door. I feel so exposed, but I let her in. She's facing away from me, she pauses, staring at the pile of books I have on the coffee table. I try not to show the worry and panic. Nobody ever comes here, so I leave everything and anything out with the exception of the day I killed Lizzy – then I had scrubbed the floor, bleached every surface, and gotten rid of just about everything else.

'Do you want a drink, something to eat?' I offer, knowing there is nothing but bread in the cupboard.

'I'm not hungry.' She turns to face me then, and I can see her eyes are filled with curiosity, wide and alert. Being on my turf changes the dynamics. Then I tell myself I shouldn't care that my home is not like hers, the only thing that matters is that she's here. She cared enough to come see me.

'You look tired,' she says in that calm, breathy tone. Her voice is always so even, so nice, but I wonder what it would take for the calmness to fall away, hear her shout, yell, how far would she need to be pushed?

'I just woke up,' I say. I hate how timid I sound.

After a moment of staring into space, she brings her attention back to me. I excuse myself for a moment and go to the bathroom. I catch a glance of myself in the mirror looking very far from perfect. I need to pull myself together, I put a dollop of toothpaste on my toothbrush and clean my teeth at speed to rinse away the stench of morning breath. I splash my face with cold water. Even if I don't look fantastic, I feel a tad better and it removes a small amount of vulnerability.

'I care about you, but I can't be open about us.' She doesn't look me in the eye.

'But why?' I say. I hate myself for it. My tone is loaded with desperation. She doesn't answer and I see the cracks between us start to widen.

'Is it because... because I'm not in your league? I don't fit into the designer life you have, is that it?' There is some part of me that wants to put my hands on her neck and kiss her while I feel her gasp for air.

I allow myself a moment of silence, self-pity, whatever it is before she moves toward me.

'I'm not like that and you know it. I'm not ready to tell the world and I thought I made that clear this morning after we slept with one another.'

I take a deep breath and try to pull myself together. I wish I didn't feel the way I do. Then it wouldn't hurt.

'I don't want to be here,' I say. 'Give me ten minutes to get dressed and we can go for a walk.'

The sky is a dark canvas of grey and gloom. We walk to the park, dry leaves crunching beneath our feet. We find a vacant cast-iron bench, my body aches from the chill I'd caught the night before. The coolness of the October air wraps round me – as if I were always cold. We sit in silence, the death of summer has occurred and it's as if there was a tremble of anger from the trees as they shook off the browning leaves that gather in the wind and swirl across the grass and mud.

'Have you ever been with a woman before me?'

Her question catches me off-guard, and my immediate reaction is to lie, but I catch myself. 'Once. But that was a long time ago.'

'I really don't care where you live or how much money you have. If anything, it makes me like you more.'

'I don't understand.'

'All my life I have been surrounded by vapid people with more money than sense. People who think they can snap their fingers and change the world to their will because they have money. People who think they can run others down because they have money. My father – I love him – but *he* is one of those people. I'm tired of being expected to talk in a certain way, dress in a certain way, but with you, I feel like I can let that expectation go and just be myself. Do we really have to label everything? Why can't we just enjoy this for what it is – do we need to tick-box our relationship like we are completing a bloody form?' The weight of confusion hangs in the air. I resist the urge to kiss her.

'I understand if you want to walk away. Honestly, I do.'

By the time we leave the park and make our way back, the sky has fallen through and given way to another torrential downpour. We managed to get into a coffee shop nestled on the corner close to the sea. It feels cosy and welcoming with the sweet tang of chocolate croissants warming and the rich aroma of coffee. We don't say very much but our legs are intertwined under the table. At points, I feel light and happy and then it's replaced with a sharp sinking feeling in my stomach. I don't tell her how I feel. I sip my coffee and eat my croissant. When the rain stops, a shard of sunlight beats on the glass, the glow bouncing off Grace's skin. She is so beautiful.

In the weeks that follow, my life is pure bliss. We go out to the cinema in the afternoons when it's quiet, we steal kisses as the lights dim. We walk along the beach, sometimes running into the waves crashing into the shore. I prefer to be at her house, but on occasion we do spend time at the flat. It offers us privacy for the most intimate moments when the thrill of getting caught isn't needed – for when we just want to melt into one another and escape the outside world. The flat feels so different with her in it, as if she has breathed a new life into a place that has always been so dark and oppressive. It doesn't matter what happens on the outside, because in this bubble I am happy for the first time in my life.

I finally understand what it means to be in love.

CHAPTER FORTY-THREE

JENNIFER MACK

I lay on the cot, its springs digging into every tight-knitted knot of stress, deepening into my neck and shoulders. The weight of the situation has pulled me into a state of disbelief. I have two questions that whirl in my head: Why can't I remember anything? How the hell did I get here?

If only I hadn't drank that night. This is a wicked punishment of the cruellest kind, I had only just resolved to become sober, but the short-lived whim of it all has driven me here.

I go back to the fact that there is nobody in my life to call. But not in the sense of needing comfort, rather, survival, a way out.

When my journal was stolen. I knew the words that were in it. My most intimate, private thoughts were now in the hands of the police. *Handwriting experts for fuck's sake.* I am under a microscope, every single part of me exposed – and Lilith, the ferocious wild beast I know she is, has turned on me. There's blood in the water and she won't stop until she can come in for the kill. I'm likely to be held in police custody for the maximum time possible; murder is a serious charge. It messes with my head. I'm like a rabbit caught in a trap – no way out. After the first twenty-four hours, I wake up from a restless sleep and suddenly my body is in panic mode and I know I need help. My mind races. I have some savings, but not nearly enough for a criminal lawyer. There's the flat, of course, but that will take too long to sell.

I need help. Now!

Danielle!

Why didn't I think of it before? I'd turned down her crazy offer to be the better person but look where that got me.

I'll give her whatever she needs if it means getting out of this cell.

I'm alone for what feels like forever when the door finally opens. Detective Arnold walks in with another policeman who barely looks old enough to drive, let alone be an officer of the law. If the situation weren't so dismal, I'd laugh.

'You're going to be released on bail.' I look up at Detective Arnold, his face crumpled and voice taut. He doesn't want to be giving me this news.

'You mean I can go?' My voice is meek, tired.

'There are bail conditions. You're still a suspect, but until we get the evidence we need, you're free to go, for now.'

I unlock the door to my flat, my fingertips numb with cold. Inside is no better, the heater has been off for days. The first thing I do is press the booster button on the furnace; it is a relief to hear the roar of the boiler ignite with life. There is a three-day-old newspaper on the kitchen table, untouched from when I was last in my home. Nothing has changed within my surrounding walls, but everything has changed within me. My phone has been returned to me, its battery drained from the police digging into it, trying to gather more incriminating evidence. I put the phone on charge and run a hot shower, I'm desperate for the fugue of jail to be washed away from my skin. After my shower, I lay on my bed, enjoying the softness and comfort it offers my aching body. My eyes close but just before that moment of hypnagogia, the gentle transition between wakefulness and sleep, the buzzer rings on my intercom. I jolt from the bed in a panic. I go to the door with unsteady movements, only this time I am stone-cold sober.

She stands with her arms hugging her body. She looks different, her buoyant presence replaced with a sombre expression, her eyes wounded and worried.

'Olivia, what are you doing here?'

'I was worried about you.'

'I'm okay. I think.' *But am I?*

My first thought is one of action. I'm sure Jacob has sent Olivia to my door to prey on me at my weakest, most vulnerable ebb.

'So can I come in?'

'Yeah... yes, sure.' I step aside and she steps into the flat, warming her hands against the radiator, which is now piping hot.

'Freezing out tonight, probably frost in the morning.' She rubs her hands together and blows into them.

'Olivia, what are you doing here?'

She pauses. Her gaze fixed on me like she's seeing me properly for the first time.

'Did you do it?'

Despite my tiredness and the last desperate forty-eight hours, I baulk at her question. Suddenly awake and alert, I feel repelled and furious that Olivia has come here to ask me that. I turn away from her and walk into the kitchen to flick the switch on the kettle. I can't be bothered to offer her anything.

'Do you *think* I did it?'

'No, but I wanted to hear it from you.'

'I have no memory of the night Hayley was killed. I went for a drink, which turned into many more, and the rest is blank. Without an alibi, my head is basically being lined up for the guillotine.'

'What if I told the police you were with me?'

The hot water I'm pouring from the kettle into my mug spills onto my hand.

'Fucking hell!' I quickly run cold water from the tap and let it work over my skin.

'Why would you do that?'

She walks toward me, her hand on my shoulder, and whispers into my ear.

CHAPTER FORTY-FOUR

THEN

It's a Saturday night. The rain is thrashing against the windows and the wind violently shakes the trees. In the safety of Grace's bedroom, we curl into one another, our bodies intertwined and content. We're watching an old film about Tom Hanks getting sacked from his job because he has AIDS.

'Things haven't really changed much,' I say after the film has finished.

'Oh, I don't know. I think they have,' Grace replies in a sleepy doze.

I bolt upright. 'How?'

'Sacking someone because of an illness would not happen now. Everyone is so much more open and accepting now compared to then,' Grace says.

I know our worlds are different by status but the alarming distortion of this off-the-cuff statement makes my insides fuse together. We are in hiding as a couple, we don't share affection publicly, not a single soul knows about our romantic relationship.

I hope my face shows the disgust Grace made me feel.

'If that's the case, if things have changed since the eighties, then introduce me to your parents as your partner. Let's tell your mother tonight, when she gets home.'

Grace shakes her head. 'It's not that simple.'

'So tell me how have things changed?' My voice is raised now. I feel heat building up in my cheeks and then it's back:

She doesn't love you! If she did, she'd openly tell the world. You're nothing but a disgusting habit. A drug she craves but won't admit she depends on you.

It's as if I heard glass shatter. It's the moment we become undone.

We've been together for six months. I've played the game her way because I believed there would be a light at the end of the tunnel, but, as if seeing things for the first time, there would never be an end to it. If I wanted to keep her, we'd never be open.

'I forgot to say, I can't see you next weekend. I've got dinner plans with some old friends.'

'I'm not welcome?' I snap.

'Oh, don't be like that. It's good to have other interests outside each other.'

'That may work for normal couples, but we aren't normal. According to the face we put on for the world, we are just friends, so why, as your *friend*,' I say with air exclamation marks, 'can I not come?'

'Come on. This isn't fair. We've been together constantly. Is it wrong to want a bit of breathing space?'

'I'm suffocating you now, is that it?' My chest tightens, like a boa constrictor squeezing the air from my lungs. I thought I was enough.

But you're not enough. You'll never be enough.

I pace the room, Grace edges to the end of the bed and puts her head in her hands.

'I care about you, but I do need my own space. Lately I feel like we are always together and if we carry on like this, we'll run out of things to talk about and just blur into one person and lose a sense of who we are.'

'I'm not bored. Are you bored?' I hate the sound of the unsteady wobble in my voice.

'Did I say bored? Look, I just need space. I want you to be part of my life. Not all of it.' Her words sting. I realise I'd been harbouring the hope that she'd never want to be away from me, that we'd be partners always. I blamed Imogen, but it should have been Grace.

I feel exhausted and bone cold. I stand at a distance from the restaurant – following her had seemed like a good idea at the time. It seemed logical to know who my competition was. We'd been to this restaurant together: Harry's, an American-themed burger bar, decked out with a retro sixties theme, cushioned booths, and giant milkshakes – we'd had fun here, but now the memory would be marred with her betrayal.

I go into the restaurant and am seated at a small table by the window. I'm lucky I get a clear view of the comers and goers but nobody can see me. I've worn black, my hair hangs loosely over my face. Grace walks in with three other girls and a couple of guys I've never seen before. She's all dressed up. Her face glowing with bronzer and shiny lip gloss: she doesn't go to those extreme efforts for me. One of the girls is devastatingly pretty, in the sense that she looks otherworldly – model-like. I watch her flip her thick raven ponytail like a fucking show horse. One of the guys looks like he works for Abercrombie and Fitch, all built up, clean and shiny like a new toy. He nestles in close to Grace, so close his body is pressed right up against her.

Grace likes him, she wants to fuck him.

Tonight I'm starting to see everything in a different light. The world I thought I'd carefully cultivated has been tarnished, no longer safe.

The pretty boy laughs a lot; he likes to be the centre of attention and Grace is eating it all up with a spoon. I order a cheeseburger and fries, it's left to go cold. I don't want to keep watching, but I can't tear my eyes away from her and the fun she's clearly having. Eventually, their plates are collected, and they don't opt for dessert. Grace gets up to go to the toilet and I quickly duck my head into my bag like I'm looking for something. She walks straight past me without so much as a small glance in my direction. My pulse is in my skull, the throbbing sensation giving me a pounding headache.

When she returns to the table the attention is drawn back to her. My dear Grace.

She's loving the attention. Hasn't even looked at her phone once to see if you've called, texted. Tonight, you do not matter.

I reach for my phone and send her a text.

> Do you want me to come over after you get home?

I hit send and wait.

I watch as she reaches into her bag and then looks at her phone. She cradles it in her hand but instead of replying, she places it back into her bag and regroups with her friends laughing at something one of them has said.

I am beyond hurt.

She's purposely ignored me.

I put down money on the table to pay for my meal and get out of the restaurant as fast as I can.

A wave of nausea hits me like a tsunami.

The chill of the night air sobers my thoughts as I walk at a brisk pace, each thunderous stomp of my footsteps on the pavement driving me into a rage. The craving of vengeance is too overwhelming to handle.

CHAPTER FORTY-FIVE

JENNIFER MACK

I am sure that I've lost my job. At this point, I don't see any other outcome. Jacob gave it to me straight. *One chance.* I had one chance, and since that time I've been arrested for my colleague's murder.

I can't face the judgemental eyes and elbow nudging, so we agreed to meet at the park.

Jacob stubs out a cigarette with his shoe just as I arrive, the smell of it still lingering in the crisp air.

'I don't have a job anymore,' I say.

He shakes his head. 'I wasn't expecting this. A murder, delivery of body parts, with *you* a suspect.'

'It's all bollocks.' I'm past trying to save myself. He holds out his pack of cigarettes and I politely decline.

'You haven't lost your job.'

My face must give away the shock. He is surely joking, right?

'To be frank, the paper is on the map because of you. And for what it's worth, I don't think you did it. Some would call me fucking insane to keep you on, but you have the killer's attention. And that means the paper has attention.'

Jacob leans back on the bench and stretches his legs out in front of him.

'Keep writing to the killer. Keep them engaged. One of the things I've always liked about you is your tenacity.' But he has no idea how afraid I have been, how I simply bottle it all up and drink my worries away... okay, maybe he knows that part.

'So how do we handle this? Am I supposed to come back into the office and pretend everything is normal?'

'You can't pretend. None of us can do that, but you don't need to be in the office. You can investigate anywhere. That's the beauty of the twenty-first century, my dear.'

'And the arrest?'

'The police needed somebody to blame, make them look like they are actually doing something. All a load of fucking bollocks. Yes, you wrote something in your journal about wanting her dead – I want my brother dead because he's a low-life little prick but it doesn't mean I'll *actually* kill him. There's none of your DNA, no evidence at the scene. I can write in a journal and say I am Michael Jackson, doesn't make it true.'

'So what do you want me to do?' I ask Jacob.

'Keep doing what you're doing. Find out who the killer is and lay the fuck low. If we get any further "deliveries" for you, I'll let you know.'

I nod. 'But how long before another reporter gets hold of the fact I am a suspect?'

'Let me handle that. Now go do your job. Call me when you've got something.'

I head home on foot. My body is bone cold and tired, thoughts whirling through my head. My stomach growls in protest; it feels hollow and empty. I haven't eaten properly in days and the combination of exhaustion, stress, and hunger is taking its toll.

I arrive back at the flat. There's a parcel on the doorstep. My heart stops as I notice the familiar thick black tape lopped over the box. The same bold writing with my name written on a crisp white label. I try to cool my prickling anxiety. I look around and see if there is a sign of anybody watching, but it's all quiet except for the distant sound of a few cars and the chill of the cold wind. I'm of two minds whether I should call the police or if I should pick up the box and find out what awaits me.

Without further hesitation I pick it up, the weight much lighter than I expected. I take one last glance over my shoulder and slot my key into the door. My skin is damp with sweat, and I place the box down by my feet and decide to play it safe by grabbing some marigolds and a kitchen knife. Thoughts flash in my head like the pop of a camera bulb. What will I find? Another hand, a head, some other gruesome body part?

The box is layered with foam balls and as I delve deeper my hands reach a manila envelope. I take a sharp breath and carefully pry open the paper with caution. It takes me a few moments to process the images; copies of my own handwriting, entries I'd made in my journal, carefully glued against photos of Hayley. Whoever sent this to me has put a lot of effort into it. I start to read the entries I'd written.

> *I want her dead.*
> *I imagine her cold, lifeless body and it gives me a sinister thrill. That must make me a bad person.*

If only I could recall the memory of what happened after I left Lilith.

CHAPTER FORTY-SIX

THEN

The sun burns away the thin layer of clouds that blanket the horizon. I loudly slurp the remains of a watered-down Diet Coke from a McDonald's cup to get her attention. I use the straw to stab the ice at the bottom. I imagine the cold blocks are my wounded feelings; chipping away at them makes me feel better. Grace keeps her gaze pinned to her phone. It's as if I'm her shadow; with her, but not acknowledged.

We have reached a dangerous point. Our arguments explosive, heated, and I desperately try to claw my way back. Acts of desperation and a wedge between us that won't budge because I am losing her.

Her nights out without me have become more frequent and I am growing tired of watching and waiting. I try to be patient, then use guilt trips but in the end nothing works. It has been two weeks since we've slept together, and whenever I reach for her, she pulls away: headaches, period pains, tiredness. *Every. Single. Excuse.* But she is always well enough to go to a party, to meet her girl gang for dinner. Feelings of love and hate overlap.

In the distance, a couple walk along the shore, their hands intertwined. It makes me yearn for affection. I slip my hand on her knee and run it down the top of her leg, the softness of her skin intoxicating.

'Not here!' she snaps.

'Then where? When?'

She laughs at something on her phone. The anger within me is like a curtain of red mist. I can't see straight.

I grab the phone clean out of her hand and run. She shouts, but I blank her out. I pull back my arm and fling her phone into the sea. It sinks into the dark waters and I feel a wave of satisfaction.

'You're a fucking coward. You can't admit who you really are. *Liaaaaaar!*' I cry.

Grace is silent, the light breeze whipping golden strands of hair across her tear-stained face.

'I don't know how many times we have to go over the same thing, if you feel like this isn't enough then break up with me.' Her words stick to me like mud.

'You don't mean that!'

'Oh but I do. I am so sick of this. You're clingy. I'm not allowed to have any interests, your jealousy is crippling, the way you criticise everything I enjoy that isn't about you... *Jesus fucking Christ, I can't breathe!*' She brings her fingers round her neck for dramatic effect.

It is like a bomb has detonated within me; rage unleashed.

I slam my fist into the side of her face. Her mouth is gaped open in a state of shock. This is it. The nail in the coffin. She takes a step back, trembling like a fragile bird. My body numbs, time slows.

She holds her cheek with the palm of her hand, her head tipped back, hard gasps of breath.

My knuckles still feel the clash of her cheekbone. A wave crashes against the shoreline and onto my legs. The waves unsteady my feet, like the ocean is reprimanding my behaviour.

Her hard gaze moves over my body, pupils dilated, her cheek now blooming into deep pink. Her expression is unreadable.

'That is the last time you will ever touch me.' Her words like a knife through hot butter slice through me. The familiar softness in her face has hardened. She is unreachable.

'You say that like I've been able to touch you. Every time I come near you, I'm shoved away, discarded like trash, you–'

'*Stop*! Just. *Fucking*. Stop!'

'It's over.' Two words have such power: the trigger of a gunshot through to my heart.

***

The weight of grief sits on my chest. In the quiet of the bedroom, I barely breathe. I wish for Death to come and snatch me in my sleep. It has been thirty-six hours since she left, since the couple on the beach came to her after they'd witnessed our fight. I haven't tried to make contact; her phone is at the bottom of a seabed, useless and alone, like me. And much like the phone, I too would be replaced. I thought about our final moments together. Looking back, the signs were there but I thought I'd be enough. Losing somebody to death is better than losing them to life. That's what she'd been doing. Systematically carving me out of her life one bit at a time until there was no part of me left. My rage was the showstopper. I handed it to her on a silver fucking platter.

Now I am here without her.

Lost without her.

The only time we are together again is in my dreams, lucid dreams, where I still feel her, still hear her.

My stomach grumbles and I wander into the kitchen and remove a knife from the drawer. My hands welcome it, like an old friend. I pull up my sleeve and gaze at my creamy skin. I dig the point of the blade into the fat of my forearm, feel the sharp pointedness. I stab through the flesh like a raw chicken, then molten blood rises to form a crimson bead. It slowly falls down my arm like a teardrop. Solace engulfs me like a cloak, shielding me from the vibrations of heartbreak.

I enjoy the sting of the fresh cut; it's refreshing to feel physical pain instead of grinding emotional turmoil.

I don't know when it is that I pass out. I don't feel myself let go, or my body hit the floor.

Am I dead?

So what if I am?

CHAPTER FORTY-SEVEN

JENNIFER MACK

I root through the kitchen cupboard in search of pain relief to stamp out the tension clustering at the base of my skull. My vision is blurry as waves of nausea wash over me like the sea coming into shore. It's as if all the stress of the past couple of weeks has congealed and fired tiny nodules throughout my back. My phone rings. I expect it to be Jacob. He's the only person who calls me, since he thinks text messages don't form an appropriate conversation. But I pause, hold the phone in my palm and see the caller ID. I have a few moments in which to decide whether to take the call or let it go to voicemail. I admit, he's been so far from my mind and the last time we were together feels like a lifetime ago. So much has happened.

'Hello.'

'Hey... I'm sorry I went all weird on you before, I just...'

'It's fine,' I mumble.

I hear his heavy breath, like he is building up to tell me something. I wait.

'I've been dealing with a few things.' Pete sounds different, the ease and bounce in his voice isn't there and I wonder, with the changes of the last few weeks, *do I sound different too?*

'Is everything okay?' The words get stuck in my throat. He is a good actor; I'll give him that.

'Can you meet? I have something I need to talk to you about.'

'Oh-kaaay... sure. Where and when?'

'Let's meet somewhere private.'

'Pete? What is this about?' I can hear Olivia's voice in my ear and I wonder if he will surprise me and come clean. Unless there is something else. I've had more than enough surprises. I'm not sure I can take anymore.

Unshaven, hair unwashed, the faint smell of alcohol lingers in the thick air. Pete looks incongruous against his perfectly kept home. The last time I'd been here, he'd greeted me with a wide smile and a welcoming warm hug; nothing at all like the preternatural atmosphere I now find myself in.

Pete takes my coat, his gaze drawn away from mine. He offers me a drink. What I loved about Pete was his easy persona, his cheeky carefree happiness. Tonight, that has vanished.

He gets up and opens the fridge, I see a bottle of sparkling rosé. He doesn't move, just stares into it like it's showing a movie inside.

'Pete?'

'Right, yeah sorry.' He reaches for the bottle and places it on the table, he takes a glass from the cupboard and sets it down in front of me.

I unscrew the cap and take the sweating bottle in my hands, enjoy the sound of the glug as it pours into the glass. I close my eyes, sip, savour the taste, let the wine sit in my mouth and enjoy the sensation of the bubbles popping against my cheeks; it offers a calmness I desperately crave. We sit at the kitchen table.

Weeks ago we had shared a meal here, talked freely and without awkward gaps in conversation.

'Where's Max?' I ask, suddenly noticing his absence.

'He's at the vet. Getting snipped.'

'Ugh, poor boy. But isn't that a day operation?'

'Overnight for observation,' he says, deadpan.

'Tell me.' He shuffles forward, elbows on the table, gaze averted. 'The police. Are they any closer to finding the killer?'

'I don't know. Lilith and I are...' I don't know how to form the words. I sigh, place my hands in front of me, and take a deep breath.

'How do police use DNA these days? Are there cameras in public places? Are we being watched all the time? Can the police basically account for every moment of our lives?'

He's rambling, like he's on fast-forward.

'I don't know the ins and outs of it,' I say. The night Hayley died, I have no memory of where I was. What if the police know more? I pause. They would have detained me if they had more, that I am sure of. *I am sure, aren't I?*

'Do you know where the public cameras are? You must have some insight into how this all works, right? You must know.'

'Pete, I don't. Why...'

He sets his hands on the table and I notice the knuckles on his right hand are swollen, red.

'You're scaring me!'

He drifts off again into a tangent. 'Just say, a person was walking through a public path, got attacked... would the police be able to zoom in, see their face?'

I hug my arms round my body. My heart thudding in my ears, I want to leave, but I can't move.

'What is it? *For fuck's sake*, there is *something* wrong, that much is clear. So just man up and spit it out.'

He takes a deep breath, runs his hand to push back the hair on his forehead, sweat oozing from his pores.

'I took Max out for a walk last week. Saw Hayley. I called out to her, she quickly walked away when she saw me, but I went after her. She was acting strange, like she was up to something, so I warned her to, you know, stay away from you.'

Pete loosens the collar of his shirt, pulling it as if it's strangling him.

I'm on my feet, pouring myself another glass of wine and I gulp it in one go, heat rises to my cheeks, the entire room feels hot, I'm aware of every little sound, the hum of the fridge, drip of the tap, Pete's fingers tapping the wood on the kitchen table.

'She said your days were numbered. I didn't know what she meant. So I asked her. Her face was dark, ice-hardened, like when she broke into your flat. Like she had more in store for you.'

'Like what?'

'I don't know, Jennifer. She wanted to hurt you somehow, and it crossed my mind that maybe she was the killer. Max got off the lead, ran into the toilets, and I chased him to put his collar on...'

'Wait!' I hold my hands up. 'What do you mean toilets? Where were you?'

'In St George's Park.'

Suddenly the woven threads are starting to pull together.

'As I was crouched on the floor, trying to put Max's collar on, I felt a blow to my head. Hayley stood over me, rock in hand. I pushed her off me. Max ran off. We struggled. She clawed at me like a fucking lion. I grabbed her by the shoulders, pushed her back into a cubicle.' His Adam's apple seems to shake. 'Her head cracked like an egg on the toilet. She lay still, eyes glazed and then a pool of blood. I killed her. I didn't mean to though. You have to believe me. I *fucking* swear it, I didn't mean to.'

My body numbs.

'Do you know they arrested me for her murder? They think I did it. She had my journal with her. Things written that basically frame me. I even thought it could have been me since I have no memory of that night. I was drunk. Pissed. Paralytically pissed. You need to go to the police.'

'They let you go, didn't they? They clearly don't have the evidence.'

'You need to go to the police!'

'I can't. My sister. My niece.'

'So, hang on... you're asking me to be your scapegoat, to–'

'There isn't any evidence!' His tone is high-pitched, desperate.

'Only my fucking journal saying I want her *dead*.'

'It isn't enough to convict and you know it.' His voice is shaky, uneven.

For a few seconds, I feel like I am in a bad nightmare.

'Max isn't at the vet, is he?' I ask.

'No.' His mouth is drawn into a hard scowl, his eyes glazed with a feral panic. 'He bolted, and I haven't looked for him because I am so scared that somehow it will tie me to that night in the park. I'm surprised the police haven't already knocked on my door since I had the altercation with Hayley at your flat. But we both know it's only a matter of time.'

I shake my head. *How did it come to this?*

'You need to go to the police, Pete. Tell them everything that happened.'

'I can't! My sister is dying. If it wasn't for you...' He stops.

'Go on. Say it,' I mutter. '*Say it!*'

'All I see is her face every time I close my eyes. I am not a murderer.'

'You killed her!'

'I did *not* mean to.' Pete's body crumples like paper.

'By telling me this information, I am now an accessory. I'm *obligated* to tell the police.'

'You can't.' He gets up, moves towards me.

'Please step back. You're scaring me, Pete.'

'Scaring you? You want to end my life, take me away from my family.'

Fear becomes a living force within me, like a beast, ready to swallow me whole. Is this how it ends? I'm immobilised, my own body holding me captive. I take two small steps backward. The pulse beating in my ears blocking out all other sound, his voice, mute.

All I hear is Olivia's whisper replaying in my mind. The truth that Pete knows Hayley, has known her all along. He's lied to me. Tricked me. I want to tell him I know but I can't.

The colour has drained from his face. I can't decide if he fears me, or if this is the last expression Hayley saw before he killed her.

CHAPTER FORTY-EIGHT

THEN

Seventeen days. That's how long it's been since I last saw her. I went to her house several times, knocked, but no answer. Curtains drawn, no signs of life. It has been that way for over a week. I went to the places she spent nights with her friends. They were there, she wasn't – it's as if she's vanished. In those seventeen days, I walked a lot, my shoulders weighed down with a grief that didn't make sense to me. I felt unplugged. One of the things I loved about Grace was how alive she made me feel; I still have her red cardigan which I wrap around my body at night, pretending it is her. Despite the raw hurt pulsating through my body, there were still mundane issues I had to deal with. Money was running low and I knew I needed work. In the November weeks, jobs in Cornwall are almost impossible to find unless you work in an office, but the small café on the beach, 'our beach', is still open and they had a sign on the door that said they were looking for staff. On the particular morning I went to the café, I had more energy than usual, I plastered a smile on my face and opened the door to the café hoping I'd leave with a job. A young woman with an extended baby belly was spritzing the small round tables and wiping them in a rhythmic motion. She was wearing a tight Lycra top with a visible tattoo around her belly button, the overly processed canary-yellow bleach hack-job on her hair cheapened her.

'Hi, I'm here about the job,' I said.

'Ma! Somebody here to see you,' she shouted over her shoulder and carried on cleaning the tables, forgetting about me.

Soon, a rotund woman appeared from the kitchen. She wore a too-tight dress which clung to her body in all the wrong places and her rounded face reminded me of the moon, with a yellowish tinge to her acne-scarred skin.

'Can I help?' she asked, her tone disconnected.

'I'm here about the job posting.' I tried to sound upbeat, but how fervent can you be for a minimum wage job – at least this café came without a boss like Ian.

'Any experience?'

'Yeah, I worked in a café in town for over a year. Serving customers, cleaning up, the usual.'

'And you left because?'

'My boss didn't need me anymore, money troubles, I think.'

'My daughter is due to give birth next month, same time she should have been taking her exams, you know, to better her life.'

The pregnant girl shook her head and muttered something under her breath. Her mother shot her a look loaded with daggers. It clearly wasn't a planned pregnancy.

'It's the off-season, which means it's quiet, but all the same, I can't handle it all by myself, bloody back.' She placed a flat palm on her lower back and followed up with a stretch and a grunt.

'I can handle busy and quiet, I'm available to start whenever you need me to.'

'Trial at 8am sharp tomorrow morning.' She walked behind her daughter and placed her hand on her shoulder. 'Aren't we lucky that...' She nodded her head in my direction.

'Amelie,' I said. Rarely do I give out my real name. It sounded foreign on my lips.

The daughter stood rooted to the spot, her face scrunched up like she was repelled by her mother. I can relate.

'Marie will show you the ropes in the morning, how the espresso machine works, inventory of the deliveries – that sort of thing.'

'Thanks. I'll see you tomorrow.'

I turned to leave when the woman's chalky voice called.

'Need your national insurance number too. We do everything above board here, and bank details.'

My heart stopped. 'I... I don't have a bank account.'

I do, but as soon as money gets paid into the account the social will take away some of my benefits and I can't afford to lose a single penny to those damn bloodsuckers.

'Right, well, just your national insurance number then. If it works out, you'll need to get a bank account. I'm not one for cash in hand, prefer to keep my accountant happy. Anyway... see you tomorrow.'

'What's your name?' I had her down as a Margaret or a Sue.

'Beryl.' But Beryl suited Moon-Face perfectly.

In the distance I hear the waves crashing against the shore. The rain shoots down from the sky like pellets. By the time I turn the corner into Drakes Road I am soaked through to the core and bone cold. The walk up the uneven steps to the café feels treacherous, one slip and my neck could snap – just like that.

The door is locked when I arrive. Through the steamed glass I see Marie with her mobile phone in her hand. I can't hear her, but her eyebrows are knitted together and she has a scowl on her face. Whoever she's on the phone with is getting the brunt of her fury. Not that I thought it was possible, but the rain falls harder. The clatter against the handrail makes me cover my ears. I knock on the door, desperate for shelter, but Marie can't hear me. She moves out of my vision as a wave of panic beats in my chest.

How long do I wait here?

I make a fist and knock hard against the wooden frame, my thoughts beginning to turn angry.

No answer.

I bang harder, the vibrations of the force behind my knock tingle up my arm.

Marie appears and unlocks the door before continuing her heated conversation on the phone. A pool of water gathers by my feet and I'm shivering. I move myself by the radiator pumping out heat that offers me a short amount of solace.

'You're early.' Marie's voice is clipped, like I've inconvenienced her.

Marie has one of those faces. Common. Slutty. Cheap with an attitude to match.

'I thought the buses might run late because of the weather, so I left earlier than I would've normally.'

She sucks her teeth, which makes me want to reach across and slap her hard.

'It's not rocket science. Coffee pot is there, card machine is the most techy thing in this shithole, but Mum won't let you handle the till until you prove you can be trusted anyway, so she can show you that another day. Right now, the dishwasher needs to be unloaded.' We go to the kitchen, which is cleaner than Ian's café was. The smell of bleach is in the air.

She's enjoying this. Having authority over me. I swallow the hard lump forming in my throat and push back the desire to tell her to fuck herself and this job, but I need the money.

'I'm due in a month.' She waits expectantly for me to

respond, but when I don't, she huffs past me and pulls open the dishwasher door with force.

'Empty all of the plates and cutlery. When you're done with that, you can take out the bins.'

She marches out of the kitchen and I couldn't be happier she's gone.

Beryl arrives when I am done placing the last mug on the shelf.

'Where's Marie?'

'I haven't seen her in a while.' I clamber down from the ladder and wipe my hands on a towel.

'She left you here, by yourself?'

I shrug, choosing to stay out of a family argument.

'That girl.' Beryl throws her hands up in the air. 'She's not ready to be a parent. And I told her, I warned her, I am not going to be the one to hold the baby when she wants to start going out again. She has no idea how hard motherhood's going to be.'

Beryl offers me a grave expression as I look up to meet her eye.

'I never want to have children.' This isn't something I've ever said aloud, nor have I ever been involved in a conversation where I would so openly share this information. The thought of another person invading my body, pushing on my organs, leeching off my blood, milk oozing from my breasts. No thank you. I always hear that tripe about the instant love mothers feel when they first set eyes on their newborn. Bollocks. How can you possibly love a shrivelled ball of skin that looks like an old man? Don't get me started on that urgent cry, as if it wasn't enough to have suckled away its mother's strength for thirty-seven weeks. But then it comes into the world, demanding more... more... more. I think about what my mother must have felt when she looked at me for the first time. But in fairness to every baby who enters into this world, they didn't ask to be here, and I can see the life Marie's baby will have before it's even started.

In the kitchen I put coffee beans into the grinder. The only cooking I'll be involved in is toasties.

Beryl watches me. 'You must be around the same age as Marie, maybe a tad older. Tell me. What would your mother do if you came home and told her you were pregnant. Not just pregnant, mind... but that there was a choice between two fathers?'

I turn on the grinder, hoping the noise will drown her out, but she holds her gaze on me.

'I'll never be pregnant.' I open a bag of sugar and pour it into a bowl.

'Yeah, I know you said you didn't want children, but let me tell you how many women have said that before. Suppose it wasn't planned and then...'

'I don't want children and I don't like men. I'm gay.'

'Oh, right. Well then.' Beryl looks to the floor and starts folding tea towels.

'And before you ask, my mother doesn't know I am gay because she's dead. But if she was alive, she'd be too self-absorbed to notice. She let a lot of things go on around her.' I've said too much, I drop the tin of coffee beans which crash to the floor and spill in every direction. I immediately start to tidy them, glad of an excuse to interrupt the menial conversation.

CHAPTER FORTY-NINE

JENNIFER MACK

Dazed by the shock of Pete's confession, I try to imagine the outcomes to so many possibilities. None of which end well. I have walked for hours, the night slowly giving way to morning. The clatter of shop-front shutters being lifted open draws me out of my thoughts as I drift toward the corner shop. A jolly Asian man greets me with a warm smile.

'First customer of the day,' he happily tells me. I follow him closely enough to smell cigarette smoke clinging to his jacket. A tinny sound of a breakfast show blasts out from a small blue radio by the till, its stainless-steel antenna revealing its age. The radio is volumes too high for my tired brain to process, and I'm just about to leave when a delivery van pulls up outside and hulks loaded newspapers. The big boys come out first: *The Guardian, Daily Mail, The Times*, and lastly, the local rags. It takes me a few seconds to process. A pause, a skip of a heartbeat. A storm pulses through my veins; the headline a knife slicing through my brain like cutting through metal.

Suddenly I feel like I'm in a fishbowl and the shop walls keep narrowing. I want to run, but I'm frozen in place. The shopkeeper bends down and snips the papers free from the plastic-braided cord. It's impossible to avoid, despite my tired state. The photo is recent, and unmistakable. *Me.*

He slowly turns his head, his gaze rests on my face, and he soon makes the connection. He rises slowly, with caution, like I'm pointing a loaded gun.

He stands straighter, his manner shifting to primal fear. He takes a step back, as if the smallest bit of distance between us will protect him. I should have known. *I'm a goddamn journalist.* A relentless creature who looks and keeps looking, unturning stones, grabbing anything, talking to anybody all in the name of a *fucking headline.* It was only a matter of time; like a boiling pan of water on the stove, lid left on too long, pressure mounting. I never cared because I'd never been on the other side of the fence. Millions of people rely on the press every day for vital, quality journalism. Once an accusation has been made, made public, the seed of opinion is planted in the readers' minds and it can grow and transform in a variety of ways.

'I should go,' I say, voice trembling. But before I depart, I reach down to the thick stack of copies of *The Gazette.* The weight of the paper feels like a bomb in my hands.

I'm transfixed. Hot and cold flashes wash over me like a wave.

Hayley Woolley murder:
Fellow journalist arrested on suspicion of murder.
Rivalry turned deadly.

Ms Wooley, 30, was last seen a week ago on the way back from drinks with a friend. A local man discovered her body in the men's washroom, located in St George's Park.

The suspect, a woman in her early 30s, is an active journalist for *The Cornwall Chronicle.*

The victim's sister, Carly Woolley, claims the two colleagues have had a competitive rivalry for years. 'It tears my heart out to know such bitter jealousy has turned such an ugly corner, and because of this rivalry my sister is dead.'

CHAPTER FIFTY

THEN

Beryl tells me more about her daughter in the following weeks.

'I remember all the hopes I had for her. This pregnancy makes her a statistic, you know. I suppose I should have seen it coming.'

I look out of the window, Beryl's voice fading into the background. My heart pauses. A girl. The same height and slim build of Grace, with the same butter-blonde hair that sparkles in the early morning sunshine. She's alone, headphones plugged into her ears, her jog a slow, rhythmic bounce. *Could it be?*

She stops, her hands reaching for her knees, her head tilts back, a striking resemblance to Grace, but her features are sharper. *It's not her.*

Where are you?

I miss you so much.

Beryl moves to the window and catches me looking.

'She looks so much like my ex. Thought it was her.' I'm startled that I said it out loud.

Beryl shifts in the way people do when they don't know what to say. If it had been a boy, a man, how would she react?

'That's Grace Matthews. Got her head screwed on, that one. Not like my darling daughter.'

'Grace!' I draw in my breath, unprepared for the emotional tug of hearing the name out loud, spoken by another person. But it isn't her, she isn't here. It's not my Grace!

'You know, it isn't natural.' Beryl hugs her chest, her oversized breasts squashing together – now that looks unnatural, and fucking gross.

Beryl is too close to me, making me flinch. 'We are who we are,' I say.

'But have you ever thought that being with a man might be better in the long run. I know that being gay is sort of the *in* thing these days, but you know... in the long run.'

'Where is your husband?' I ask.

'He died. Lost at sea during the storm back in '04. Marie was just a young 'un. Everything would've been different if my Andy was still here.'

'I've been fucked by a man before.'

'I *beg* your pardon?'

I enjoy the shock on her face, the way her eyes bulge and her double chin creases into a balloon. Then I pause, take a breath.

'He was my mother's boyfriend.'

Her face turns red, the judgement building.

'I was eleven when it started. He came into my room. I remember the hard lump between his trousers, him fondling it like a trophy, like it was something to be proud of. I'd never seen one before, not like his. I remember thinking it looked like it was sitting in a bird's nest. See, I didn't have hair and my mother shaved hers off. Said it was cleaner, more attractive that way. Back then my genitals were for one thing – going to the loo.

'But there he was, standing in my room. He smiled at me, like he was giving me something special. A toy. Something I could keep and hold on to forever, and I have, but nothing about it was special. It started with him kissing me. *"Our secret"* he called it. Because that's what made it more special. My skin hurt, you know, as his beard scratched against it. Rough as sandstone. I didn't move, couldn't move, the inability to find my voice frustrated me, still does. But looking back on it now, I realise I was quiet as a dormouse because I knew my mother wouldn't rescue me. And compared to what he did to me, that was far worse. After a while, the touching started. Palm placed on my vagina, fingers finding their way into my underwear. Then... on the night of my twelfth birthday, he came into my room and stole my virginity.'

Beryl is stone still. Unmoving. Uncomfortable. Her mouth gapes open, baring her crooked yellow teeth.

'*Unnatural* is a grown man raping a child.' I grind my teeth at the memory.

'They should bring back hanging.' Beryl touches my shoulder and quietly walks away.

Left with my thoughts, I realise that Grace Matthews has picked up speed and jogged further down the beach. I can only see the back of her.

Two days in a row, faux Grace takes the same route. I study her movements from the safety of the café. The days pass in a blur, but the sighting of faux Grace gives me a reason to get up in the morning. I am a spectator in my own life, watching from afar. There is a part of me that enjoys it. I've never been able to tell another soul about 'our story'. I want to let go, but can't. I can't take any of it back. Broken and bruised, she gave me happiness only to snatch it away from me. Once again, I have no control. It's invoked that all-too-familiar feeling of being taken advantage of. It's as if I am being haunted by her. Unable to forget. It's the cruel trick that is my life. How am I expected to move on? I have no choice; I need to find a sure way to remove the memory. But I don't know where she is. She's gone.

It's just after lunchtime, and very few customers have come in today. The sharp turn in the weather means visitors to the beach are few and far between. I am free to take my break. I pour hot steaming tea into a flask and take it to the beach. My eyes are transfixed on the white caps on the sea's surface; there's a light spray of rain, enough to soak the top of my head, but I don't care. As I am about to get up and return to the café, she comes into view. This isn't her usual time of day to run on the beach, and my stomach knots being this close to her. It isn't Grace, but she is so like her, and this is what we are now. Strangers. She briskly walks past me, looks past me. It is irrational to think the universe is throwing this my way as some sort of sign. Not that I would ever believe such bullshit, but it feels like this is happening for a reason.

The sand becomes alive with venomous snakes rearing their heads and hissing, synchronising with the crashing waves against the rocks. In the middle of the serpents, she stands with her hands outstretched, head down. I go to her only when she lifts her head. It isn't her, it's faux Grace. She laughs an evil laugh, a deep cackle with an intention to mock and taunt. I bolt upright, sweat pouring from my skin. I pant, reach for the water next to my bed, and cast my eye on the bedside clock: 2.20am.

It's late, but I figure it's my chance to see if Grace, my Grace, has returned home. I dress in dark clothing and call a cab from my phone. In the dead of the night, the journey to her house is quick and easy. I stalk the road, quiet and still, most lights switched off except those of the gated driveways and the tiny blinking lights of security cameras. I stand at the end of her driveway, the driveway I've walked up and down a hundred times and I feel so removed from the past I spent with her – it's as if the house itself is warning me away, repelled by my presence. The car's gone, much the same as the last time. I look around, then hear a door opening. A familiar looking man stands in the doorway, a scowl plastered on his face. I know him.

'What do you want?' His voice is pinched, drenched in privilege. He looks at me like I'm a rat raiding his pantry. 'I know who you are. The obsessed friend. Grace isn't here. You would do us both a favour if you could just pootle along now and kindly fuck off before I call the police.'

He looks older in person than he does in the pictures in the house. Fatter too.

'I know who you are too. The unfaithful husband, the man Grace wishes dead because of what you've done to your family. I was the one, you know, the one who was there for her, wiped her tears.'

He shakes his head and the security lights turn on as he steps forward.

Grace never told me she wanted her father to die, but I say it for effect.

CHAPTER FIFTY-ONE

THEN

I hover in the kitchen chopping vegetables, living a meaningless existence. Marie is a constant irritation, always looking for sympathy, and with Beryl, my ears ring at her constant complaining. I've reached the point where everything is imploding within me. At this moment, I cannot imagine that everything will ever be 'all right'.

It is a Tuesday afternoon, and Beryl has trusted me to run the café. She acted like it was a fucking privilege and I should bow down to her fat feet. It is Marie's last midwife appointment. Nearing her due date, she is putting her birth plan in place, details which bored the shit out of me, but I couldn't help but think of that poor unfortunate soul who will have that pathetic Marie as a mother. I once read a newspaper article about culling deer to control the population. It said it was necessary in order to maintain the number of deer and prevent overgrazing, which would result in starvation. An interesting concept, one that humans would be good to adapt. There needs to be order in humanity; children born to incapable parents, doomed to a life of neglect and poverty could be prevented if we looked at things in the same order of conservation. When the gruesome twosome finally left after much bickering, I made myself a sandwich and a cup of tea, and I am sitting in my spot overlooking the beach. Here, I am able to be a spectator. I watch a little girl run through the sand, and when the wind blows, her hair rises round her head like a golden halo. It contradicts my earlier thoughts of children; I guess some are wanted and loved. It is just after noon, and as soon as I see faux Grace my heartbeat quickens with renewed strength. I close my eyes and for a moment I pretend it is her, my Grace, coming back to me. I marvel at the pace in which she runs, today her usual slower pace was transformed into an elegant movement, just the way *my Grace* moved. A wild thought crosses my mind. If I can't reach my Grace, I'd have a stand-in. A rush of euphoria ignites my insides, as if a match had struck and a flame burned bright. I was in luck. Faux Grace stops and takes a sip from her water bottle. I open a tab of reason in my mind – how could I start a conversation with her? What would it be about? I am too fixated on these little details to get myself out onto the beach and grab my opportunity when she starts to continue her run. On the table, Marie has left behind a silver chain with an anchor pendant. Usually, she never takes it off, but as fate would have it, she did today. I scoop it up and dash down the uneven steps leading to the beach. She is a little way ahead now, so I have to pick up pace.

'Hey!' I call out.

She doesn't hear me.

I shout louder. 'Heeeeeeey!' And jog toward her.

She stops and turns to look at me with a confused look on her face.

I stand waiting for her to meet me halfway, breathless.

'You... you dropped this,' I say and dangle the silver chain on my fingers. I was right, she looks like Grace, but up close, in the harsh light of day, the stark differences between them are obvious, but it is undeniable, the two could pass for sisters, cousins at a push.

'It's not mine.' She is unapologetically blunt.

'But I saw you drop it.' I'm grasping at straws trying to find a way to keep her with me longer.

'Nope. Not mine. Sorry.' She turns on her heel and continues with her run. Meanwhile I stand there like a goddamn idiot.

I've worked out that faux Grace takes her run along this route of the beach between 1 and 2pm and that it is never to the minute. Beryl had given me her full name 'Grace Matthews' and after a quick search on Instagram I found her. Her profile open, she isn't hiding, she *wants* people to see and like her pictures. She isn't quite the aloof girl on the beach, after all. The girl in those small square boxes lives in a privileged social bubble. Here's what I learned: she wears pink a lot, it's her signature colour. Her boyfriend is called Harry, best friend Bobo. She likes to surf, there are hundreds of photos of her in Newquay in various shades of pink wetsuits, she holds a surfboard with pride like it's her wings to the sea. She's fresh-faced, wears little make-up, she also has a thing for baby rhinos (weird). She has a big following, but her circle is small and compact, she loves her mum a lot and uses the hashtag #mymumisbetterthanyours in a cringeworthy finger-down-throat kind of way. Then there's her cat Scarlett, with excessive white fur, blue eyes, and a scrunched face that looks like it has been hit with a frying pan. I give myself a good faux Grace education before I put my plan in place. Marie has a bike in the storage cupboard which hasn't been used in forever, so I ask Beryl if I could borrow it for a while to save me taking the bus.

My plan is to wait for faux Grace and I'll take to the pavement and follow her. I'll admit, having a new purpose is exciting. By the end of the second week, I've worked out her movements, and it shouldn't have come as any surprise this was another rich girl who lived in a house bigger than my Grace. The property is set back behind cast-iron gates, three gleaming cars sit in the curved driveway: a Range Rover, Jaguar, and Bentley, more value in those cars than any money that's ever passed through my hands.

I wait on the corner of the street for faux Grace to leave the house. She is later than usual today, which irritates me. When she is finally in my sight, I cycle up to her as fast as my feet will allow me to pedal.

'Grace?' She turns to me.

'Yeah?' she replies.

'You don't know me, but it's about Harry and us girls. We gotta stick together, right?'

'Who are you exactly?'

CHAPTER FIFTY-TWO

JENNIFER MACK

The police station doors make a loud bang as I shut them behind me, a testament of the decision I made. Outside, the dark, cold sting of the air hits me in the face; a sobering moment despite not having had a drop of alcohol in hours. The headlights of the oncoming cars blind my vision. I've walked up and down this street hundreds of times, it's a place I call home. But now everything feels distorted and unfamiliar. The heavy clouds give way to another downpour, and by the time I reach the top of my road, I'm soaked to the bone, drips of rain running beneath my jacket. My heart sinks as I approach my front door. Pete.

He's huddled up on the doorstep, his eyes bloodshot and swollen.

'What are you doing here?'

'My sister has a week to live. Two at best... I came here to beg you not to say anything to the police. My niece is falling apart having to see her mother slowly decline. It's the worst fucking thing in the world. Her dad isn't capable. I'm all she's...'

My head is to the floor, I cannot meet his gaze, can't let him see the truth.

'I've been here for hours. Tried to call you but your phone's been off. Where've you been, Jen?' It's the first time he's called me Jen.

'Pete, you know that by telling me what you did that–'

He rises to his feet, hands grabbing my shoulders with such grip that I wince as he shakes me. The physical force of him overpowering me. He pushes me to the ground, his crushing weight pinning me down.

'Get off!' I shout.

'You've already fucking gone to them, haven't you? That's where you've fucking been all this time!'

His hand reaches over my mouth. His breath smells putrid, his breathing ragged. The sweetness of his kind face I've known for these past few weeks has completely dissolved. I kick as hard as I can, but the strength of him is too much.

Suddenly, I imagine Hayley and what must have been the face she saw before she took her last breath. Thoughts flow through my mind at rapid speed.

'You're going to get up quietly and open the door. If you don't do exactly as I say, I will fucking kill you. Do you understand?' Heat radiates from his body, his voice low and clear. It is a voice of authority. He means what he says.

'Please... Pete... let's talk about this,' I plead.

His expression is vacant, unreachable, like he's possessed. It's impossible to reach the Pete I cared about, if he ever was that person.

He gently removes himself from my body, and I rise unsteadily to my feet, my hands trembling as I reach into my pocket for my key.

I hear footsteps behind me. Pete's arms grip my waist.

My neighbour, the nurse.

'Everything okay here? I just got back from my shift and heard shouting.'

'She's had a bit too much to drink and is feeling a bit, uh, over-emotional right now,' Pete explains.

I look to my neighbour, hoping she'll see the fear set within my face, see that I need her help.

'Well, so long as everything is okay, I guess.'

Pete pinches the top of my leg.

'Yeaaaah, fine.' My words come out slurred, and it's believable, but nothing's ever been further from 'fine'.

CHAPTER FIFTY-THREE

THEN

Trust is a delicate thing. It takes years to build but only seconds to shatter. It takes one simple comment to cast a shadow of doubt even to the most seemingly social-media perfect couple. The trouble with society, and social media, is that everything we show the world must look like a movie, but it's no fucking secret that life isn't perfect and if you look close enough, you'll see the cracks. It wasn't hard to get her to come to the café when I told her the evidence was on my laptop. She eagerly followed. *It was that fucking easy.*

Marie is officially on maternity leave and Beryl is out buying supplies, it is perfect.

'I guess you've had your suspicions about Harry for a while, huh?' I ask, hovering behind the counter to make us a cuppa. I give her the hot-pink mug, a perfect fit for her pink obsession. When she's not looking, I reach into my pocket and drop the powder in, leftovers from precious Imogen. I take a teaspoon and stir it until the white powder dissolves and there is nothing left but the colour of beige tea.

'So, can you please show me the photos you have?' she asks.

I place the hot-pink mug of tea in front of her, the steam rising. She blows the top of it as I wait for her to lift it to her lips.

'Are you sure you want to see them? They're quite upsetting. Same thing happened to me; my ex cheated on me.' My mind flashes to that night when *she* was with Abercrombie and Fitch but I'll never know what really happened. What I do know, however, is that's when she started slipping away.

'I want to see them,' she says with conviction.

Her long, slender fingers wrap round the hot-pink mug, hands like my Grace. I wonder if they feel as soft as hers. I can still feel Grace's hands in mine. On the nights when it was just the two of us in our own world, happy times. The memory stings. It's a grief I cannot move past because she's out there somewhere, living on without me.

Was I nothing to you?

'I'll just go get the laptop,' I say.

Just as I go behind the counter, she lifts the mug to her lips and takes a sip.

I'm back in the game.

CHAPTER FIFTY-FOUR

JENNIFER MACK

He opens my fridge like he's in his own home.

'I'll never understand the competition between you and Hayley. You were both as bad as the other.'

'How so?'

'You complained about her... she complained about you. You both had a fantastic opportunity to work together on the Grace murders, but you got the scent of success and you wanted it all for yourselves.'

'I don't understand.'

'You know, for a journalist, you really aren't all that good at putting the pieces together.' He takes out a bottle of wine from the fridge and pours a glass for himself. 'Want one?'

For the first time I really don't. I need to be as clear-headed as possible.

He puts his hands together and rubs them. 'This will blow that tiny mind of yours.'

'You don't really have a dying sister, do you?'

'You got me!' A sinister smile spreads across his face.

'Hayley and I. We went way back. Met in London, she had

a bit of a thing for me back in the day... and you know, I gave her what she wanted every now and then.'

I feel sick.

Stupid.

'I found out you knew her. Don't think you had this watertight, because you didn't.' I bang my palm against the wall for good measure. Then, I pause for a moment and look straight at Pete. 'The Grace murders? Were you involved with another person?'

He throws his hands up quickly and says, 'Can't take credit for that one. Nothing to do with me, or Hayley so far as I know. There really is a crazy lunatic out there.'

'But you did kill Hayley?'

'It was a complete accident. Everything happened like I said it did. She came after me in the toilets, but she was incensed about the time we'd spent together. Thought I actually had feelings for you. I wasn't supposed to sleep with you, but come on, it had to be realistic.'

'What the fuck was your game? Both of you?'

'Well, in London, work had dried up, could barely afford my rent. Hayley got in touch, offered me a place to stay, but you know Hayley, everything comes at a price.'

'Me?'

'Hey, well done! You're finally starting to get it.'

'What was the point of it all?' My head is whirling.

'The point being, she wanted to take the story, this would be the making of her career, she had BIG plans, but your bosses entrusted you. So, my role was to come in and steer you away from work, make you fall in love with me. The point is to give information back to her.'

'You're fucking crazy.

Why did you kill her?'

'An accident. She did fall against the toilet and she did crack her head open. It wasn't intentional, but you understand now I've got a big fucking problem on my hands.'

'Why did you even tell me you killed her? You could have just–'

'I didn't know you would go to the police. I thought you were too weak, that you'd protect me. I panicked. I had to come up with something.'

'The hand... oh my God. Did you send me Hayley's hand?'

He runs his hand through his hair and sighs. 'Wasn't planned, but I thought it would throw the police off the scent, make them believe it was the killer. Pretty clever if you ask me.'

My blood feels frozen. 'So, you happened to be carrying a knife, but you accidentally killed her, have I got that right?'

'You want to hear the truth about something? Hayley was smarter than you, she fooled you, when it comes to the race, she's the one in first place. But it is what it is.'

'Please... just let me go. I will tell the police I was drunk, that you didn't confess to me... I–'

'Too late.'

'But it doesn't have to be.' I get up and move toward him.

'Sit back down.' His voice has changed. Deeper. Darker.

His gaze travels down my body, stopping right at my breasts. I want to scream, but my voice is lost.

He puts his hand on my shoulder and lets his fingers trail up and down my arm, somewhere from the back of my throat is a piercing cry.

God... please no.

My whole body is overcome by a thunderous tremble.

I spin around and grab the first thing I see, a table lamp and throw it at his head. It has no impact but it's enough to put distance between us for me to get to the door. I pull the handle, but he's already behind me, the full weight of his body pinning me. He grabs a fistful of my hair and pulls my head back, my neck feels like it's about to snap.

'Let me go.' Hot tears run down my face, my vision is blurred, it's like I am watching this happen to somebody else. I can't believe this is happening to me.

He puts his hand over my mouth and with full force I bite into it until a metallic taste hits my tongue. He falls back, which gives me time to open the door. I manage to get out and yell for help, but my voice drifts off into silence. Where are my neighbours? I need somebody to hear me. He grabs me by the ankles and I fall flat on my face, my head knocking onto the concrete.

Then everything goes black.

I can't move. Everything hurts. Where am I?

The familiar swirly pattern is the first thing I see, and it tells me I am in my bedroom.

My arms are spread out and tied with silk scarves to the bedposts.

'See what you did to my hand.' He holds it up, a flash of red stains the white paper towel.

'What now?' I say.

'I don't know,' he replies.

A horrible thought creeps into my mind. Nobody will come to look for me.

He leaves the room. I don't know what he's planning but I begin to tug at the scarves to loosen the grip but it's no good, the knots only get tighter the more I try to free myself.

I drift in and out of consciousness. I hear a knocking sound. I dismiss it. Until Pete is at my side whispering into my ear.

'Expecting anyone?'

'No,' I say.

Another knock. Only harder.

He disappears out of the room for a few moments and then rushes back.

'I'm going to untie you but if you try anything, I'll fucking kill you.' He's holding one of my kitchen knives in his hand.

'The fucking police are outside. Fuuuuck.' He paces back and forth, body jittery, like a boxer about to go into the ring. He pulls me into the living room and pushes me onto the sofa, he gets a bottle of wine out of the fridge.

'Fucking down it. Then lay the bottle on top of you,' he demands.

'Jennifer, can you open up? It's Loretta.'

'Don't say a fucking word.'

'She knows I'm home, she saw us,' I hiss. A wave of nausea hits me hard and fast, the combination of the head injury and the wine he's made me drink. I scream, and I keep screaming.

The door bursts open and four uniformed policemen burst through.

Pete goes to run, but they pin him to the ground, forcing his hands behind his back so he cannot move.

Loretta rushes to me, places her arms around my shoulders, and pulls me in close.

'I saw everything. I saw him hurt you.' My body falls limply onto hers, I cry out of fear, relief, hurt, and everything in between.

CHAPTER FIFTY-FIVE

JENNIFER MACK

Four weeks later

My head is crystal clear. I haven't touched a drop of booze since the police arrested Pete. I see how easily my life could have been taken from me. I looked for the truth and found I hadn't been living a life at all. The dangerous game Hayley and I had played had cost her her life. Luckily, I had Lilith, who has been a pillar of strength for me during these weeks.

'We all get things wrong,' she said. But she never apologised for arresting me for Hayley's murder. However, now there is an invisible respect that flows between us.

I'm back in the office, the newsroom, in the hub of the action. Olivia told me she'd seen Hayley and Pete together; she knew they were planning to ruin my life and that's why she'd offered to give me an alibi. Of all the people I thought I knew I could trust; I've since found friendship in the most unlikely of places. Now my focus is on the Grace murders. There haven't been any more victims, but that offers little comfort to the victims' families. It's my job to navigate this to justice, to bring some closure and hopefully stop the killer striking again.

It was late on a Thursday when a typed letter arrived on my desk addressed to me.

I didn't think much of it at first. Until I opened it and realised who it was from.

```
Print me!
    You don't know my name, but you know
who I am.
    You give me all sorts of labels:
psychopath, evil, sociopath, murderer,
serial killer. I like the last one best,
it kind of gives me an edge, don't you
think?
    But I am who you seek. The Grace
Murderer. You must know by now that
there are those who are born this way,
and those who become this way. I was
born to the devil. A mother who allowed
her boyfriend to touch my eleven-year-
old body in a way that no child should
ever be touched. Evil lived in my home.
I can't help who I am, what I do. I need
it the way a writer needs to write, a
painter needs to paint. I have the
wisdom to hide who I am, because I enjoy
shocking society, but as much as you
call me 'the Devil' I also play God, I
get to decide who lives and who dies,
and if you piss me off, you die. There
is no power greater than being the hands
```

that drain life away. Control, that's what it is. I was foolish once, I tried to play normal, be part of something called 'love' until she left. With no way to trace her. So, what did I do once my control was taken? I went to the next best thing. I went to the women who mirror her. I loved Grace. But Grace broke me. This bloodshed is because of her, she has blood on her hands, she's the reason for the pain and suffering caused. But she has given me something I rather enjoy, my new little hobby, getting away with murder. 😉

A chill runs down my spine. I hold the piece of paper in my hand and stare at the words of a killer. I drop the paper down on my desk, knowing I shouldn't handle it too much. I'll be calling Lilith and handing this in as evidence. Jacob's door is closed, I see him through the glass, on the phone, and cross the office as fast as I can. He waves me away, but I take the phone out of his hand and end the call.

'What the–'

'The killer! They sent another letter.'

'Fuck.'

Jacob gets up from his chair and follows me to my desk. I pick up the letter, hold it at the edges and Jacob reads it.

'Reminds me of the Jack the Ripper letters.'

'That was a long time ago,' I say, a little irritated that Jacob is comparing this to something from over a century ago.

'Bloody sinister.'

'Jacob, we've got work to do. I'm gonna call Lilith and get this to print.'

I go back to my desk and call her. There's a nagging feeling in the pit of my stomach that the killer is much closer than we all think.

The clock is ticking.

CHAPTER FIFTY-SIX

THEN

Faux Grace's head rests on her hands. She's out cold. I lug her body into the store cupboard. She's light, so it isn't hard to move her. I lay her body on the floor, surrounded by tins of baked beans and tomato soup. Beryl advertises her winter warming soup as home-made; *we all have our secrets*. I let my fingers map her face. I used to do this with my Grace when I told her I knew her features better than I knew my own. Sometimes, at night when I'm alone in bed, I close my eyes and imagine her next to me. I use my own hand to touch the top of my thigh like she used to do and pretend it's her. Sometimes I whisper into the dark, tell her I love her. Sometimes I scream into the pillow, asking her why she hurt me? How could she leave me alone like this? Physically gone but not forgotten. I tried everything I could think of to find her, but she left, not a trace of her to be found. None of her friends know where she is, or so they claim. And when I told them I was her girlfriend they looked at me, stunned, and said, 'Grace wasn't gay, much less in a relationship.'

The phone rings. Faux Grace doesn't stir. I quickly answer it.

Beryl is out of breath, her words tumbling out in broken sentences.

'Marie is in labour. There's complications. Lock up the café. We'll close for now.'

I cannot believe my luck!

I wish Beryl luck and almost skip back to the store cupboard. When I go to open the door there's a weight behind it. It won't budge.

I hear a snuffle. Fuck! She's awake.

This shouldn't happen. I used half the dose I used on Imogen; a full one was enough to kill her, half should absolutely be enough to knock her out for a spell.

'Open the door,' I gently say. 'You passed out when you saw the photos of Harry.'

I try to push the door open, but she tries to push her weight against it, but can't, she's too weak, too fucking weak.

The reality of it all is I am being pushed away, again.

I cannot let this happen.

I will not let this happen.

It takes all my strength, but I make it through the door. She falls backwards, the tins of canned soup falling from the shelves on top of her. I throw my body onto her, my hands reaching for her neck. I finally take hold and I squeeze so hard that she's gasping for air. She kicks hard, writhes. The fight turns down a notch, her body no longer resists, but I don't let go until I see the life drain from her face.

As night draws in, I have a decision to make. Take her apart or let her go in one piece?

I don't think I want to carve up her body; she's too pretty to ruin, too much like my Grace. But I do have to get rid of her. I sit with the body for a couple of hours and talk to her, like I am talking to Grace, my Grace. I tell her how much I miss her, the life we could have had, the reason why she's dead, which is, to put it bluntly, completely her fault. If she hadn't left, this would have never happened. She drove me to it.

I go to the kitchen, take an apple from the fruit bowl, and peel its skin with a sharp knife. I return, look down at her body. I go back to her, play with her earrings, swirls of blue shades, too big for her narrow face. The blue matches her eyes, I can see why she picked them. I gently remove them and decide to keep them as a souvenir. I lean down and kiss her on the forehead, as I do, the glint of the knife catches my eye.

'What can I do to make you really mine?' I ask her.

I try to imagine what my Grace would say. I try hard to hear her velvet voice.

It's nice, being here like this, just the two of us, the fear of her running away eradicated by my own actions, control. There is nothing better. Nothing could be sweeter except having my Grace with me, but I've come to realise sometimes we have to take second best.

I lay next to her. Just like I used to do with my Grace.

I allow my body to merge into hers. Like we are one.

I kiss her again, this time on her ice-cold lips, a strange sensation, like kissing a statue, but I let my mouth linger there anyway. Watching her feels intimate, the quiet knowing that I am the only person who was with her during the last hours of her life and the last hours after her death.

'Have you thought about it?' I whisper. 'Come on, tell me. What can I do to make you mine?'

Tattoo me. Make me yours.

'That's what you want!'

I flip the body over, lift up her pink jumper and expose her back, I take the knife with its remnant of apple peel and wipe it gently against her jeans, then above her bra strap I gently push the blade of the knife into her skin.

GRACE NUMBER 1

CHAPTER FIFTY-SEVEN

JENNIFER MACK

I awake to darkness filling my bedroom. Pitch black, not a flicker of light. Fear sets in, every shadow, every sound shifts my mind into overdrive. This cruel trick of the mind has been present since I started working on the Grace murders and it set in fully when Hayley broke in. Since Pete and thoughts of what could have happened if it wasn't for Loretta's interference, I often wonder what would have happened if she hadn't been there. I tap my phone to check the time: 02:46. I close my eyes, but sleep does not return. The violation of all these encounters has not left me. I've made the decision to sell, I've installed one of those doorbell cameras, which is both a blessing and a curse because it alerts me to every passer-by, but without it I am too exposed, too vulnerable. The killer's letter will go to print tomorrow and I am (somewhat) prepared for the backlash I will receive from the victims' families, from the public. I've given the killer a voice and some might view that as twisting the knife – there are some who will doubt the authenticity of the letter, but the criminal team think it is the killer. In the past couple of weeks, I have picked up my interest in serial killers again, the hows, the whats, and the whys of it all. I imagine what it would be like to sit opposite a killer, to hear how they view the world. I've not admitted this to anybody, but on some level, I get it. I'm not suggesting for one moment I could bring myself to carry out the act itself, but when I think about Hayley I have come to a bitter truth. I'm not sad she's dead, I'm not sad she was murdered. But I am sad for me, for the underhanded tactics she used to triumph over me, for the way she and Pete conspired against me, how my life could have been spent in prison. It blew up in their faces. Do I feel bad one of them is six feet under and the other will be behind bars? No. But I'll never tell anybody that. Not many of us are guilty of the act of murder, but how many of us are guilty of thinking it?

I am guilty.

As the sun came up, I awoke from a restless sleep and a pain in my cheek from where I'd grinded my teeth and bitten the inside of my mouth. The paper is published, online and in print. I ditch my morning run and head straight to the office. I feel like I'm preparing for battle. There are a few other reporters in when I arrive, and they nod their heads in my direction, bleary-eyed and fuelling up on caffeine and toast. The red voicemail light flickers on my desk. Usually I check voicemails last, but today is a day I should probably check them first. There's a couple of uni students asking for work experience, and since *The Chronicle* played a huge part in the Grace murders, everyone wants a piece of the action. I hear a muffled voicemail, like a hand is over the receiver and I strain to hear the message. I turn the volume up to try and gauge a better sound. It's probably a *nothing* message, but I have a feeling it is *something*.

Logic is part of the game in journalism, but so is a gut feeling.

I've had similar moments to this in the past. When my grandmother (my mum's mum) was about to die when I was ten, the night before she did, somewhere deep in my core I knew I'd be part of something huge – and then I was living it. This is the feeling I have now.

I hear intermittent words like 'I know', 'identity', 'killer'. It is enough to set my brain on fire. I stand up and keep hitting replay over and over, like pieces of a puzzle. There's no number attached to the call. I scribble the words down trying to make a clean sentence out of them, and when I finally do my nerves become barbed wire.

'You're in early.' Jacob's voice.

'We've got a new lead,' I say, pointing to the phone and then to my frantic illegible scroll.

'What do you mean?'

'I mean, Jacob, that somebody knows who the killer is.'

Jacob rolls his eyes. 'Jennifer, you're going to get a hundred crackpots calling you with crazy allegations. This is just how it's going to be for a while.'

'Maybe...' I pause, quiet my raised voice and whisper, 'but what if it's not? And Jacob, the killer isn't a man, it's a woman.'

CHAPTER FIFTY-EIGHT

THEN

Her body floats, unseeing eyes upright to the moonlight casting a diluted glow on to the ocean. I support the weight of her with my arms under her back, recreating a memory of when I was with my Grace. I think of the last time I saw her face. In a way, this feels like her funeral. I'm saying goodbye on my terms. I've been lost without her, thinking about her all the time. Isn't love overrated anyway? This is so much better. The chill of the water bites through my skin, my body covered with goose pimples, but I feel so alive, so alive that I want to do it all over again.

'We're back at the beach. This is where it all started. But this isn't where it ends.'

Her skin is ashen. Body drained of life. Lividity set in.

Her hair is white as snow.

She looks like an angel.

Even though she's been dead for several hours, here I am, still talking to her. I wish I could stay here all night, but it's too cold. I don't think I'd survive it.

Slowly, I pull my hands away from her body, letting the water engulf her.

A baptism. Not for her. For me.

When her body is surrendered to the ocean, I wade back to the shore. I take a moment to look back, imagining the sea has now swallowed her.

Back home, I make myself a hot cup of tea and use the rest of the water to prepare a hot water bottle. I wash my face, stare into the bathroom mirror, and grin. What an incredible achievement, the overwhelming feeling of power pulses through my veins. I pull my shoulders back, stand taller.

The briny scent from the ocean still clings to my skin, underneath my nails are dry remnants of her blood. The knife was surrendered along with her body. Next time, I'll use a different knife.

The next morning, I wake to the sound of a joyful tune from my mobile.

It's Beryl. It's also my day off, but then I suddenly fear I've left something behind in the café. I take the call.

'Sorry to call you on your day off. But something awful has happened.'

Now I must pretend to show concern.

'Oh no, what's happened?'

'They pulled a body from the water. They think it's Grace Matthews. I can't process it all. That beautiful girl. Her whole life ahead of her, I feel sick to my stomach.'

'Oh...' Pause. 'That's awful. Did she drown?'

'They think she was murdered. Rumour has it the sicko carved up her back. Wrote words, even. What kind of sociopath could do such a thing?'

I take the phone away from my ear and try not to laugh. It's funny hearing Beryl so hysterical. I can imagine her pacing up and down the beach desperate to discover every last detail.

'I told the police you were here last night cleaning up. They want to talk to you, want to know if you saw anything.'

'I went in the afternoon. Only saw a mother and child, maybe a dog. That's it.'

'But they may want to know if those people saw something, best you come down.'

'I can't.' A knot forms in my stomach.

'Why not?'

'I'm sick.' If she only knew how sick I was, but that's not something I'm ready for her to learn just yet.

London was unfamiliar territory. A while after I'd killed Grace number one, faux Grace, the media blew up. My mark had left quite an impression. I worked long hours at the café and squirreled away cash so that when the time was right, I could take the train to London. I told Beryl my aunt had died (I'm not lying if I never said *when*, am I? Poor Aunt Lizzy!). I had never left Cornwall before. There was something so enticing about travelling to a new city, a new discovery. I stayed in a Travelodge for a couple of days, went to gay bars in the evenings, where finding lesbians was like taking your pick in a toy shop. Instagram is pretty much a killer's catalogue. Filter a name and place and *poof!* Like magic a whole dreamy collection appears. I knew where she was going to be because so many people spill their entire lives out on social media, I even knew what she had for breakfast that day. You would think people would be more careful, because there are people like me, watching, waiting and really if you are going to lay yourself out like a piece of meat, expect the wolf to devour you. The Village is where I found her. I wore a short blonde wig and long patent, heeled boots. I absolutely looked like a prostitute but playing another character was fun. It added to the excitement. Surrounded by a group of friends, 'Grace Number 2' and her pals were like a pack of wolves on the prowl. It reminded me of the early days when Imogen was still around. I watched her throw her hands in the air and dance; finally, her pack dispersed, and she was left alone at the bar. I took this as my chance. I bought her whisky and tequila, told her my name was Emma and I'd just come out of a shitty relationship with still-in-the-closet Becky, who cheated on me with a man to prove to herself she wasn't gay. She bought the story, took pity on me, and we left together. She was vastly different to Grace Number 1. Far grittier and I didn't have to persuade her. If anything, she was all over me. I found the forwardness off-putting. We kissed in an alleyway behind a kebab shop; the smell of chicken fat and doner escaped from the vents and the overflowing dustbins permeating rot and decay made the perfect setting for her desperation to please me. We moved to a couple of other bars. She downloaded her shitty life as if I gave two fucks, but I was good at pretending. Fused with alcohol and maybe a line or two of coke, we found an old, abandoned video shop to get more handsy in. She complained of feeling sick, hey presto, I took the opportunity to give her one of my 'here's one I made earlier' bottles of water with a magic pill and waited for her to slip into unconsciousness. The ceremony was just that: an act.

'London has been fun, hasn't it, my love? Such a shame these old video shops are abandoned. I can relate. Once they were the place to be, until something better came along.' She couldn't hear me.

The song 'Video Killed the Radio Star' popped into my head and I began to sing it.

After a short conversation, I took my hands to her neck and

it was enjoyable, like switching her off.

When I pulled her top up to tattoo her, I saw marks on her arms that showed she was already a cutter.

Seems I did her a favour.

Just as I'd finished carving 'number 2' into her back I heard footsteps. A rustle. I paused. A person? Rat?

I hid behind a video rack, a homeless man making his bed for the night. It was too dark to see another exit without passing him. I had to risk it, slowly, slowly. I crawled on my hands and knees; the crunch of plastic alerted him. Fight or flight. I pushed one of the heavy video racks to the floor and bolted.

LSD was my drug of choice to take to Earth Rabbit. Newquay is known to be a hotspot for partygoers and people who are just out for a good time. Her Instagram handle was Gracie Elizabeth, and she had her own online fashion boutique. It was easy to gain her trust from a few social media exchanges. I have learned that most people fall for flattery, because in our own way we are all looking for acceptance. I never purchased any of the clothes from Gracie Elizabeth. I am not stupid enough to leave a trail – but I did comment how they were exactly the kind of thing my boss would love to feature in her new reality show. I told her my boss was a well-known celebrity, but of course I couldn't say who, not until we met in person. It really was that easy for her to fall into my lap, like sprinkling a bucket of blood and guts into shark infested waters. They will come. Just like they always do. It turns out that Gracie wasn't nearly as pretty in real life as she was in her little square boxes – I almost felt like I was the one who'd been lured under false pretences. The word 'catfish' sprang to mind when I laid my eyes on her for the first time. I have to admit, my hope of getting that hit of pleasure during and after the kill evaporated quickly leaving an empty chasm in my chest. She was dull and blunted and the world really wouldn't miss her.

While eating dinner at the café, Beryl mentions the latest happenings with the murders. She places *The Cornwall Chronicle* in front of me.

'All those poor girls. Grace Matthews. Oh, I can't imagine what their families are going through right now. It's a right sin is what it is.' Her chin is shiny with bacon grease. 'One of them is alive, but she'll never be the same again. Can you imagine going through that ordeal, reliving that moment over and over? Poor girl. I hope she gets the help she needs.'

She wasn't supposed to be alive.

There's an old box TV in the corner of the café which sits on a food trolley meant to serve dessert. Beryl turns it on, it's slow and takes ages for the picture to come into focus. A thick sheet of dust is settled on the top, she uses her fat index finger to remove it and wipes it on her gingham apron. The news is on. Jennifer Mack is in the background; hungry, alert. I like her, she's got tenacity, fire in her belly. She isn't exactly what I'd call pretty; her face is reddened, on-screen she looks older, but it might just be the lighting from the camera. She looks more like an art student than a journalist, reporter, whatever it is they call themselves.

The Redbricks look different in real life to how they look on TV. The quiet area is now brimming with activity, crawling with police, press; all this because of me.

She survived.

Beryl flicks the channel to another news station, repeating the same thing.

It makes me a little sick to know the ritual had to be abandoned. This is a mark of failure, my failure, but I tell myself even the most prolific killers have made mistakes along the way. I wish I had known how much she'd fight back; I would have given the bitch an extra pill.

CHAPTER FIFTY-NINE

JENNIFER MACK

L ilith switches off the tape machine.

'Let's end it there.' Beryl nods, tears filling her eyes. She chews on her fingernails, to the point there is barely any nail left to bite. She's told them everything she knows. Another police officer comes in and tells us they've located the address of Amelie Jones, and that of her former lover Alice Watson, formerly known as Grace Anders.

'My grandson and my daughter live with me. I'm worried about what she'll do, if she'll come after us.'

'Would you like us to find you somewhere else to stay?' Lilith says.

Beryl nods. She's trembling, her breathing hard and laboured.

'You know, I always knew she was a strange girl, but after everything she told me she's been through, well, it was bound to mess her up.' She points her finger to her head, signing madness.

'We will not reveal your identity, Beryl, we will keep you and your family safe.'

When Beryl leaves with two policewomen, Lilith looks at me.

'As soon as we get what we need, you can go to print, okay? But for now, every movement we make has to be cautiously executed.'

'You have my word.' I want to catch the killer as much as she does.

A warrant to search Amelie Jones' flat has been granted. I've been given permission to ride along, but not to enter the premises. I begged, pleaded, but I am told the law is the law. We leave the police station by the back door and step into the bitter November air. I see my breath as I breathe and my heart beats against my ribcage. I am a part of something big. Entering the beast's lair. I slip into the back of a police car, sitting next to an officer who smells of fried food and has bright pink cheeks. He doesn't talk to me. In fact, he is giving me distinct 'fuck off' vibes telling me I shouldn't be part of this operation, that I am the hair in his soup.

We are joined by two other officers who sit in the front. They start the engine and as the car pulls away from the station, nimbostratus clouds knit together forming a heavy blanket of grey in the sky. Soon, sleet begins to fall and the windscreen wipers spring to life. When we arrive at the Grahame Warner Estate, the sleet is coming down in sheets. It makes the tall high-rise towers appear menacing, like the headquarters of hell. We enter the block and I'm first taken aback by the stench, the putrid rot of poverty, urine, and poor choices. I go to the lift. The officer who I sat in the back of the police car with glowers at me. 'We're taking the stairs. Use your brain. If we get stuck in the lift we're screwed.'

I take his point and follow the armed officers up the stairwell. When we reach number 75 my mouth is completely dry. That night with Pete I felt fear, but this is a different kind of fear, because it's mixed with both adrenaline and excitement.

'Police! Open up!'

Hard knock.

'Police! Open up!'

Silence.

Bang!

They break open the door and enter the dwelling. I stand in the doorway but don't step inside. The flat is clean and orderly, open-plan so the kitchen and the living room are one, there is nothing glaringly obvious to suggest this is the home of a murderer. No dead animals, no body parts being cooled in the fridge. Temptation gets the better of me and I edge far enough in to see more details. On the coffee table is a neat pile of books: *A Good Marriage* by Stephen King, *Monster* by Aileen Wuornos and Christopher Berry-Dee, *Women Who Kill: Profiles of Female Serial Killers* by Carol Anne Davis. Lilith is joined by another pair of officers.

'Hey, look at this,' I say, pointing to the books.

'That's not evidence,' she says.

'But it shows who she...' Lilith holds up her hand and cuts me off.

'What if we came in and saw she had a big showcase of Disney DVDs, then what? It's circumstantial at best. This tells us nothing. Jennifer, I need you to stay back, you know you can't be in here.'

The police pull apart her bedroom drawers, blankets, underwear, a sex toy the handling officer shows no embarrassment toward as he tosses it onto the bed.

In the wardrobe is just rails of clothes, everything has a place, it *seems* 'normal'.

When the police lift her mattress, I drift in the kitchen. *Think, Jennifer.* If I were a killer, where would I hide the evidence? It's a full thirty minutes before the police begin to draw things to a close when an annoying fly buzzes around my face. I draw my head upwards to swat it with my phone. Lilith calls the team and points to the kitchen ceiling; a tile is dislodged. She grabs a dining chair and stretches her arm to shift it but she cannot reach.

'Ma'am, can I help?' the officer nearby asks.

'Look, there. You're tall, you can reach it. Get a torch,' she says.

His eyes flicker, showing he is nervous. He grunts as he steps up onto the chair. The weight of him makes the chair protest with a creak.

He reaches to his belt and pulls out a baton, uses it to poke the tile. He turns on his torch.

'Ma'am, we got something here,' he calls out.

Like flies to shit, the entire team gathers, making the walls of the small kitchen feel like they are going to close in. The tension in the room heightens as an old shoebox is lifted out from the ceiling.

The box is placed on the kitchen table. Lilith snaps on some gloves and is the one to lift the lid.

Inside, a blue earring, a bracelet, a pack of Softmints! A small notebook patterned with green butterflies; Lilith flicks open the pages, her expression not telling anything.

'Can I get an ETA to Bristol? And dispatch to the Bristol Special Crime Unit.'

On her command, the action happens.

'What is it?' I ask.

'This, I believe, is her ex-girlfriend's address, it is written in the notebook. And since our suspect is nowhere to be found, I'm guessing she's on her way over. We need to get there before it's too late.'

CHAPTER SIXTY

AMELIE

The lights are on. You haven't pulled across those expensive mechanical shutters yet; what are they for? To shut out the world or shut out me? It doesn't matter because I see you. I have always seen you. You're with me every single day. You move with ease around your habitat, like a ballerina, supple and elegant, dancing a story. *Our story.* You've cut your hair, I imagine the snip of the scissors slicing away parts of your golden strands, like a reptile shedding its skin, becoming anew. The choppy bob ages you, but in a good way. It's added an exclamation mark to your sophisticated style, emphasising how you want the world to see you. But they don't know you like I do. All smoke and mirrors. You hold a glass of red wine with those slender fingers, and you still have that habit of twirling the ends of your hair with your thumb. You are still there. Nobody can erase all of themselves, there are always splintered fragments left behind, built within us like the coding of our DNA. You said you felt sorry for me, but I know who I am. Do you?

You can change who you are on the outside, but you will never change who you are on the inside. Aristotle once said,

'*Knowing yourself is the beginning of all wisdom.*' Try to remember that, it'll help.

You reach for a book. I can't see what it is, but I know you have always preferred real books to e-readers. You always said we need to experience the written word, the smell of the paper, the weight of a story in your hands. I love the way you sniff a book before you dive in and read. I wait a couple of seconds and laugh; there you go, your nose pressed up to the pages like clockwork. The crisp white shirt you're wearing hangs loosely around your slender frame, the memory of what's beneath it takes my breath away. Your silky skin; it's one of the things I loved most about you. You set the book down and jump up, reaching for the phone. Who is calling you this late? It must be someone important to you. I watch you throw your head back and laugh. I miss that sound. We had a lot of laughs, didn't we? Now someone else is firing you up, making your insides light up. You take the phone to another room and slip from view. I let myself imagine I'm on the sofa, waiting while you make us both a drink. I can see us in the apartment, happy, content. It suits the couple we were supposed to be. Your job isn't enough to pay for all of this, but that's the way it's always been for you. Money comes easily. You told me not to worry, that I was enough and money was just a thing. But if that was true then why do you need the leather sofa or the expensive Art Deco bullshit on your walls? Why is it so important that your coffee machine has ninety-nine settings? You love to pretend to be humble, and I think you want to be, but you just can't let go of the good life. I get it. I longed for it too. But I deserved it far more than your pretentious, spoiled friend did. I'm glad she's gone.

You stay on the phone a while. A hard lump that I cannot swallow forms in my throat like a piece of coal. I've been replaced. It's painful to watch you for this long, but now that I've finally found you, I don't want to let you go.

What would you do if you saw me?

Run?

Scream?

Hide? But you're already doing that. We've been playing this game of hide-and-seek for a while now. I came close to finding you before, but you always changed tactics, my clever girl.

I have so many questions; how this all came to be, how two people so connected, so in love could have yanked it all away? Our love was like a mirror, such a beautiful reflection, but it came under strain. It remained intact until it cracked, and once a mirror is broken, the cracks will forever be visible, impossible to repair, but I could live with the damage if it meant I still had you. If you still wanted me.

My soul hurts.

You fall away from my view again. It's like I'm watching you on the TV and it went to a commercial break. I eagerly await your return; you're gone for ten minutes. Now the cold has snaked around my body and I feel the bite of the night air. When you come back you walk to the window, dressed in a white linen two-piece pyjama set. Your hair is pulled away from your face in a neat headband. You return to the sofa and sink into it, reaching for the book again and sinking down lower. The book covers your face and I can only see your long, slender legs. So many of our nights were spent with your legs draped across my lap, you enjoyed the way I stroked them so much you'd close your eyes and drift into a deep sleep. Hours later, I'd wake you and take you to bed in your dozy state, your voice drenched with sleep as you'd ask me to put a glass of water next to the bed. It was my duty to look after you. How could you forget that? How was it not enough? I reach out my hand, longing to touch you, but your eyes are fixed ahead. I don't want this to end. I am still immersed in your beauty. I want to get inside your apartment. Get inside you.

Can you feel me?

I'm right here.

In my bag is a knife, a special blade; expensive, just like you. I go to the door; you have one of those fancy doorbells with a camera on it and a bright security light. I take a cloth from my pocket and drape it over the camera. I ring the bell and wait. It takes a few moments before I hear your footsteps, you open the door with the chain still on.

'Can I help you?'

I always thought you'd know when I was close to you, the connection we once had has been bashed as well as my heart.

Can you feel me?

I'm right here.

You rest your gaze on my face, mapping it together and then it clicks, oh how it clicks.

You *can* feel me.

You know I'm here.

'Amelie?'

'My Grace.'

'How did you find me?'

'I never stopped looking.'

'Please go.'

'We belong together.'

'Amelie, please leave. I won't tell anybody you came here, but you need to leave me alone. Right now.'

Is she crying?

She doesn't want you, the voice in my head says. But I won't believe it. I refuse.

'Shut up! Shut up! Shut up!' I bang the side of my head with my fist.

You try to shut the door, but I put my foot against the jamb. I'm wearing hard-toed boots.

'If you don't open the door, I will kill your fucking parents.' I pull out the butcher's knife and hold it up in plain sight.

'You'll never find them, you psycho!'

'Your mother lives at Barren Lodge, Theobald Road. Your father, 67 Shepherd Lane.'

Your hands are trembling. You try to unlatch the chain, but you're all fingers and thumbs.

'Hurry up.' I've waited long enough for you.

Finally, you open the door and I step inside to the life of Alice, but now I am an unwelcome visitor, not the girl you used to spend hours kissing, holding, touching.

A moment of stillness, as if time itself cannot be measured. Then you take a step back from me, like I am the fuel and you are the flame. I reach out my hand, but you move like a bullet. Your body connects with the glass table behind you and a crystal vase falls, a million shards of sharp silver glitter around your bare feet.

You're unsteady as you move away from the broken glass. You fall backwards as I try to reassure you that it's just me. You know me. You love me.

'Why do you have a fucking knife?' You're hysterical. Unhinged. And you say I'm the crazy one. Ha!

Your face looks ghastly in the dim light, eyes wide and animated. I think you're over-dramatising it all.

'You should know just how much I love you.'

You shake your head, as if you struggle to understand.

'No... if you ever loved me you wouldn't want to hurt me.'

'I hit you once.'

'Have you got amnesia? You hit me far more than once. Not just with your hands but with your mouth.'

'I don't want to hurt you. I want you to understand. Why can't you just *understand*?'

I will not scream, I will not cry. You've taken enough from me.

'I do understand, I do.' Your voice softens, oh, how I have missed that velvet voice.

'What is it you understand?' It's a test, of course, it would be easy to fall for your sudden change of heart, but I know you are trying to pacify me, protect yourself.

You don't reply, fear thinning your skin.

'I asked you a question, Grace. What is it you understand?'

'I understand I hurt you. And... and I'm really sorry for that.'

'But?' Because there is always a but!

'Love shouldn't hurt. Love shouldn't mean you can't live a life without that person, it shouldn't mean you have to be all of my life, but you wouldn't allow me to...'

'Allow you to what? Act like you're single? Be with people who aren't deserving of you? Or allow you to hide me like a dirty little secret. To be ashamed of me?'

The old emotions that near enough swallowed me whole now rise to the surface.

'I wasn't ashamed.'

'Liar!' The beast is out. I cannot bear your lies anymore.

'I need to ask you a question.' My heart is beating so fast, chest tight like a boa constrictor is coiling its thick body around me squeezing tighter and tighter. 'If I had been a man, would you have hidden me?'

'That is an impossible question to answer.'

'No. It. Fucking. Isn't.' I stand over you, your knees tuck into your stomach, arms shield your face.

You sob.

How did it come to this?

CHAPTER SIXTY-ONE

JENNIFER MACK

The house is silent and still. The lights are off. There's over twenty police officers on the scene now. They circle the perimeter of the property as I stand next to Lilith watching the scene unfold.

'Can't they just go in?'

'We have to assess the entire situation. One wrong move and that's it,' Lilith says in a hushed voice.

'Do you think she's inside?'

'My gut tells me she is.'

My heart is thudding so hard I feel like it might explode.

A loud crash alerts everybody to the fact the house is not empty.

'Break the door down!' Lilith screams.

Three officers are immediately at the door and smash it wide open. One of them flicks a switch. The white marbled hallway illuminates. Shattered glass covers the floor, crunches underfoot. The police fall in line and enter the grand kitchen, a spray of colourful flowers sit in the middle of the island. Another light is turned on.

Blood. So much blood. *We're too late.* She got to her before we could. Bile rises to the back of my throat. Soon the street and the house is alive with red and blue flashing lights. Sirens cut through the midnight air, the symphony telling listeners something terrible has taken place. Face down, her top is covering half of her back, drops of blood thin and streaked, like that of an artist's paintbrush.

Lilith lifts Grace's top.

There is the familiar scroll written by the hands of the Devil herself.

My Grace.

A moan, a shift.

'*She's alive,*' Lilith says. I grab hold of a kitchen towel to staunch the bleeding. Soon paramedics dive in and start to repair the carnage that has been inflicted on Grace's body.

In the utility room a shadow lurks in the corner, huddled into a tight ball. Hooded eyes. Blood-soaked clothes and knife in hand.

The Grace Killer.

We meet for the first time. Her face is twisted and contorted, she makes a low grunting sound, malicious and wild, almost supernatural. She is a woman possessed. But by what? Love? Rage?

'Nice to finally meet you, Jennifer Mack.'

My gaze is fixed on her. Being face to face with the killer invokes all kinds of feelings within me, fear being the dominant one. I have to be calm, so I try to respond but the words won't form.

I am shoved aside with a jolt and my shoulder slams into the door-frame. Armed police grab hold of Amelie, she is like a piece of elastic, her body bending in total submission.

'Her life has ended, but I will love her forever.' Clipped and off-kilter, she sounds inhuman, so far gone. So, so far gone.

'She didn't die,' I tell her. Suddenly Amelie's face turns sour and the blood drains from her cheeks. Her smile falters and then I see it, the reality she will be forced to live with for the rest of her life. Regret. Suffering. Failure. Three little words. One powerful hit.

One Month Later

I've never been in love, but I know love shouldn't change who you are. Evolve, yes, but don't rewrite their story, the character you decide to play life out with. Acceptance is key, or so the romantics say. To love is to love the whole person. We are all flawed, not one person is perfect. When a human or animal is trapped, our natural instinct is to break free. Well, that's true for most of us. Amelie Jones has been diagnosed by her medical team as having ASPD. In layman's terms, it means she's a sociopath. They typically engage in behaviours that harm others for the benefit of themselves without remorse. I guess you could say we all have a bit of a sociopath in us. People who are diagnosed with this can still function in everyday life, hold down a job, have a family (imagine that!).

There will always be the Hayleys who want all the attention no matter the cost.

There will always be the Petes in life who love to play games in order for personal gain and benefit.

We are a society of selfish fuckers. Always wanting more.

Amelie wanted one thing. Control. As I peel away the layers of her personality, I am not surprised to learn we are only one bad thing away from being just like each other. Life served her a ton of shit. But don't believe for a second that the murders were a symptom of the abuse she suffered.

My flat is completely packed up. The removal men parked

up in their vans. This is the end of my chapter in Cornwall and the new road to London awaits. I didn't want to be a local journalist, I always thought I was too good for it. There is an ego in us all; but I am so glad I did work at the local paper. I have learned so much about who I am because of this journey, the mistakes I've made, the education I needed. So, the difference between Amelie and I is that she is a person who will always justify her mistakes and will never grow and never learn.

SAVING GRACE
JENNIFER MACK

Meet the Grace Killer. The 5'5", slim, long-haired brunette may not be the depraved, pernicious monster you imagined. Yet, in the shadow of her 19-year-old innocent façade hides the sociopath responsible for the gruesome murders of Grace Matthews, 22, Grace Martin, 18, Grace Elizabeth Joseph, 19, and the attempted murder of Grace Phelps, 18.

Amelie Jones was born on 5th March 2000, to single mother Deborah Jones who died of throat cancer when Amelie was about to turn 17. Jones describes watching her mother die as 'deeply satisfying'.

Jones claims she suffered sexual abuse from the age of 11 at the hands of her mother's on/off boyfriend Derek Steed, 'She knew what he was doing to me, and she did nothing to stop it,' Jones said in a shocking confession. Steed was known as a heroin addict and died of an overdose in 2017 while holidaying in Spain. 'Am I happy he died? Not at all... because I wasn't the one to cause his death.'

Jones survived by working low-paid waitressing jobs. She grew up on the notorious Grahame Warner Estate, infamous for its reputation of gangland violence, drugs, and prostitution. Some might argue Jones' abhorrent childhood paved the way to her committing these harrowing murders. Regardless of what the truth may be, when you talk to Amelie Jones you no doubt ask yourself, 'Are some people born evil?'

Jones is being detained at HM Crossfield Prison in Hull, which holds Category A female criminals. HM Crossfield is dubbed as holding 'the worst of the worst' female offenders, including notable inmates such as Bernice King (Black Widow), who is serving a life sentence without parole for the butchering of three of her husbands to collect their life insurance, and Jan Hart, the nursery worker who was part of the 2011 Shrewsbury paedophile ring.

On 16th May 2019, I met with Amelie Jones at HM Crossfield, hoping to discover what drove her to commit the unspeakable acts and the particularly chilling encounter where she sat with her first victim, Grace Matthews, for several hours after she'd died. In 2016, Jones met the young girl she describes as the love of her life, Grace Anders, who was wealthy and privileged. The unlikely couple were worlds apart, but despite their differences the two became lovers. Grace, however, was not yet ready to reveal her homosexuality to the world, thus increasing the tension in their relationship. Over time, Jones grew jealous of the time Grace was spending with other people. Grace broke up with Jones following a bitter argument that resulted in a physical altercation. 'It's as if she disappeared off the face of the earth. I couldn't call her, couldn't see her. She was just gone.' After several weeks of nursing a broken heart, the killings began. There were three, but Jones hints there may be more blood on her hands. Jones wrote letters to me, she wanted her words to be out for the world to see. *The*

Cornwall Chronicle became both her sounding board and her downfall. When a letter was published 6 months ago, she'd included information which Jones had shared with Beryl Pattinson, a former boss at a café Jones worked at on Briar Bay. Beryl contacted both *The Chronicle* and the police when she connected the pieces together. She was certain Jones was behind the killings. In late November, the police obtained a warrant to search Amelie Jones' flat on the Grahame Warner Estate, and found journal entries and drawings of the victims which showed how they'd been left to die, images and details which have not been released to the press. Jones was arrested and taken into custody. Upon her arrest, she assaulted two female officers and was placed in a segregated unit under round-the-clock surveillance. Because of Jones' high profile, she is also segregated from other inmates. Her only contact is with prison officers, her legal team, and, today, me. I've followed the Grace killings from the start. The first murder took place on the beach I played on as a child. I have studied criminology, and have sought out answers as to what makes women kill.

We all have murderous thoughts. There are those of us who think about doing it and those of us who act. The ones you really have to worry about are the ones who relish doing both. That's the making of a serial killer.

Amelie Jones will never be released from prison.

Saving Grace will air on BBC1 on Tuesday night and the book will be released in April 2022.

Jennifer Mack
BBC News, London.

AMELIE

'Until we meet again, my love.'

THE END

ACKNOWLEDGEMENTS

Firstly, thank you to my editor, Abbie Rutherford, for her extraordinary attention to detail and pushing the story in the right direction and for not judging my twisted thoughts (ha!).

Thank you to the team at Bloodhound for taking a chance on this story and making the process enjoyable and giving Saving Grace its wings to fly into the world.

Massive gratitude to my friends and family who always support my passion of writing and allowing me to share my ideas with you. To Nat for your constant friendship. To Jenny and Suzy who said this story would be in the hands of readers even when the voice of doubt told me otherwise, "roots" ladies. To my sister, Johanna, nobody makes me laugh like you do.

To my parents, Benna and Rob for continuing to support my dream of writing and who encouraged me ever since I was little to keep at it and never quietened my overactive imagination.

To my children: Everything is nothing without you.

Finally, thank you to my husband, Adam... thank goodness for that empty dancefloor!

A NOTE FROM THE PUBLISHER

Thank you for reading this book. If you enjoyed it please do consider leaving a review on Amazon to help others find it too.

We hate typos. All of our books have been rigorously edited and proofread, but sometimes mistakes do slip through. If you have spotted a typo, please do let us know and we can get it amended within hours.

info@bloodhoundbooks.com